DARK HARVEST

FROM *MANCHESTER EVENING
NEWS* OF MAY 24, 1946

Germs, more deadly than an atomic bomb, can be used in a secret spray gun devised in the United States, members of the Appropriations Committee of the House of Representatives stated in Washington today.

One member said: 'The Navy has developed a weapon that can be used to wipe out all form of life in a large city; if the germ is sprayed from planes that can fly high enough while doing it to be reasonably safe from ground fire. It would mean quick and certain death to a city, as the germs are highly contagious, and the effects would spread rapidly. One operation would be sufficient.'

The member said that the spray dropped on fields would destroy all crops even to seeds in the ground.

Congressman Albert Thomas (Democrat, Texas) who was a member of the Appropriations Committee, which heard secret evidence from high Navy officials, told the House of Representatives that the U.S. Navy had 'something more deadly than the atomic bomb today—not to-morrow—and it is in usable shape.'

JOHN CREASEY

Dark Harvest

WALKER AND COMPANY
New York

CONTENTS

ONE

OLD FRIENDS MEET

'I WILL inquire, sir, if you will please wait here,' said the footman, and, to the visitor's surprise, walked out of the front door into the sunlit grounds of Brett Hall.

There was no sound inside the house except the impatient tapping of the visitor's foot. The cut of his clothes, his rimless glasses and the square toes of his highly polished shoes proclaimed, to the English eye, that he was an American—as had his voice when he had spoken to the footman.

He became aware of watching eyes. His lean, tanned face grew set and his body seemed to become rigid, although the movement was almost imperceptible. His gaze riveted on a doorway opposite the staircase.

When he saw who was watching him, he relaxed, smiled broadly and strolled forward, over skin rugs and polished wood. The watcher was a little girl of about nine or ten and, although she looked timid, she came to meet him.

'Good morning,' said the child, formally.

'I thought you were watching me,' the American told her.

'I must apologize,' said the child, 'it was very rude of me.' She was a little elfin creature, with long, slim legs and a pointed face. She added, reflectively, 'I am afraid you are going to be unfortunate, sir.'

'Oh,' said the American, startled.

'I overheard you ask for Dr. Palfrey,' said the child, 'and you are not likely to be able to see him for some time.'

'That's a shame,' said the American.

'You see, grandfather's eleven is batting.'

'Batting,' said the American, with some relief. 'I think I follow you now. Dr. Palfrey is playing a game.'

'Why, yes, cricket,' declared the child.

'I've never seen anyone play cricket,'' the American confided.

'You—haven't?'

'They don't play it much where I come from,' he told her.

The dark-clad footman re-entered the hall and said, apologetically: 'I am afraid that Dr. Palfrey is engaged indefinitely, sir. I have left a message for him, and I am sure he will come as soon as he can.'

'Why, thank you,' said the American, and glanced at his watch. 'What's the latest time he'll be in?'

'A little after one o'clock, sir.'

'All right, I'll wait.'

'If you will come with me, sir, please,' said the footman, and led the way into a high-ceilinged, airy room, flooded with sunshine, where there were easy chairs and books and magazines.

The footman went off. Not once had he acknowledged the existence of the child, who had not followed them, but in the hall the American heard him say:

'Miss Hilary, shouldn't you be in the school-room?'

'No,' said 'Miss Hilary', 'Mam'selle is not well this morning, you see, and I am allowed to be in the garden.'

The footman sniffed, probably at 'Mam'selle'.

'This is not the garden,' he declared, and walked away.

The little girl made no reply, and the American smiled, then shook his head wonderingly as if he were reflecting on the curious habits of the natives of this island. He sat down and picked up a magazine. Presently a shadow fell across his feet, and he looked up to see Hilary standing by the open french windows.

'Something has just occurred to me,' she told him.

'Well, then—let's hear it.'

'If you come with me to the pavilion, we can wait there for my uncle, and as soon as he is out—if he comes out before lunch, that is—you will be able to see him. Of course, I leave it entirely to you,' she added, politely.

'It's a grand idea,' said the American. He jumped up, and soon she was leading the way through the roses beyond the beech hedge. The branches of the cedars beyond almost touched as they spread out, and the American, although not a tall man, had to lower his head as he walked underneath them.

Dr. Palfrey was having a good morning.

He had been dropped in the slips and at cover in his first over, but since then he had not looked like getting out. He batted with a casual, almost lazy, ease which made the thing seem simple. The American seemed fascinated by the quick footwork, the easy strokes and the complete command the man seemed to take of the bowling.

'You never look at anyone except Uncle Sap,' Hilary commented.

'Well, we're old friends,' the American told her, 'and we've never met in England before; I haven't seen him at home. It doesn't matter what he touches, he's good, isn't he?'

'I believe he is rather capable,' agreed Hilary. 'Are you sure you wouldn't like to go to the pavilion? I should not like you to get thirsty.'

'Thirsty?' He looked at her, startled. 'But I—oh, sure. I could do with a drink,' he added, hastily, and Hilary looked pleased.

'This is the quickest way,' she said, and led him beneath the cedars again. 'You see, the thick hedge at the end of the ground won't allow you to pass through.'

'I see,' said the American.

The scene lay vividly before his eyes—the little, thatched pavilion opposite the cedars, the small buffet on which glasses and bottles glinted in the sun, a few dozen people sitting in deck-chairs, a few sprawling full length on the grass, all absorbed in the game. Near the pavilion was the score-board, where a small boy was standing by the side of a very old man; and at either end of the field were big white screens—'sight-screens', Hilary confided.

'We pass just behind that one,' she said, pointing. 'We mustn't move if the bowling is from this end, though, or there would be an awful stink.'

There was a shrubbery at the end of the field which they were approaching, a maze of shrubs and small trees, with the sight-screen just in front of it. Hilary led the way towards the shrubbery, and soon they were hidden from the view of everyone near the ground itself. As they reached the screen there was a sudden, fierce roar, which sounded like 'Howzatt' and made the American start.

There was another, sharper sound.

'You needn't——' began Hilary.

Then she stopped abruptly and gave a little cry.

The American was looking towards the shrubbery with the alert expression which he had shown when the child had first met him. He hardly heard her exclamation. He stared at the bushes, and his right hand slipped inside his coat.

'Please,' said Hilary.

'Quiet a minute,' he answered, sharply.

9

The little girl looked at her arm. There was blood on it, and the blood was spreading.

'*Please*——' she said again, with a frightened note in her voice.

He glanced round at her, impatiently, and saw the slender, brown arm stretched out, with the blood oozing half-way between the wrist and elbow. He uttered a fierce exclamation, snatched her into his arms, and then dropped on to the ground with the child beneath him.

The crack of bat on ball came again, and there seemed to be an echo, but a much sharper sound. Something splintered the wood of the sight-screen. The American kept his head low and pressed Hilary tight against the ground, so that she could hardly breathe. Then he wriggled backwards, muttering:

'That damned board.'

No one else seemed to pay any attention, and at last the American was satisfied, and straightened up. The child raised her head, but he pushed her down gently.

'Just a minute, honey.'

She lay breathing heavily, her face white, and averted her gaze from her wounded arm. The American took a handkerchief from his pocket, let her sit up, wiped away the blood and then tied the handkerchief round her arm.

'It's all right,' he said, 'you've nothing to worry about now.'

But the tone of his voice belied his words. He knew that he had been the target, and if he carried Hilary to the house she might get hurt again, for whoever had fired that shot would not worry about hitting her, provided they got him. Once they reached the cover of the cedars, he thought, they would be safe. He held her closely, and ran. . . .

The portly, red-faced captain of the visitors decided to have a gamble and put on his slow bowler, a man unreliable in length but who might toss one up which would flummox Palfrey. So the field spread out to patrol the boundaries, and Dr. Palfrey glanced round to take in their new positions.

He saw a man running, carrying Hilary.

He did not wait to reason.

There was the man, a stranger as far as he knew, hugging Hilary close to him. Palfrey let out a bellow and, to the astonishment of fieldsmen and spectators alike, rushed towards the cedars. Then the others saw what was happening. The fields-men near the cedars jumped to life and raced towards the

American; the other batsman followed Palfrey, who made better speed than most of them, his eyes raking the grounds beyond the trees.

The fieldsmen were near enough to Hilary for her to be in no danger, so Palfrey concentrated on looking for other intruders. He thought he saw a dark figure between the cedars and the shrubbery. Two men were at his side, and he pointed with his bat.

'That way.'

They obeyed without question, and the three of them rushed towards the dark figure. As they ducked beneath the cedars, which slowed them down, they heard a sharp crack—the crack of a shot. Palfrey had heard a similar sound twice before that morning, but had thought nothing of it. Now he saw that the dark figure was standing and firing. The others also saw the man, who was taking careful aim; three more sharp cracks echoed about the grounds and the now empty playing-field.

Palfrey said: 'Be careful, but go straight for him.'

He himself ran off at a tangent. Not far away was the long drive from the lodge gates. If the man with the gun had a car, he reasoned, it would probably be parked near the lodge, and the man would run along the drive. Palfrey hoped to cut him off. He did not give a thought to the incongruity of racing wildly across the uneven grassland in pads and gloves, with his bat swinging in his right hand.

He lost sight of his quarry, but went on until he came within sight of the drive.

He had guessed rightly.

The gunman was running quickly along the drive, without looking behind him. Fifty yards or so away, half a dozen white-clad men were in pursuit. There were a few bushes between Palfrey and the fugitive, and Palfrey waited, breathing hard, trying to judge the moment when he should spring from his cover. He held the bat ready to throw and trip the other up.

But the man caught sight of him.

Palfrey saw the gun raise towards him, and threw himself down. There was one shot, and a bullet went over his head. He thought he heard the click of an empty revolver, and straightened up: the man was past him. Palfrey flung the bat, but put too much force behind it, and it sailed over the man's head. Palfrey put on speed, but the pads were rubbing against each other, handicapping him. Soon two of the fieldsmen passed him, running easily, but the dark man was well ahead and

11

disappeared behind some trees. Palfrey kept going until he reached the trees; from there, on the drive, he saw a small car and heard its engine. The fugitive jumped into the car, which moved off immediately; the two fieldsmen got between it and Palfrey and blocked his view so that he could not quite see the number.

The car turned right at the drive gates.

'Yes,' said Palfrey, into the telephone, 'it headed for Reading . . . Of course it may have turned off,' he agreed, somewhat testily. He was flushed from his exertions, and still wore the pads. He was telephoning from the lodge, which was nearer than the house itself, and the lodge-keeper was staring at him in alarm. 'Yes, a small car, a two-seater, probably a Morris, and the first letters of the registration plate were XR . . . No, we couldn't get the rest . . . I tell you that shots were fired . . . Yes, I am speaking from Brett Hall!'

The lodge-keeper opened a bottle of beer and filled three glasses.

Ah, that's just what I wanted,' Palfrey said appreciatively, and drank deeply. Then he wiped his forehead and dabbed his neck. 'I hope Hilary's all right,' he remarked to the two players with him, then lifted the receiver again and motioned to the bottle. 'Have one yourself, Morton.' The lodge-keeper poured himself a drink, and Palfrey, after some delay, spoke to a footman at the house. The man was out of breath, sure evidence of the disturbance, but he was also reassuring.

'I believe Miss Hilary is only slightly hurt, sir.'

'That's good,' said Palfrey. 'Send a car out for me, will you?'

'Yes, sir, at once.'

There were half a dozen cars parked outside the garage, and soon one started down the drive.

A knot of cricketers and spectators were gathered outside the front door of the house, and the men with Palfrey joined them while he hurried inside.

An old, white-haired man was standing near the door of the morning-room, and moved forward as Palfrey entered.

'Hallo, Christian,' said Palfrey. 'How is Miss Hilary?'

'I don't think it is really serious, sir, but Dr. Ebutt is on his way out. She was slightly wounded in the arm.'

Palfrey's frown deepened.

'Well, we got one of the beggars, anyhow.'

'As a matter of fact, sir,' said Christian, who had been the

12

Marquis of Brett's butler for countless years, 'I don't think we have. I understand from Simm that the man whom you saw had called here to see you, and he did in fact carry Miss Hilary out of danger. I am not fully acquainted with the facts, however.'

'Oh,' said Palfrey. 'Where is this hero?'

'In the library, sir, with his lordship.'

'I'll go up,' said Palfrey, and started for the stairs.

'I wonder if you would care to change your boots?' suggested Christian. 'I have had a pair of shoes fetched from your room.'

Palfrey smiled. 'That's a thought,' he admitted, and sat down to change. Christian undid one boot while Palfrey undid the other. 'Who is the caller?'

'All I know is that he is an American.'

'And he came to see me,' mused Palfrey.

He did not think much about it as he went upstairs, glad of the comfort of the house-shoes and of the freedom from pads. He visualized a picture of the man in a light suit rushing away with Hilary, but kidnapping, it seemed, was out—unless the American had caught the dark man in the act of snatching the child away.

The library led off a spacious landing. He heard voices as he opened the door, and saw Brett sitting at a leather-topped pedestal desk in one corner. Next moment he saw the American, who was lying back in an easy chair, with a glass by his side.

'Hallo, Sap,' said the Marquis.

'Sap!' exclaimed the American.

'By all the curry in India!' exclaimed Palfrey, and met the American as he jumped from his chair. Their hands gripped. 'I should have guessed it was you. You always were rescuing damsels in distress.' They eyed each other for a moment, in mutual regard and satisfaction, and then Palfrey turned to the Marquis of Brett.

'How *is* Hilary?'

'Only slightly wounded in the forearm,' Brett assured him. 'I've seen it myself, and there's nothing to worry about. It frightened her, naturally.'

'Frightened!' exclaimed the American. 'The way that kid was hurt and the way I fell on her ought to have made her scream to high heaven, and she hardly let out a murmur.'

'I suppose someone was after you,' said Palfrey. 'When he sneaked through the grounds and saw you against the screen he took a pot-shot.'

13

'You're about right,' agreed Donald Lannigan. 'And I was after you. You always said I'd never be able to get out of a jam without you, and am I in a jam! You've seen something of it, you can judge how bad it might get. But the thing I'm pleased about right now is that Hilary wasn't badly injured. I was by that white board with her; we were like two sitting birds against it. The man who fired those shots ought to take lessons. That reminds me,' he added, with a humorous lift of his eye-brows, 'did you get him?'

'No.'

'Isn't it time you said "police"?'

'I've telephoned them,' said Palfrey, and explained more fully. As he finished, there was a tap at the door, and Christian entered.

'Luncheon is served, my lord.'

'I'll have to lunch with the others,' Brett said, 'but you two will want to talk. I'll take your apologies, Sap,' he added, and went out.

'I know what you're thinking, Sap,' ventured Lannigan. 'I don't like a man who doesn't care whether he hits a kid so long as he hits his man. But these people are like that. I suppose I shouldn't have come here, but I found you weren't in London and it seemed as quick as any way to see you. I didn't want to talk openly on the telephone.'

'Let's go downstairs and talk over some food,' Palfrey said. 'I'll have to be ready again by two-fifteen.'

'You're going to play on?'

'I don't see why not.'

'I guess you're right,' he conceded; 'you never gave up easily, did you? And after being chased off by a pack of wolves in white, Manuel isn't going to come here again in a hurry. I guess he's never been so scared.'

'Manuel?' murmured Palfrey.

'It's the name I've given the guy,' Lannigan said, 'I don't know what he calls himself.' He spoke slowly, taking off his glasses and polishing them, while the sun gleamed down on the rimless edges. 'I'm getting worried about myself,' he added.

'Is this business getting you down?'

'I wouldn't put it that way. I'm getting worried because I thought I'd slipped Manuel in London. I didn't know the man existed who could follow me if I wanted to get away from him. He's smart. I'm not so smart.' He paused, then added seriously:

14

'I didn't want to bring trouble here, Sap. But there is trouble. I don't know how big.'

As they walked across the impressive landing and down the wide staircase, Lannigan looked about him appreciatively. Doors and windows were open, and they could hear Brett's voice as he gave a welcoming speech to the guests. Lannigan's smile broadened.

'Cricket's kind of formal,' he observed.

'Not a bit,' Palfrey denied. 'This is a little pleasantry which has gone on for so long that it's difficult to stop. Today is the first day of the week.'

'Are you playing every day?'

'I hope to.'

'Where's Drusilla?'

'She's coming the day after tomorrow,' Palfrey told him. 'She's gone north for a day or two.'

Christian met them in the great, picture-filled dining-room. A cold buffet was on the sideboard. Palfrey told Christian that they would help themselves.

'Come and sit down,' said Palfrey.

'Sure.'

Palfrey thought of another summer's day, much hotter than this, in Southern Italy. It had been during one of his unchronicled journeys during the war, when he had served Z.5, a small branch of Intelligence, under the guidance of the Marquis of Brett. Brett had conceived an Allied Secret Service organisation, and during the war it had worked well, with representatives from all the big powers and often from the smaller ones. Palfrey did not know just how, but he had become the active leader, and on that day in Southern Italy he had met Lannigan for the first time.

The American had performed one of the war's greatest heroic feats.

Lannigan broke his silence at last.

'Very busy, Sap?'

'Not really.'

'Doctoring again?'

'I've been on the Continent for a few months, helping out at some of the hospitals,' Palfrey said. 'I'm not practising in England. I have a consultation now and then, but——' he broke off, and shrugged his sloping shoulders.

'Restless?' murmured Lannigan. 'I hoped you would be.

I think I can interest you in a little mystery that will get the jitterbug out of your system.'

'You might be able to,' admitted Palfrey, 'but interesting Drusilla will be a different matter. Little Hilary is on the way. Or little Lionel, as the case may be.'

'Why, that's wonderful!'

'Oh, I don't know,' murmured Palfrey, with a faint smile. 'But Drusilla isn't exactly looking for what you might call excitement. And she won't be anxious for me to dabble in any.'

Lannigan shrugged.

'It was only a hope, anyway.'

'What's it all about?'

Again Lannigan grinned, but Palfrey felt sure that he was disappointed by the news, although he tried hard not to show it.

'I'm looking for a dame,' he said.

'Beautiful, I presume?'

'She was,' Lannigan said, slowly. 'I don't really know what she's like now. She's been missing for nine months. That's a long time. I think she's in England, but I'm not even sure about that. Manuel gives me some hope. Would Manuel have trailed me out here and used that gun if I weren't getting pretty close?'

'It doesn't seem likely,' said Palfrey. 'Did you know Manuel was so dangerous?'

Lannigan laughed. 'I had an idea. Did you know I'd left F.B.I. and started for myself?'

'I knew you'd left the F.B.I.,' said Palfrey. 'I didn't know you were a lone wolf. Congratulations!'

'Congratulations don't feed me,' Lannigan said, with a grimace. 'I didn't intend to get a licence, I thought I'd try to become a foreign correspondent.'

'Just your mark,' Palfrey said.

'No editor thought so! I came nearest with *World Citizen*. Has that been published over here yet?'

'I haven't heard of it,' said Palfrey.

'It's a big noise back home just now. It came out first three or four weeks back; with a splash. The first world newspaper. Special correspondents in every place that counts, news from an international angle—that line.'

'It sounds first-rate,' said Palfrey.

'Only they wanted experienced men, not F.B.I. agents who couldn't take discipline and thought they could scribble. When I couldn't get a job, I started out on my own. But I had a lot of trouble getting work until this came along. I received a down payment of a thousand dollars on it, and spent that long ago. The balance comes only on results, and I don't look like getting any results. It's one of those simple cases, Sap—so simple that when I first looked at it I said it was easy money. I knew the girl—slightly. I didn't think much of her. Spoiled since she was so high, high-ball crazy, new man, new gown, new thrill every night—you know the kind. But rich, and so is her old man. She disappeared one night after a big party and went off with a new friend and didn't return. You don't read any of our newspapers, do you?'

'No.'

'It made a splash,' Lannigan told him. 'It looked like kidnapping. Her old man paid ten thousand dollars in ransom, and another ten thousand, against the advice of the police. Then he hired me. I thought I knew who was behind it, and tagged along for a bit. Then I found out that I didn't know who was really behind it. The man I checked on had taken her and collected the cash, but he'd done it on someone else's instructions. Have you heard of Little Whitey?'

Palfrey shook his head.

'All right, call him Al Capone,' said Lannigan. 'He was that good—or bad! But he was scared of the man who told him what to do with the girl—so scared that he wouldn't say a word when he was picked up for the kidnapping. I know when a man's frightened,' declared Lannigan, soberly, 'and Little Whitey was stiff with fright. The police did a crazy thing. They thought of letting Whitey out on bail and finding out where he checked in. He wasn't out twelve hours before he was shot. Whitey's friends all acted the same way—sizzling with fear, Sap. They didn't like the man who had given Whitey that job and they didn't know where the girl was. I got one squeal, just one squeal so soft you could hardly hear it, from a man who had bought two airplane tickets for London for a guy. I checked that a man and a girl, who might have been the one I was looking for, had caught the airplane on those tickets three days ago. That was when I went crazy. *I* flew over. I lost some time because I went to Ireland first, but I wasn't more than twenty-four hours after them. And I thought I had some luck. This couple went to the Merchester in Park Lane and I found the rooms where they'd checked in. I got into those rooms. I had a look round, and I didn't find anything worth seeing, except—Manuel.'

'Oh.' said Palfrey.

'He came in when I was finishing,' Lannigan said, 'and we had a few words. He's really smart. He'd heard me inside. He covered his face so that I couldn't see him properly; and he had a gun. I didn't like the look in his eyes and I didn't like the gun. I made out I was seeing what I could take away with me in ready money. He didn't believe me. He knew who I was and what I was doing. I thought my number was up, Sap, because I saw from the way he handled his gun that he knew how to use it. What *he* didn't know was that he was standing on a rug which would slip. It's an old trick, but it worked. I got out. He followed me, and since then I've been trying to get away from him.

'That's the run of the story. I can't be sure the girl I'm looking for is in England, but I think she is. I can't be sure that the guy she was with is the guy Whitey and his friends were scared of, but I think he is.' Lannigan toyed with the stem of his claret glass. 'On the strength of what I've told you I wouldn't have come out here, though.'

Palfrey offered cigarettes, and asked:

'Well, what haven't you told me?'

'The man at the Merchester is a British Embassy official in Washington,' Lannigan said. 'How do you like that?'

TWO

OF KENNEDY LEE

PALFREY did not like that at all.

Lannigan etched in more details, reiterating that he could not be wholly sure that he was right; but obviously he felt reasonably certain. The girl had come from America with the Hon. Kennedy Lee. That was a name to conjure with; Lee was a member of a family as old at Brett's, one with an unblemished reputation. He was not a high official; but then, he was a young man as diplomats went—in the early forties.

The girl's name was Grayson, and her father was a wealthy Seattle shipping merchant. Now that he knew the names, Palfrey remembered reading of the kidnapping in the English papers.

He thought of what the newspapers would make of the

18

story if Kennedy Lee, whom he knew slightly, were mentioned. There were other implications; if a British Embassy official were concerned in the disappearance of an American girl, every isolationist in the United States would use it as a baton for a crescendo of protest.

Lannigan stood up and went to the window.

'I thought maybe you could help me to get a line on Lee,' he said. 'You're out, I know, but a line——' he broke off, hopefully.

'I'll try,' promised Palfrey. 'The Marquis probably will, too.'

'I'll leave it to you.' Lannigan hesitated, and then asked lightly: 'Is Z.5 still running?'

'More or less.'

'That's no answer at all.'

'It's the right answer,' said Palfrey. 'There's a move on foot to revive it as the nucleus of a United Nations Secret Service. How far the various governments will play I don't know, but Brett's trying hard. It's badly needed.'

Lannigan said slowly: 'This *might* be a job with international complications, Sap.'

'It might be the opportunity Brett's looking for,' admitted Palfrey. 'Does the F.B.I. know about Lee?'

'I don't think so.'

'That's probably as well,' said Palfrey. He glanced at a clock; there was a sudden burst of conversation outside. 'It's five past two,' he said. 'I'll tell Brett that you want a word with him. Tell him the story from start to finish, and get his reaction.'

He told Lannigan where to wait and hurried into the grounds. The fieldsmen were already taking their places and he buckled on his pads hurriedly.

Palfrey's score stood at sixty-one when they resumed play, but, perhaps because he wanted to be with Brett and Lannigan, he took risks which should have proved fatal sooner than they did. In twenty minutes he was in the middle nineties. Then he skied a ball and was taken in the deep.

He put on his blazer and sauntered towards Brett and Lannigan. Brett looked at Palfrey with a faint smile.

'What do you make of this story, Sap?'

'It's interesting,' said Palfrey.

'I'll make some inquiries about Lee,' Brett promised, 'and if it's possible I'll tell you what I find out, Lannigan.'

'What will make it impossible?' asked Lannigan.

'Diplomacy,' declared Palfrey, darkly.

'Well, I don't want to start another war,' Lannigan said, 'but I would like to find out if Lee brought Valerie Grayson over with him, and what he's doing with her. There's one thing I forgot to tell you, Sap, but I told the Marquis. The girl with Lee didn't *look* like Valerie, but Valerie has a birthmark which a lot of people wouldn't notice. Just below the neck-line of all nice dresses,' he added, with a grin. 'This girl has such a birthmark.'

'How do you know?' asked Palfrey, pointedly.

'I'm on my own this side, but I'm not on the other,' said Lannigan. 'If I get the breaks, I'll send for my secretary, who's good—very good, Sap. The squeal I got named Lee, and this girl who's with him in England was seeing a lot of him, so I put my secretary on to her. She managed to take a peek—don't ask me how. And the girl is different to look at but has certain of Valerie's characteristics which seem to tie up. If it's Valerie, she's lost weight, and—but what's the use of talking?' he added. 'If the Marquis will find out what he can, that suits me. Sap, do you have to play cricket tomorrow? If Drusilla isn't coming until the next day, you and I could have a day in London, looking around. You could show me places! Maybe you don't realize it, but this is my first trip to England and I find it strange,' he added, plaintively.

'We've a strong side out tomorrow,' remarked Brett. 'If you'd care to let someone else have a game, Sap, that's all right with me.'

Lannigan stayed at the Hall that night, and during the evening Brett made several telephone calls to London. His part in secret diplomacy before and during the war was outstanding, and he was liked and trusted by all sections of political thought in England. Behind the scenes his influence was perhaps as great as any man's, and, though he was getting old, he worked ceaselessly towards the full co-operation of the nations of the world. His dream of an Allied Secret Service had been rudely shattered soon after the war, but he was not prepared to admit that it was a hopeless proposition.

At half past eleven he entered the billiards room. Palfrey sauntered over to him, looking very thin in his dinner jacket. 'Any luck?' he asked.

'Lee spent much more money in America than he could afford,' said Brett, 'and it's suspected that he gambled heavily.

There's some suggestion that he won't be returning to Washington,' Brett added, 'but whether it came from him or was officially inspired I don't know. There's a hint of mystery about it.

'Lee presumably had something in his suite at the Merchester which Lannigan might have seen. At least, Manuel thinks he saw it and, to prevent him from telling others, he trailed Lannigan and tried to murder him. It's pretty hot, And, I suppose, properly speaking it's police work.'

The police had been out that afternoon to photograph the bullet holes in the sight-screen and to question Lannigan. They had not traced the small car, and the only useful clue was the calibre of the bullets, which had been fired from a .22 automatic. There had been no footprints, and so far as the Reading police were concerned, there was little hope of getting results.

'Yes, it's police work,' Brett said, 'but if they're told the full story, Lannigan will be in trouble for breaking into the Merchester. I think we'd better leave that for the moment. Find out what you can about Lee tomorrow.'

'I will,' said Palfrey, 'but I'm not going to take Lannigan about with me. Manuel may pick him up again ; it will be just as well if I'm not associated with him yet.'

'I quite agree,' said Brett.

Palfrey reached London at half past ten and lost no time in making 'inquiries'. Gradually he formed a mental picture of Kennedy Lee. Lee had brought expensive presents home from America, his generosity was a by-word, he looked well and more contented than ever in his life before, he had a host of friends, it seemed likely that he was going to get married: Kennedy, a confirmed bachelor!

Descriptions of the girl varied ; some thought her beautiful, some thought her sad. The 'sad' caught Palfrey's attention, and as it was repeated several times he thought of Valerie Grayson, who surely had reason to be sad. The girl's name, it appeared, was Diana—what could be more English than that?—and generally it was assumed that she was a nice girl. One or two regretted that Kennedy was thinking of marrying an American, others thought it a good thing. No, there was no official engagement, but it was generally believed that it would be announced on Friday, when Kennedy was giving a party at the Merchester.

At a quarter past one, Palfrey went into the Merchester, where Lee was lunching with his lady.

Palfrey could only see his back, but when Lee moved he

could see Diana—or Valerie. He agreed with those who called her sad, and with those who said that she was lovely. It was a classic loveliness. She had dark hair, wound round her head in plaits, and it made her look rather old-fashioned. Her eyes were tragic. Lee, bronzed, good-looking, seeming younger than his years, had a deep, laughing voice; Palfrey remembered him as a man whom most people liked but of whom the discerning felt a little shy.

He stood up, and stared overlong at Diana. Lee glanced at him, frowned, and then smiled broadly.

'It's Palfrey, isn't it?'

'Yes,' smiled Palfrey. 'Kennedy Lee?'

'That's right. Diana, here's an old friend of mine,' said Lee, expansively, and Diana smiled and offered her hand. Lee seemed to welcome Palfrey and asked him to take coffee with them in the small lounge.

Kennedy Lee was telling Diana that Palfrey's was a name to reckon with, and talked much about his wartime adventures.

Palfrey interrupted with a smile. 'He's exaggerating, of course.'

Lee chuckled. 'You're nearly as well known in the States as here,' he said. 'Are you busy on Friday,' he added, as if with an afterthought. 'You must come here to our little party in the evening. Quite small—mostly family. Bring your wife—I haven't met her, have I?'

'Probably as a long-legged school-girl,' said Palfrey, and glanced at his watch. He pretended to be startled. 'Here, I must go!' He jumped up and bowed low over Diana's hand.

'Friday, then,' said Lee.

'I'm looking forward to it,' beamed Palfrey.

He went out, leaving them together. He was thoughtful, and convinced that if Lee had any guilt on his conscience, the man felt quite sure that he was safe from exposure. But Lee, hearty and handsome though he was, had made nothing like such vivid impression on him as Diana had. There was something worrying her, she was not quite normal; she behaved almost as if the world about her were unreal.

He wished he had a photograph of Valerie Grayson. Lannigan had one at the small hotel where he was staying and where, he had said, he felt quite safe from Manuel.

Palfrey telephoned him.

'Any luck?' asked Lannigan, eagerly.

22

'I don't know,' said Palfrey, 'but I think we've got something to talk about. I'll come and see you.'

'Right now?'

'Are you doing anything?'

'I've a date in ten minutes,' said Lannigan. 'I picked up an old friend who might be able to help a little. Will an hour make any difference?'

'None at all,' Palfrey assured him. 'I'll be there at four o'clock.

Lannigan was at a small hotel in a turning off Shaftesbury Avenue. Palfrey reached there at four o'clock—an hour and a quarter after he had spoken to the American. Palfrey made his way up the narrow staircase, walking on a threadbare carpet.

He tapped on the door of room 27, but there was no answer. The reception clerk downstairs had said that Lannigan had not left the hotel that afternoon.

He tapped again, and thought he heard a movement. He waited expectantly, but only silence followed. He tried the door; it was not locked.

He stepped into the room. 'Don,' he called, softly.

Lannigan was there, but he did not answer.

He was sitting in a small armchair, his head on his chest, one leg thrust straight out, the other bent. Palfrey's heart seemed to turn over. He glanced swiftly about the room. There was no sign of a disturbance, and there were only two places where anyone could be hiding. He looked under the bed and into the wardrobe, where a single suit was hanging. He turned to Lannigan, his heart thumping, and slowly lifted a limp hand to raise the American's head.

He winced.

A long needle had been driven into Lannigan's right eye.

Palfrey shivered, although the room was warm. The window was wide open, but there seemed no air. He crossed to the window, trying to think clearly, and as he stared at the blank brick wall of the building opposite he heard a movement at the door.

Palfrey recognized the man on the instant as Manuel, but recognition was unimportant compared with the gun in the other's hand.

Manuel closed the door gently behind him and took a step forward. 'This is, perhaps, a friend of yours?' he asked.

Palfrey forced himself to speak. 'Yes.'

'I am sorry,' said Manuel. 'Who are you?'

'Just—a friend.'

'That is not good enough,' said Manuel. His voice was thin and had a slight lisp, but he had no recognizable accent. His dark hair, over-long and heavily greased, fell in waves which looked artificial. His broad features were ugly. 'I must know who you are, because I am interested in Mr. Lannigan's friends.'

'I am interested in his enemies,' retorted Palfrey.

'Really? That is unwise,' said Manuel. He smiled, showing rows of white teeth. 'Your name, please?'

Should he gave a false name?

'Your *real* name,' said Manuel, and smiled again. 'I shall search your pockets and find out whether you have given me the right one; please do not be foolish.'

If the man made him take off his coat he could not very well resist, unless as he took if off he flung it at Manuel. That might provide the chance he needed; but should he give his real name or take a chance at being proved a liar?

Yes; his real name.

'Palfrey,' he said.

Manuel's eyes narrowed.

'*Dr.* Palfrey?'

'Yes.'

'You have been staying at Brett Hall, have you not?'

'Yes.'

'So Lannigan came to see you there. Did he tell you why he was in England, Dr. Palfrey?'

Here was a chance to lie and get away with it.

'Not really,' Palfrey said. 'He had come on business. He was an American private detective and was looking for someone. He asked me to help him. I came to hear the full story,' said Palfrey.

'You were going to help him, you were going to interfere,' said Manuel. 'That is true, is it not?'

'I was going to advise him to see the police—again,' said Palfrey, heavily. He thought it best not to let Manuel know that they had met before; the man had probably not recognized him as he had fled along the drive.

'Again?' echoed Manuel.

'Someone shot at Lannigan in the grounds of Brett Hall,' Palfrey said, 'and the police were called in. A child was hurt.'

'So I believe,' said Manuel. 'It is in the paper this morning. The child got in the way. So you know only a little of what

Lannigan knew and others cannot know very much.' He smiled again. 'I am sorry,' he began. His gun moved up.

Palfrey realized the man was going to shoot. He flung himself sideways, snatching at a tray on the dressing-table, desperate to get a missile; but the glass slipped under his fingers. He heard a soft, hissing sound, but no explosion. There was another sound, a sharp crack as something hit the mirror on the dressing-table. He fell on the floor, shouting at the top of his voice. As he reached the floor he turned over and stretched out his hand, clutching at Manuel's ankle. Manuel staggered backwards; there was another hissing sound, followed by a thud. Manuel pulled his leg free.

Someone outside said in alarm: 'What's that?' Then a door slammed and heavy footsteps sounded in the passage. The footsteps faded, but excited voices were raised. •

Palfrey got up, and something dragged his sleeve. He glanced down and saw a long needle exactly like the one which had killed Lannigan. He remembered the hissing noise, as of an air-gun. He pulled the needle free and stood holding it between his fingers. Manuel must have come to the door, taken careful aim at Lannigan, and fired; and he had hoped to kill Palfrey in the same way. Palfrey examined the point of the needle; it was covered with something tacky. He did not touch it; he did not doubt that the needle was poisoned. This was a refinement of the blow-pipe weapon—a refinement of barbarism.

A thickset man came in, agog, but stopped speaking when he saw Lannigan, gaped, swallowed hard, and then averted his face.

'Have you sent for the police?' asked Palfrey, levelly.

No one knew the man whom Lannigan had met. The hotel staff remembered that he had had a visitor before Palfrey; a small, thin American who had not given his name but had been directed to Lannigan's room. There was no other clue to the man's identity, and the police inspector whom Palfrey saw seemed pessimistic.

After making his statement, Palfrey went to his flat. Bitterly angry about the murder, he was unable to think constructively. He felt responsible: he knew that was nonsense, but the feeling remained. When he thought of the desperate life Lannigan had led during the war, of the narrow shaves, the frequent imminence of death, it was sharp irony to think that he had died like this.

Surely the police would find Manuel now. They had a detailed description of him, and presumably he was still in London. Whatever success they had, it was a matter for them; there was nothing Palfrey could usefully do in London; he had made all possible inquiries about Kennedy Lee——

There *was* one thing he could do: see Lee, tell him the whole truth and judge his reactions. He telephoned Brett. It was good to hear the firm, calm voice. Palfrey put the suggestion bluntly.

'I think it might be a good move,' said Brett, after reflection.

'You're a free-lance, Sap, and you're not obliged to consult anyone about what you do. If Lee is concerned, he already knows about your interest, and if he isn't, no harm will be done.'

'That's how I'd reasoned,' said Palfrey, relieved. 'I'll go straight away.'

'But you'll come back here tonight, won't you. I'd like to talk to you.'

Brett vouchsafed nothing more, but coming from the Marquis the request was tantamount to a command.

Palfrey telephoned the Merchester just before seven o'clock and asked for Lee.

It seemed a long time before a soft voice answered him— Diana's.

'This is Dr. Palfrey,' said Palfrey, in a friendly voice. 'Is Mr. Lee there?'

'I'm afraid he is out.'

'When do you expect him back?'

There was a pause before she said: 'To tell you the truth, Dr. Palfrey, I did not expect him to go out this evening. He had an urgent message and said that he would not be long, but he has been away for an hour.'

'I see,' said Palfrey. The girl sounded worried; or was that his imagination? 'Do you think I might come round in the hope that he'll soon be back?' he asked.

'Please do,' said Diana ; and this time there was no doubt of her eagerness.

She was dressed in a black evening gown, cut high at the neck and gathered there with a single diamond brooch. Her braided hair seemed as black as the gown. Her arms were white, perhaps a little too white, and certainly too thin. She greeted him eagerly as if he were an old friend. There were drinks on a small table and she indicated an easy chair and sat down herself. A quarter of an hour passed, and Lee did not return.

She stood up abruptly.

'Will you have more sherry?'

'Thank you,' said Palfrey, rising. He watched her pour out the drink, and imagined that she was glad to have something to do.

'You're worried, aren't you?' asked Palfrey.

She looked at him for a long time, and then slowly she nodded and sat down on the arm of her chair. Her eyes seemed to grow larger.

'Yes,' she said, 'I am very worried about him. He is in some danger; what it is I do not know. He—he was talking a great deal about you after we met. He said: 'If I knew Palfrey better, he'd be just the man.' I asked him what he meant, and he laughed and passed it off, but he seemed—obsessed by you. He actually took me to a newspaper office in Fleet Street and looked up some files in which there were stories about you. And then—the message came.'

'Who brought it?' asked Palfrey.

'A man whom I have met several times,' said Diana, leaning forward. 'I dislike him intensely.'

'Let me describe this messenger you don't like.' She stared at him without speaking; he thought that she caught her breath. 'About five-feet six, with a broad face, dark hair and a very white parting——'

'You know him!' she exclaimed.

Palfrey said: 'I've met him, Miss Leeming.'

'But—how did you know he——' she broke off in confusion.

'I made a guess,' said Palfrey. 'Do you know this man's name?'

'No.'

'We call him Manuel,' said Palfrey. He stood up. 'It's a long story, but I will give you an outline.' He watched her closely, his hopes rising. 'A friend of mine from America, a man named Lannigan, followed you and Kennedy Lee from Washington. Lannigan had a curious idea that you were not Diana Leeming but Valerie Grayson.' He paused again. She continued to stare at him, white-faced, but did not interrupt. In some disappointment, because he had not forced a more conclusive reaction, he went on: 'My friend came here when you and Lee were out the second day after your arrival. Manuel was here, and threatened him. He got away. He came to me and I told him that I would try to help. I wasn't much good,' he added, abruptly.

'Lannigan was murdered by Manuel in his hotel this afternoon.'

'Are you sure it was Manuel?'

'Yes,' said Palfrey. He held out his arm and pointed to the tiny tear in his coat sleeve. 'I was there. I saw and talked to him after Lannigan was killed.'

She walked to her chair and sat down; and this time her words took his breath away.

'Who do you say I am?' she asked.

He stared; she waited tensely.

'Lannigan thought you were Valerie Grayson,' he said, with an effort. 'You lived in Seattle and spent a lot of time in Florida and New York.' He stopped abruptly, although he was beginning to think that he knew part of the explanation of this girl's strangeness. He smiled at her, and then asked gently: 'Don't you really know who you are?'

She shook her head. 'No, no, not for sure.'

Palfrey got up and went towards her. He rested his hand on her arm and smiled much more cheerfully.

'Don't worry about that,' he said. 'I'm a doctor—but you know that. I might be able to help or to recommend someone who can. Loss of memory is common enough.'

'It's horrible.'

'But curable,' Palfrey assured her.

'I don't know that it is,' said Diana. 'I always feel that there is something dreadful, something I shall never want to remember, somewhere in the past. It's always near the surface of my mind, yet I can never recall what it is. It—it frightens me.'

'Does Lee know?'

'He knows—I'm not well.'

'But he doesn't know what it is,' said Palfrey. How strange this situation was! Why had she not told Kennedy Lee? Was there any truth in the story that they were going to get married?

'No,' she answered slowly, 'I haven't told him. I—daren't tell him. I shouldn't have told you, but it's with me all the time. It's not only that I don't know who I am, I don't remember anything that happened in my past—except—except the last few months. It seems ages. It——' She broke off again. She wanted to tell him everything, and yet was reluctant; afraid to unburden herself. Palfrey did not think it would be wise to press her then.

'I remember waking up one morning in a nursing home,' she said, suddenly, in a taut voice. 'I was in bed; nothing was

28

familiar. Most mornings I have that same feeling. I feel as if I belong somewhere else. It isn't until I see Kennedy that I forget that. You see—I love him so much.'

Palfrey did not speak.

'I did not meet him for some days,' went on Diana. 'I was tended by a nurse, who was friendly and charming and who told me that I was recovering from a serious illness. She told me my name—Diana Leeming. It did not seem right, but nothing seemed right, and I suppose that she knew what she was talking about. She told me that I had been in an aircraft which had crashed in Florida; that my parents had been killed, that I was being looked after by a family friend in New York. And I believed it; I couldn't remember an aeroplane, I couldn't remember a crash, but—well, she actually showed me a newspaper with the story in it, there was a photograph. It looked like me. I *had* to believe her.'

'Of course,' said Palfrey.

'After a few days I was allowed to go downstairs, and after two weeks I went out, meeting a few people whom I was supposed to know; but I knew none of them. The first man I met——' she broke off, and stared at him; and he thought that tears were about to well up in her eyes again. She forced them back. 'The first man I met was the "friend" who was looking after me. I disliked him on sight. I came to hate him!

'His name is Karen—just Karen. He was friendly; I wished there was no need for me to see him again, but he was often at the nursing home and when I left I went to live at his apartment. His wife lived there, there was no reason why I shouldn't stay, but all I wanted to do was to get away. If I had not hated him before, I would have done after I had come to know his wife. She was terrified of him. She shook whenever he spoke to her.

'I ran away,' went on Diana, 'but I had no money and he sent a man to follow me, a man who brought me back. He was always friendly towards me. He seemed to think that it did not matter what he did to his wife provided he treated me well. And, you see, I was completely lost. She—she wanted me to stay, too; she said that it was better since I had been there.

'Then, after a month, Kennedy came to the house. I was attracted to him from the first. He was to me too. That delighted Karen. He made an excuse to leave us together for most of the evening, and when Kennedy was gone he seemed very pleased with himself. I don't know why—I still don't know why.

'It was just afterwards that we had another visitor who called himself a psycho-analyst. Karen told him that I was suffering from acute depression and neurasthenia, and I suppose he was right. The doctor came just once. He told me that I must not try to remember anything that had happened in my past; it was better forgotten. I wish I could talk as he did,' Diana burst out, passionately. 'I wish I could let you understand the hateful suggestions he made, how he filled me with horror at something he said I had done. I can't forget it, it's with me all the time. I thought when Karen agreed to let me come to England with Kennedy that it would mean freedom, but it's no better, because the man you call Manuel is here.'

'Did you know Manuel in New York?'

'He worked for Karen,' said Diana, and caught her breath again. 'He is the man who followed me when I ran away. But— before I left New York with Kennedy, Karen talked to me. He said I had a chance to marry the man I loved, a man with a good position, respected, well liked. He warned me that if I ever told Kennedy the truth about myself, if I let him think that I did not really remember my past, that there would be no hope of—of a future with him. So I have kept silent. He told me that I must not let Kennedy know that I knew Manuel; and he made it clear that if I disobeyed him he would divulge the truth, that horrible unknown truth, that the doctor had hinted at.'

She took her hand from the mantelpiece, and her voice was so low-pitched that Palfrey only just caught the words.

'What could I do but obey?' she demanded. 'What could I do?'

THREE

PLIGHT OF A LADY

'NOTHING,' said Palfrey. 'Nothing at all.'

'Do you really think that?'

'Of course,' said Palfrey. 'You were quite right.' He wanted to break the tension, for, having told him so much, he felt sure she would fill in the details later. 'Don't you think we should have dinner now?'

'He isn't back yet,' observed Diana.

'He won't expect you to wait for him,' Palfrey assured her, and pressed a bell.

'Will you order?' asked Diana.

She gave a fleeting smile, picked up her bag and walked toward a door at the side of the room. She moved with grace, her dress trailing on the rich carpet. She went out and closed the door, and Palfrey lit a cigarette, thrust his hands into his pockets and swayed up and down.

As he thought of her story and of Karen and the 'psycho-analyst', he felt a sharp anger. He remembered, too, Lannigan's story of Little Whitey's fear. Now he had heard the story of Karen and the fear that he inspired. Was it jumping to conclusions to assume that Karen had frightened Little Whitey? Lannigan had not reached Karen, but might easily have done so through Kennedy Lee and Diana; it did not seem too much to assume that Lannigan had been killed so that Karen would not be named.

There was a tap on the door.

It was the floor-waiter with the menu. Palfrey ordered *hors d'oeuvres*, chicken, apple charlotte, and champagne; champagne might bring more colour to Diana's cheeks.

The man bowed and hurried out, and Palfrey stepped to the door and looked into the hall. No one was there. He tried to laugh at his fears, but it was not easy to laugh at Manuel or the man who had frightened Little Whitey. He looked at the telephone, then went to it and picked it up. He gave a Mayfair number, and did not replace the receiver, although the operator would have called him. He heard the ringing sound and began to tap his foot impatiently. When he was beginning to think that the man he wanted was out, he heard a deep voice which held a laughing note; in fact, the man finished laughing before he spoke, and that simple act did Palfrey good.

'Brian Debenham speaking,' said the other.

'Hallo, Brian,' said Palfrey. 'It's——'

Debenham's voice rose. 'Is that you, Sap?'

'Right in one,' said Palfrey. 'Are you particularly busy tonight?'

Brian paused. 'I—er, no, not particularly. Why?'

'You've read about the business at Brett Hall, haven't you? It's concerned with that. I wondered if you could pick up

Charles Lumsden or someone equally energetic and come along to the Merchester. Suite 14. Just to keep a weather eye open while I dine with a charming lady.'

'Yes, of course. I'll be right over.'

'And you might ring Scotland Yard and report that Kennedy Lee has been missing for some hours,' Palfrey went on. 'Tell them I'm with his girl-friend.'

'Right-ho,' said Brian.

He rang off, and Palfrey, feeling easier in his mind although a little rueful at what might be much ado about nothing, pondered over the girl's story and all its implications.

The waiter came back with another man and they laid the table. Diana came back. She had made up afresh ; he thought she looked brighter eyed, and her smile was certainly more natural.

'Have you been laughing at me?' Diana asked him, when they were alone.

'Certainly not,' said Palfrey. 'You've impressed me so much that I've sent for some friends to help. They'll be here soon.'

'How can they help?' asked Diana.

'Manuel might come back,' Palfrey said, 'and I don't feel like tackling him on my own.'

They were half-way through dinner when the telephone-bell rang.

'That's probably for me,' said Palfrey, jumping up.

It was Brian Debenham, who had brought Charles Lumsden with him and was waiting downstairs. Palfrey asked them to come straight up, then left Diana and met them in the outer room. It was good to see them.

Palfrey lost no time in outlining the situation. He described Manuel and told them that he thought it just possible that there would be trouble during the evening ; their task was to stay on guard.

'Here?' asked Debenham.

'One of you here, one outside,' said Palfrey. 'Do you mind?'

'Mind!' exclaimed Debenham, with a vast grin.

Lumsden chuckled.

'I'll toss you who stays here,' he said, and dropped into a luxurious easy-chair.

'You can fight that out between you,' said Palfrey, and went to join Diana. She was smiling, obviously relieved that the others were outside.

Nothing happened up to half past ten, and Kennedy Lee

had not returned. By then Diana was getting really agitated, and Palfrey was thinking that he would have to telephone Brett and tell him he would not be able to return to the Hall that night. He was on edge; Lee should have come back. It seemed likely now that something had gone seriously wrong.

Diana got up from an easy-chair and said abruptly.

'If—if he does not come back, what shall I do? I have no friends, no money, I do not even know who I am.'

Palfrey jumped up. 'I know what you'll do,' he said impulsively. 'You'll come with me to Brett Hall.'

Brett was alone; the rest of the party, Palfrey gathered, had gone to bed. The marquis's eyes lit up when he saw Debenham, his nephew, and Lumsden. His daughter, Hilda, had taken Diana upstairs. Brett poured brandy into glasses which were warming by a tiny electric fire.

'Some secret documents are missing from the Embassy in Washington,' he said. 'I can't tell you what they're about, they're as secret as that. It seems certain that Lee is concerned, that Lannigan's mission had to do with them indirectly, and it's just possible that Lee and his friends know where they are. Attempts might be made to prevent them from talking.'

Palfrey began to toy with his hair.

'Dark business,' he said, but there was a gleam in his eyes. 'We may have to get busy.'

Debenham gave a little, crowing laugh.

'Have I thanked you for sending for us, Sap?'

'More about the mighty atom?' murmured Lumsden.

'No,' said Brett, quickly. 'These aren't atomic power secrets, I can tell you that—and also that I've been asked to have Z.5 standing by. I wish I could tell you more, but you'll have to be patient. Now let me hear your story, Sap. I've told Hilda to keep Diana upstairs for half an hour.'

'Half that's gone,' said Debenham, anxiously.

'I can manage,' said Palfrey. He gave the essential points of the story quickly, and all three listened intently.

'Our key man is Karen,' he said, 'and we want to get information as quickly as we can about him. Other urgent matters are: getting Grayson over here to identify his daughter, finding out why she was kidnapped, whether Karen really wanted to use her to influence Kennedy Lee—which doesn't seem likely on the face of it,' he broke off.

'Why not?' asked Debenham.

'How could he know that Lee would fall in love with her and she with Lee?' asked Palfrey. 'Can we assume now that it's an official matter, Brett?' he went on.

'I think so,' said Brett.

'Are we in?' asked Debenham quickly.

'Are you free to help?' asked Brett, sitting down. 'I don't know where it will lead, how long it will take, what dangers you'll be exposed to. The work will have to be done, but whether three married men are the right ones to do it is a different matter.' Debenham frowned, and Lumsden stirred. 'You know the probable extent of the danger,' Brett added, 'and you will have to decide for yourselves whether you ought to take part in the work. I expect it will lead abroad, probably to America. What do you think, Sap?'

'It depends on its real importance,' said Palfrey.

'I don't think we can over-estimate that,' Brett told him.

Debenham said, 'I'm in!'

'I don't see why not,' said Lumsden.

Palfrey thought of Drusilla . . .

Then Hilda came in with Diana, who looked flushed and excited. She found a child-like enjoyment in new experiences, it seemed, and Hilda would make anyone feel at home. But she had not been in the room for ten minutes before she yawned, laughed a little guiltily, and agreed when Hilda suggested that they should go to bed.

Palfrey wondered whether she would sleep; he wondered whether he would: and whether there would be trouble during the night.

'Is there anything more to talk about?' Lumsden asked.

'I don't think so,' said Brett. 'Sleep on it.'

'Then I'll get back,' said Lumsden, jumping up.

'You're not going back tonight,' said Brett. 'Telephone your wife and tell her you've been detained.' He smiled as he looked at Lumsden, who seemed uncertain. Watching them, Palfrey knew what was passing through Brett's mind. If Lumsden were hesitant about staying away tonight, what chances were there that he would be able to give his mind to the task if he worked on it. The struggle between loyalty to a cause and loyalty to his family was apparent in Lumsden's eyes.

'Okay,' said Lumsden at last. 'Where's the telephone?'

It was half light when Palfrey was woken up. It must be early—certainly not six o'clock. The door had opened.

34

'Are you awake, sir?' That was Christian's voice. 'I'm sorry to disturb you, sir, but Mr. Lee is downstairs. I had a call from the lodge, and gave authority for him to be admitted.'

'Oh,' said Palfrey, blankly.

'I haven't disturbed his lordship,' said Christian, 'he sleeps so soundly early in the morning, but if you think it would be wise, I will call him.'

'No, not yet,' said Palfrey. He flung back the bedclothes. 'I'll be down in a couple of jiffs.'

Lee was in the morning-room, sitting in an easy-chair, smoking. He looked pale and haggard, and Palfrey thought he had been drinking heavily.

'What the devil have you been playing at?' snapped Lee.

'Just trying to help,' murmured Palfrey.

'Help be damned! You'd no right to take Diana away from London!'

'All right,' said Palfrey. 'I'm sorry. She's upstairs, quite safe, and she can go back with you a little later in the day. There's nothing to get het up about.'

'I think there is,' snapped Lee. He had not been drinking, Palfrey decided; like so many people in this affair, he was just frightened. 'And she's coming back with me now; she isn't staying here another minute. And I warn you not to interfere in *my* affairs, Palfrey.'

Palfrey looked at him with acute distaste.

'No,' he said, 'I won't—not willingly. What are you making such a fuss about. You left her alone without sending a message, and she was worried.'

'That's my business.'

Palfrey studied him dispassionately. Lee knew something which might be helpful; all doubts of that had gone. Palfrey was confronted by the urgent need to find out what that was, and he must decide quickly how best to get it out of the man. Clearly Lee's weakness was Diana.

'Take me to her,' commanded Lee.

'You're not seriously thinking of waking her up at this hour?' remonstrated Palfrey.

'I tell you——' began Lee, but broke off as someone tapped at the door.

'Come in,' said Palfrey, and Christian entered, carrying a tea-tray and biscuits. Palfrey's eyes brightened. 'That's the ticket,' he said. 'Thanks, Christian.' A thought flashed into his mind; he was really awake now. 'I'll pour out,' he said, and as Christian went into the hall, he added hastily: 'Oh, Christian, is his lordship——' he went out in the butler's wake and pulled the door to behind him. It closed with a bang, as if by accident. 'Wake Miss Leeming,' he whispered, 'take her into Lady Hilda's room, tell her there is nothing at all to be alarmed about, but that it's urgent.'

'Very good, sir,' said Christian.

Palfrey opened the door. 'But don't disturb him if he's asleep,' he added, for Lee's benefit, and went into the morning-room. He poured out the tea, and handed a cup to Lee, who took it with a grunt of thanks. 'Now look here, a couple of hours won't make any difference,' he said. 'You look as if you could do with a spot of rest yourself. Be reasonable ; let Diana get her sleep up, and go back to town after breakfast.'

'I'm going to take her with me now,' insisted Lee.

Palfrey shrugged. He uttered the next words casually, while calculating how long it would take for Christian to get Diana from her room to Hilda's. Both women would have to be woken up, that would take a little time. To be safe, he must keep Lee down here for ten minutes.

'Well, it's your responsibility. But if I were you, I wouldn't act as if you owned the girl.'

Lee started so violently that tea spilled into his saucer. He put the tea on the table, and more spilled over. Next moment, Palfry was astonished to find the man gripping the lapels of his dressing-gown, and shaking him!

Lee's face was livid.

'What did you say?'

'Eh?' asked Palfrey, standing limp. 'Say? I——'

'What do you mean by saying I think I own her?' cried Lee, and he snatched one hand away, then drove the clenched fist at Palfrey's face.

Palfrey moved his head, and Lee caught him a glancing blow, stinging but not hurting badly. Palfrey jabbed at Lee's stomach, and Lee winced and lost his grip.

'Before you break any necks, remember you might get hurt afterwards,' said Palfrey. 'Or hanged.' His voice was crisp, he seemed a different man, and Lee, taken aback, stared at him in bewilderment. 'Drink your tea, and try to behave like a human being,' ordered Palfrey.

Lee put out a hand for his cup, then snatched it away again, forcing himself to shout.

'Are you going to apologize?'

'Apologize for what?'

'Suggesting that I—that I'd—that I'd *bought* her.'

'Oh,' said Palfrey. 'Sorry. It was a figure of speech.'

'It was a queer way to talk.'

'But I am queer,' said Palfrey, with the lazy note back in his voice. The interlude, puzzling in itself, had served the purpose of gaining the necessary time for his trick with Diana. 'Everybody knows that,' he added. 'Why did it catch you on the raw?'

Lee did not answer, but sipped his tea.

'I intend to take Diana away with me now,' ne repeated.

Palfrey shrugged. 'All right, I'm not going to stop you if you insist on being tough.' He lit another cigarette and poured himself out more tea. Lee walked impatiently to the door. The ten minutes were nearly up, but it would do no harm to exacerbate the man's feelings further. When they got to Diana's room, she would not be there. With a little prompting, Lee would jump to the conclusion that she had either been taken away or had gone of her own accord. He was already close to breaking-point, and the shock might reduce him to such a state that he would talk freely under questioning.

When at last Palfrey tapped on Diana's door, there was, naturally, no answer.

They listened for a moment before Palfrey opened the door. He tip-toed in. Kennedy Lee followed.

Diana's clothes were folded on a chair near the wall—flimsy things—with one stocking on the floor by the side of the front legs of the chair. There seemed something pathetic in that. The bed was turned back, and obviously had been slept in. Lee started to speak, then stopped. He turned to Palfrey, and words seemed forced from his lips. 'If you've let them get——'

He broke off abruptly, but he had said just enough to give Palfrey the opening he wanted. Palfrey swung round on him and barked: 'Who might get her? Who would want to get her?' He took Lee's arm. 'What are you afraid of?'

'N-nothing.' Lee stared at the empty bed, and then suddenly crossed to the window. His hands were clenched by his side, his face was drawn and haggard. 'She can't have gone away,' he said hoarsely, 'she must be somewhere in the house. Look for her, can't you? Look for her!'

Palfrey joined him by the window and examined the paint. There were two or three small scratches, probably ages old.

'Someone's climbed in or out,' said Palfrey, and hoisted himself forward, looking down at the flower bed below the window.

37

'And there are footprints in that flower bed,' he added, withdrawing his head. 'I don't like this a bit. Stay here a minute.' He hurried out of the room, closing the door behind him.

Hilda's room was farther along the landing. He reached it, glanced over his shoulder and made sure that Lee was not looking out, then tapped lightly.

'Who is it?' called Hilda.

Palfrey said: 'Sap,' and went in.

There were twin beds in the room, and Hilda was sitting up in one, with a light wrap over her shoulders, Diana in the other, wearing a nightdress which had only shoulder-straps. The thought 'birth-mark' flashed into Palfrey's mind, and he smiled at Diana as he went forward.

There was a brown mark, like a rich brown stain, on the gentle swell of her right breast.

Said Palfrey: 'Diana, Kennedy's here, and quite safe. I don't want him to see you just yet. You told me that he was frightened, I want to find out why.'

'He's in the house!' exclaimed Diana.

'Yes, in your room. Don't worry—and as soon as I've talked to him I'll bring him in.'

'You won't,' said Hilda. 'You can take him downstairs. We won't get another wink of sleep, so we may as well get up.'

'Sorry,' murmured Palfrey, and patted her hand. 'Don't worry, and don't come out of the room until I give the all clear.'

Lee was standing by the window, looking out, and jumped when Palfrey entered the room.

'No sign of her, I'm afraid,' said Palfrey, convincingly. 'I've sounded the alarm; the grounds will be searched at once. Don't worry too much.'

'Don't worry! I'm distracted; you've let them get her! If she'd stayed at the Merchester this wouldn't have happened. It's your responsibility, Palfrey! You've got to find her.'

Palfrey said: 'I'll try. Who are these people you keep talking about?'

Lee said: 'They've nerve enough for anything. Palfrey, we've got to find Diana, she's in terrible danger. I'm not exaggerating—the danger couldn't be greater.'

'It looks like a simple case of kidnapping——' Palfrey began.

'Don't be a fool! Palfrey, that girl was placed in my care. I knew she was in danger. I had to bring her from America because she might—she might have been murdered at any

38

minute. It's got on my nerves so much that I hardly know what I'm doing. I thought we were all right here, until——'

He broke off, helplessly.

Palfrey said: 'Until Manuel came?'

Lee stared. 'Manuel?'

'A short, broad-faced, oily——'

Lee screeched: 'Do you know *him*?' He took a step forward and shook Palfrey's shoulders. 'What do you know about him?'

Palfrey said coldly: 'He tried to kill me yesterday afternoon, so I didn't exactly take to him. What is his name?'

'Ca—Casado,' said Lee, with a sob in his voice. 'I can't believe it, Palfrey. I can't think why he should attack you. But he's the man who's taken her away.'

'If she's really in such danger, tell me about it. I might be able to help.'

Lee looked at Palfrey with his haggard, bloodshot eyes, as if he were trying to make up his mind to talk. He reminded Palfrey vividly of Diana before she had unburdened herself.

Then Lee dropped into a chair.

'I oughtn't to tell you,' he said. 'Palfrey, I—I'm being blackmailed. Not—not for money. I haven't got to pay money, I've got to pay with—with Diana.'

Palfrey pretended that it made sense, and nodded.

'She was in an airplane crash nine months ago,' said Lee. 'Her parents were killed, she was left quite alone. I—I met her and fell in love with her. I don't know what there was about her, I—I just lost my head over her. She was staying with friends, some people named Karen.' He shivered; everyone seemed to shiver at the mention of the name Karen. 'Karen told me that she was in danger. He said he didn't know why. He said the only real safety would be if she left the States, and I—I arranged to get away from Washington. I'm not going back. I know I'm throwing up my career, but I can't help it. I can't take her back to the States, where anything might happen to her.'

'But what *is* this danger?' Palfrey demanded.

'I—I don't know much about it,' Lee said, with a catch in his voice. 'She was missing for two days in New York once. She came back, but—well, it proved how easily these people could get hold of her. I think—I think she knows something which could cause——' he broke off.

'A sensation,' murmured Palfrey.

Lee licked his lips.

'You'll have to take my word for it that it might be disastrous,' he said. 'I knew her for about four months in the States. All the time I was constantly being warned of the danger to her. Odd little things happened to her, nothing at all important, but——'

'What were they?' asked Palfrey.

Lee said: 'Well, we'd be dining and someone would bring a slip of paper to me with two or three words such as "Be careful" or "You're playing with dynamite". I could never find out who the man was who brought them. And I would get letters underneath my door, in my desk at the Embassy, with correspondence awaiting attention. It was a kind of nerve-war. I kept as much from Diana as I could, but she knew I was worried. Then I decided to throw everything up and bring her here. Karen kept saying it was the only safe thing to do.'

'Why did you leave her alone at the Merchester tonight?'

'I had a message from Casado,' said Lee, 'and I just had to go to see him. But he didn't turn up. That's the kind of thing that happens, Palfrey. I was all keyed up to talk to him, and when I got to the rendezvous he wasn't there. He'd left a message to say I was to wait. I waited until half past three, and still he didn't turn up. Then I telephoned the Merchester and learned that Diana had gone. I—I was never more terrified in my life. I rushed there, found your letter, and came straight down here.'

'Lee, I'm going to be brutally frank. Brett and I are always interested in any mystery which concerns the diplomatic service,' Palfrey said. 'And I've heard rumours about you that don't make pleasant hearing.'

Lee stood up, slowly.

'What—what do you mean?'

'You've been splashing money about everywhere,' said Palfrey, 'and you're not a rich man. You're mixed up with the mystery of Diana; you've allowed yourself to be victimized in at least one way. How have you got your money, Lee?'

There was a long pause; and then Lee muttered: 'If you think I know anything about the trouble at the Embassy, you're wrong. Someone told me last night there had been a spot of bother over some missing papers.' He tried to make light of it. 'They'll turn up; we're always getting scared when a bag gets mislaid—it's spy-mania. I know nothing about it beyond that, Palfrey.'

'Then where do you get your money?'

40

'For—for looking after Diana,' said Lee.

'Who pays you?'

'This man—Karen.'

'And he pays you enough to enable you to live as you're living?' marvelled Palfrey. 'He's so interested in Diana that he'll do that, but he won't do anything himself to help her. Does it make sense?' he demanded.

'It—it's true.'

Palfrey studied the man and, in spite of the improbability of the story, he was inclined to believe him.

'You've not been paid for anything else?'

'Damn you, no!'

'All right,' said Palfrey, and offered cigarettes. Lee's fingers were unsteady as he took one. 'What does Diana mean to you?'

'You—you ought to know.'

'A good income?' asked Palfrey, cuttingly.

Lee jumped up. 'That's an insult, Palfrey! I—I'm in love with her, I have been from the moment I first saw her. All I wanted to do was to help her. It just happened that I could help her this way, that's all.'

'Does Karen know what's happening over here?'

'I haven't told him yet,' said Lee. 'I thought I'd wait until I knew what Casado wanted.' He licked his lips. 'Palfrey, you're playing with me. Have you any idea where Diana is?'

'She's been here all the time,' said Palfrey. 'No, don't flare up! I had to find out what you knew, Lee. These lost papers are more important than you seem to think. Someone stole them. Apparently they were missed just after you'd left. A lot of people will jump to conclusions.'

'I didn't touch them!'

'I don't think you did,' said Palfrey, judicially, 'but I had to inquire. You'd better have a bath and shave before you see Diana.'

'You're not fooling this time? She *is* here?'

'Yes,' said Palfrey.

He convinced the man, who fell silent, looking heavy-eyed but less on edge. Palfrey took him to his bathroom, supplied him with a razor and shaving soap, and left him while he went downstairs.

Diana was already in the morning room. She was wearing a tweed suit of Hilda's which was much too big for her; and she reminded Palfrey rather of Hilary.

'Where is he?' she asked eagerly.

'He'll be another quarter of an hour,' said Palfrey.

Hilda came bustling in, fresh-eyed and important. 'Where is your young man, Diana?'

'He'll be down soon,' said Palfrey. 'Take Diana for a walk, will you?'

'That was my intention,' said Hilda. 'I *always* have a walk before breakfast.' She took Diana's arm and led her away, and Palfrey chuckled as he went upstairs and back to his room.

He heard nothing from Lee, and was surprised that he had not finished his bath. He waited for a few minutes, feeling hungry, but sure that Christian would see that breakfast was served early.

Brett usually woke up soon after seven; there would be quite a story for him.

Palfrey went to the bathroom door.

'Going to be long?' he asked.

There was no answer.

'Lee!' He raised his voice as he flung the door open. 'What——'

His voice trailed off.

Lee was in the bath, and his head was under water. There was no ripple of sound or movement.

FOUR

PALFREY GETS A TELEGRAM

DR. EBBUTT straightened up. He was an elderly, grey-haired man, a busy country practitioner, who always looked tired. But there was a sharp gleam in his eye as he looked at Palfrey.

'I don't like this,' he said.

'No,' agreed Palfrey, 'nor do I.'

Brian, who was standing by the window, said sharply:

'What do you mean?'

'I think we shall find that he died of narcotic poisoning,' said Ebbutt. 'The police will have to be informed.'

Brian turned and looked out of the window. 'That poor kid downstairs!'

Palfrey smiled bleakly.

'She isn't having a good time,' he agreed. 'But it might be better for her in the long run. I'm not sure that Lee would have

42

been good for her. I'd better go and break the news,' he added, and turned and went out of the room.

Diana was upstairs in her room, with Hilda. Palfrey was in the breakfast-room, with Brian, Lumsden and the Marquis. None of the cricketers who were staying at the Hall was up yet, for the day's match did not start until half past eleven, and for most of them it was a holiday.

No one spoke very much.

Palfrey had a vivid picture in his mind's eye of Diana when he had told her of Lee's death, gently but bluntly. He could remember the way she had caught her breath and turned away from him, standing rigid, with her hands clenched by her side. Hilda was just the right companion; he need not worry about the immediate future. But 'Diana Leeming' was penniless and without relatives, a visitor to a strange land. If she were really Valerie Grayson, much would be eased for her, but it would be some days before that could be proved. 'Can't anyone say something?' asked Brian, abruptly.

Palfrey smiled. 'Twice in twenty-four hours I've opened a door and seen a dead man, and as the first was certainly murder——' he shrugged his shoulders. 'Now start disagreeing,' he said.

'Go on,' encouraged Brett.

'Robbery at the Washington Embassy,' murmured Palfrey, as if talking to himself. 'Important papers stolen. An Embassy official with a lot of money he shouldn't have, thus becoming an obvious suspect. He tells a tall story about being paid to protect his girl—who in the wide, wide world will believe it? We might get evidence from Karen to confirm, but I don't expect it—by the way, are you getting in touch with New York?' he asked.

'I've arranged for that,' said Brett.

'Trust you.' Palfrey smiled. 'Karen will probably deny all knowledge of Lee's income. The evidence will mount up that Lee took the papers, was handsomely paid for the job, came to England with a fantastic-sounding pretext and, when he realized that he wasn't likely to get away with it, committed suicide.'

'It sticks out a mile,' said Brian.

'But supposing Lee was murdered. Supposing he had a drink or two when he was waiting for Casado, who didn't turn up.'

'Casado?' asked Lumsden.

'Manuel to you,' said Palfrey. 'Morphia takes quite a while to work. The time taken is according to the strength of the dose, of course. He drove down from London and reached here at half past five. On the empty roads, and driving as he would drive, it would take him no more than fifty minutes. He'd been here another fifty before the stuff took effect, so it's reasonable to assume that he took it in London. It wouldn't have worked quickly enough if he'd swallowed the dose after I'd talked to him. There's the one weakness in the suicide theory; in London he had no reason to think that he wouldn't get away with it.'

'Oh, yes, he had. He knew you'd taken Diana away,' objected Brian.

'A possible answer,' conceded Palfrey. 'But I'm not satisfied.'

'Why should they murder a man who was helping them?' asked Lumsden.

Palfrey laughed. 'My dear chap, he'd served his purpose by bringing Diana here. I think they wanted Diana abroad. We can work on that as a fairly reliable theory. But they wanted something else—to make it seem certain that Lee was the thief at the Embassy, hence his "suicide". No one will look further for the thief, no matter how far they look for the papers. And in Washington the real thief may be sitting pretty, ready to do his work again.'

A footman came in. If there were a criticism levelled against the Marquis, it was that he lived in a style almost forgotten; a relic, said many, of a bygone age. But so great were his services to the country that such criticism was always made good-humouredly; and he went on in his own way, unperturbed.

'Yes,' he said.

'For Dr. Palfrey, m'lord,' said the footman, and handed Palfrey a note on a salver. 'A telegram which has just been telephoned.'

Palfrey unfolded the slip of paper, and read. He widened his eyes, then frowned, and read again, aloud. *'Please try to meet me at Reading Station, eleven-twelve.'* He paused, and then added: *'Drusilla.* Hmm.'

'What's odd about that?' asked Lumsden.

Palfrey raised his eyebrows. 'Oh, nothing much,' he said, and glanced at the top of the paper. 'Handed in at Chester at half past eight. 'Silla got up early!' He laughed without amusement and passed the note over to Brett. 'Things are moving,' he said.

'What on earth are you making a mystery about?' asked Brian.

'My dear chap, didn't you hear? "Please try to meet me Reading Station 11.12—Drusilla." 'Silla would sign herself '*Silla*——'

'Draw it mild,' protested Brian. 'Someone else might have sent it for her.'

'Someone else did,' agreed Palfrey. 'Someone who didn't know that nothing, except real emergency, would make 'Silla ask me to miss today's game. If she had to spoil it, she would telephone me. But we haven't started yet,' he added. 'We now reach the real evidence. To reach Reading from Chester by eleven o'clock in the morning would mean getting up at an unearthly hour, for which there is no need at all. And'—he grinned—'she's travelling by car, anyhow!'

'So it's warming up,' Lumsden said, slowly.

'I don't know that I want it any warmer,' said Palfrey, with a sudden frown. 'I do know that someone would like to see me at Reading just after eleven——'

'And will be disappointed,' said Brian.

Palfrey touched his hair. 'Oh, I don't know,' he said. 'Some things do come before cricket. And if the interview is over quickly, I'll be back before lunch—well before lunch——'

'Why not cut out all argument, and telephone Drusilla?' asked Brett.

'There speaks the man of common sense,' said Palfrey, getting up. He put through the call from a telephone in a corner of the dining-room, and the girl who answered from the Hall exchange promised to ring back.

He stood with his hands in his pockets, looking out of the window onto a sunlit lawn.

The telegram took the edge off his anxiety for Diana only because it created greater anxiety for Drusilla. He felt quite sure that she had not sent it, and equally sure that Casado could not be working alone, since he had discovered that Drusilla was in Chester. It was just possible that Casado had traced her destination and not gone to Chester himself; but someone working with him had been in Chester that morning to send the wire, and therefore was unpleasantly close to Drusilla.

He turned. 'Can one of you go to Chester?' he asked.

'Yes,' said Brian and Lumsden, in unison.

'Thanks,' said Palfrey, appreciatively.

The telephone bell rang.

Palfrey lived what seemed an age of suspense while he moved to the telephone and lifted it.

'Hallo, darling!' said Drusilla.

'Oh, hallo,' said Palfrey, and furtively wiped his forehead 'How are you?'

'I couldn't be better,' said Drusilla.

'That's marvellous,' said Palfrey, beaming broadly. 'Absolutely wonderful! And everyone else up there?'

'Yes,' said Drusilla, with a laugh in her voice. 'And the answer, darling, is—no.'

'No?' echoed Palfrey.

'A most definite no,' affirmed Drusilla. 'At least'—a different note sounded in her voice—'I hope you'll be able to say no.'

'To you?' murmured Palfrey. 'Never!'

She laughed. 'Darling, don't sound innocent. I know what you're going to tell me about and I hate the thought of you doing anything. I couldn't be franker than that, could I?'

'Oh,' said Palfrey. 'No. You don't know quite everything. You're thinking of the spot of bother here, I suppose?'

'I didn't read about it until this morning,' said Drusilla. 'We had a day out yesterday and I didn't even glance at the papers. Hilary is really all right, isn't she?'

'She's jubilant,' Palfrey assured her. 'Darling, this is all very intelligent of you——'

'What's that?' asked Drusilla.

'I said it was very intelligent of you.'

'And what,' asked Drusilla, 'has that got to ao with it?'

'Eh?' asked Palfrey. 'Er—darling, I said how bright you were, and——'

'It isn't a very good line, is it?' asked Drusilla.

'Let's appeal to the operators,' said Palfrey, and called the Hall exchange. Then suddenly he heard her voice as clear as if she were standing opposite him.

'Is that better, Sap?'

'Much! Can you hear me now?'

'Perfectly. Darling, I've a horrible feeling that you're really trying to tell me that you're going away for a few days. I suppose if you must you must, but can't you wait until I come down?'

Palfrey's tension eased, and he sat on the arm of a chair, relaxed, blessing Drusilla, who, as he should have known, would not make difficulties.

'I'm not planning anything yet,' he said, 'but there is a bit of a mix-up and some of the people concerned seem to know where you are. You didn't send me a telegram this morning, did you?'

There was a moment's pause. Then: 'No,' said Drusilla, slowly.

'That's good. What you'd better do is to stay where you are until Brian and Charles come up for you. They'll leave here at once. I think it will be safer—you're all right there, aren't you?'

'I think so,' said Drusilla. 'I hoped I'd been imagining it, Sap, but—we were followed part of yesterday, and I think the house is being watched now. I'm not sure, I can't see the man properly, but it has worried me a little.'

'I see,' said Palfrey. 'Try and get a closer look at him, and don't worry. I'll see that you're all right. Don't leave the house until you've seen Brian or Charles.'

'All right,' promised Drusilla.

Palfrey nodded: 'Good-bye, my sweet.'

He stood up briskly as he replaced the receiver. Now all the others were looking at him, Brett as tensely as the younger men.

'Not good,' said Palfrey, crisply. 'I suppose the best way of making sure that Drusilla is watched, until you two get there, is to ask the Yard to talk to the Chester police.' He was tapping the receiver up and down. 'How much does the Yard know what's happening?'

'Ask for Superintendent Grice,' said Brett, 'he'll give you all the help you want.'

By ten o'clock, Brian and Charles were on their way to a big civil aerodrome outside Reading, and Palfrey hoped that by now the Chester police were keeping a special watch on the house where Drusilla was staying. Hilda had come downstairs and told them that Diana was asleep, but she seemed worried about the girl.

'You'd better see her, Sap,' she added.

'All right,' agreed Palfrey. 'I want Adamson to see her, too,' he added, half to himself, and went quickly to the telephone and called a Welbeck number. Adamson was a specialist on amnesia cases, and had a world-wide reputation.

At half past ten Palfrey went upstairs to see Diana, thinking that it must not be long before he telephoned Grayson, in

Seattle; Brett would look after the rest, including getting information about Karen.

Diana was lying on the bed in a darkened room. Palfrey went in quietly and closed the door.

'How can I help, Diana?'

'I don't think you can,' she said.

'I'm going to try,' said Palfrey.

'What use is—revenge?' she asked, wearily.

'Diana, listen to me. I want you to try to remember everything you can about Karen, his wife, the people who visited the apartment, and also everything you can about Manuel, whose real name appears to be Casado. It doesn't matter how trifling the thing might seem, put it down on paper. It will be good practice for two jobs,' he added, 'for telling me later exactly what you know and remembering what happened before you woke up in the nursing home. A friend of mine is coming out to see you about that later in the day. Will you give us both all the help you can?'

After a long pause, she said: 'Yes.'

'That's fine,' said Palfrey. 'And there's another thing, Diana. You and Kennedy are just two people caught up in a wicked business which spreads wide and might become really serious. Don't run away with the foolish idea that you're responsible for anything that has happened—the responsibility certainly isn't yours and it wasn't Kennedy's.'

'You're—so good,' she said, huskily.

'My dear, I'm simply telling you the truth,' said Palfrey. He squeezed her hands. 'Now I've got to go. I'll see you at luncheon.'

It was a quarter to eleven when he looked into Brett's study.

'Sit down, Sap,' Brett invited. 'How is she?'

'I've given her something to occupy her mind, and I think she'll be all right,' said Palfrey. 'Without relaxing the watch on Diana, can you lend me some useful fellows who can watch me when I'm in Reading?'

'That's easy enough,' said Brett. 'I sent for several men from London as soon as I knew about the trouble at the Embassy. I've told them to wait outside, to speak to you!'

Palfrey chuckled, and got up.

Two capable-looking men were already waiting in the hall, and Palfrey made arrangements with them quickly. They were to go ahead of him, approach Reading Station by a roundabout route, and watch the main entrance while he was at the

48

station. It should not be difficult, he said, and they showed no alarm at the prospect. Nor did Palfrey show alarm, but he felt keyed up. If what had happened at the London hotel was any guide, a single shot while he was sitting in his car might see the end of him.

Before he left, he slipped a small automatic and a spare clip of ammunition into his coat pocket.

Then he drove fast towards Reading.

Palfrey turned into the station yard and saw one of the men from the Hall standing in front of a big time-table. He did not see the other man, but for the first time since he had left the Hall he felt more confident although still on edge. He could not rid himself of the fear that this might be a simple scheme to bring him into the open so that he would make an easy target.

Trams were clattering on the road beyond the station approach, and a train was just steaming in. The brakes squealed as he neared the booking-office. A porter was standing just inside.

'Is there a train due at 11.12?' he asked.

'Just come in,' said the porter, laconically.

'Thanks,' said Palfrey. 'This is the only exit, isn't it?'

'It's the main one,' said the porter.

If someone were coming off the train to meet him, Palfrey reflected, they would surely come to the main exit. He waited, smoking, more at ease, but keeping a sharp look-out. He saw the other man from the Hall, who passed him without any sign of recognition; both men knew their job; that was a cheering thought.

Passengers were beginning to leave the station, and all seemed in a hurry. Two or three cars drew up in the station yard. A post-office van backed towards the pavement, a Carter-Paterson lorry rumbled over the cobbles. It was the ordinary station scene. No one approached him, no one seemed in the slightest degree interested in him.

For the first time it occurred to him that the telegram might have had a simple purpose—to lure him away from the Hall. He brooded over that. Another van, a local carrier's, backed into the yard near him, and the man at the back jumped down. Palfrey moved to one side. Someone pushed him. He thought it was deliberate, and swung round, but saw only half a dozen blank faces. There were more people nearby than there had been all the morning. The van-man let down the tail-board with a crash, and it missed Palfrey's foot by inches.

'Careful!' protested Palfrey.

'Sorry,' said the van-man, in turn, while another man inside the van threw out some sacking. The crowd was much thicker now, and Palfrey noticed that only men were about him, but he could not see Brett's men. He felt another surge of alarm—and then suddenly, before he could do anything to defend himself, three men seized him and pushed him on to the tail-board. Someone else grabbed him from inside the van. Next moment an evil-smelling sack was thrust over his head, and the man inside hooked his legs from under him.

The van started off. Palfrey struggled desperately, but his struggles only worsened his plight. He felt something heavy; a man was sitting on him. He felt a hand moving over his body. It reached his neck. There was slight pressure, but not enough to hurt him. He struggled afresh. He felt someone take his hand, which was free of sacking, and push up his sleeve. He tried to pull his hand away, but failed. He felt a sharp prick.

Palfrey came round in broad daylight. Although he was quite still, he had a curious impression that he was moving. There was a humming noise not far off—a low-pitched, regular hum of a high-powered engine. The odd feeling persisted, and he identified it. He was in an aircraft.

He lay there, half-conscious for a while, listening to that steady humming. A shadow loomed over him.

'Are you awake?'

He started, and opened his eyes wide, for it was a girl's voice. She was bending over him, a girl in her twenties, with big blue eyes and a snub nose and a mop of hair which dropped over her forehead.

'Do you want anything?' she asked.

'Drink,' said Palfrey. The word did not sound like drink to him, but she seemed to understand, for she bent down and took a bottle from a locker, poured water into a bakelite mug, and held it to his lips.

'Better?' she asked.

'Much,' said Palfrey. 'Thanks.'

'That's good,' she said.

It was a ridiculous conversation in the circumstances. Palfrey smiled weakly, then looked about him. They were in a small passenger aircraft, and he was on the floor between two rows of seats—there were eight seats in all, but the girl seemed to be the only other passenger. Why on earth had they left him alone with her?

He glanced at the door leading to the pilot's cabin. He could just see the pilot's head, and also that of a man sitting next to him. So he was not alone with the girl. He looked at the comfortable, upholstered seats, and tried to get up. The girl put her hands beneath his arms and helped him. He dropped heavily into a seat, and the pilot glanced round. The girl waved to him, but neither of the men came in.

'Would you like a cup of coffee?'

She took a vacuum flask out of the locker, poured steaming coffee into the bakelite cup, and then put in three spoonfuls of sugar from a small container. 'I'll stir it for you,' she said.

'It wouldn't be poisoned, would it?' asked Palfrey.

'You're rather cute,' she said. 'Most men would be tearing mad by now.'

'Why?' asked Palfrey.

'Don't you remember what happened?'

'That only makes me mad with myself,' said Palfrey.

'That's one way of looking at it,' said the girl, and handed him the coffee.

'Thanks,' Palfrey sipped. 'Where are we?'

'You'll have to find out later.'

'Oh, well.' Palfrey sipped again ; the coffee was piping hot.

'Satisfied with me?' she asked.

'No,' said Palfrey, emphatically. 'You're in the wrong setting. Open-air country girl, that's you.' She was wearing a thick tweed suit, which added to that impression. 'And if I judged from your eyes, which is a bad thing to do, I would say that at heart you're honest. No, I am not at all satisfied.'

She laughed again, rather attractively.

'I'm sorry about that,' she said. 'I'm really quite evil.'

'Oh, I know. The Devil lurks in charming places. But then, that's his best bet, isn't it? He offers you cream and doesn't tell you about the dry bread you'll get in the next world. Still, it's no use moralizing, I suppose, you being a hardened criminal.'

'It's no use at all.'

'You've got rather nice hands,' said Palfrey, glancing down. Then he looked at her throat. She wore a khaki shirt, open at the neck. 'And quite a lovely neck,' he added, and watched her flushing slightly. She sat farther away from him, on the seat opposite. 'Most connoisseurs like women with lovely necks,' he declared, gravely. 'Ask any portrait painter. Never mind the face, they say, give us the neck and we'll be satisfied. Curious, isn't it? That's what the hangman says, too, and as it means ten pounds to him every time, I suppose one can't be surprised.'

'Can't one?' asked the girl, coldly.

'Ever heard of the wages of sin?' Palfrey went on, pleasantly.

She snapped: 'What do you think you're doing? Trying to scare me?'

Palfrey narrowed his eyes.

'Can't I leave that to your employers?' he asked, and she flushed again. What was more interesting, she did look frightened.

'You talk too much,' she said, harshly.

'I'm sorry,' said Palfrey, and lapsed into silence. He took out a cigarette and lit it, then looked out of the window. There was no land in sight. All he could see was the shimmering, glistening sea and, to the starboard, a liner making its regal way. He made out three funnels, so it was probably a large, ocean-going ship. Presumably he was flying over the Atlantic. He felt sure he was being taken to America.

He was conscious of the girl's gaze upon him, and he smiled deliberately.

'There's nothing the matter with your nerve,' she said, with grudging admiration.

'Hallo!' exclaimed Palfrey. 'Are we friends again? What did you say?'

'You heard me.'

'Something about nerve,' said Palfrey. 'It doesn't do to get into a panic when some trifling thing goes wrong. What time are we due in the States?'

'You'd better guess again,' she flashed.

Palfrey chuckled.

'You're fairly cool yourself. We ought to get on well. Er—you *ought* to be feeling rather nervous, too,' he added, 'being all alone with a big strong man like me, and the ocean so far below.' He glanced at the door, and smiled more broadly. 'After all, this business has become a matter of a life for a life, hasn't it?'

'One shout and I'll get help,' she said.

He had annoyed her, and she got up and opened the door of the pilot's cabin. The noise of the engine grew louder, and, although Palfrey could see her lips moving, he could not hear a word she said. He ate heartily, looking out at the silvery ocean, feeling warm although they were at a fair height—ten thousand feet, he thought. The liner was out of sight now, and they were flying over this watery desert; and he still had not the faintest idea of where he was going.

He finished eating, brushed the crumbs from his coat and then faced the thought of Drusilla.

She, had come into his mind several times, and he had forced himself not to think of her. He could not even be sure that she was safe; they might have kidnapped her with the same swiftness and precision with which they had shanghaied him. On the other hand, there was no apparent reason why they should want Drusilla; he was the prize they coveted; with him out of England, surely they would leave her alone.

Then he glanced out of the window again, and sat up with a sudden shiver of excitement. To the starboard there was a faint grey haze, darker than the water. Land! He stared at it eagerly.

If they had crossed the Atlantic, it was likely that they were going to touch down in Canada, for a twin-engined aircraft of this size would not have a flying range sufficient to reach the United States from England. The haze grew darker; and soon he was able to see the actual coastline.

The girl came out of the pilot's cabin with a man whom Palfrey had never seen before.

'How are you feeling?' he asked, in good native English.

'Oh, fair,' said Palfrey.

'I'm told you've a lot to say for yourself,' said the man. 'I should save it.' He nodded to the girl, and to Palfrey there seemed something significant in the nod and in the smile which accompanied it. It flashed into Palfrey's mind that they were going to drug him again. He sat stiff and erect, prepared to struggle—and then the girl, standing behind him, dropped a close-fitting hood over his head. She pulled a string tightly round his neck.

Palfrey sat in semi-darkness, with light getting in at the sides of his neck and his cheeks, but unable to see anything of the land they were approaching. He felt the disappointment sharply; perhaps his emotions were out of all proportion to the importance of this move. One thing was evident: they were extremely anxious to make sure that he did not know where he was going to land.

He heard one of them sitting down in the seat opposite him.

'Don't make a fuss,' said the man, 'and we won't hurt you.'
Palfrey did not answer.

'So he's stopped talking at last,' said the man. He laughed
with satisfaction, and then said something to the girl, who
laughed in turn. Before long they were talking idly, making
small talk as coolly as if this were an everyday occurrence.
Palfrey, recovering a little from his disappointment, listened
intently and tried to gather something significant from what
they were saying, but it was only chatter.

He did not know how long they kept him there with the hood
on, but he was feeling hot and uncomfortable when at last he
felt cool fingers on his neck. It was the girl, who took the hood
off, rolled it into a bundle, and stuffed it into the pocket of her
coat.

The sun was much lower in the west; but the light was still
good. They were well inland, flying over meadows and ploughed
fields. He could see farm buildings dotted about the country-
side, but they revealed no particular characteristics from the
air. He did not think he was in England; the fields were much
too large. The farm buildings became less frequent. He saw a
series of irrigation canals, golden in the setting sun. Here the
land was all grass, and cattle were grazing in big numbers.

The man walked past him. Casually the fellow took out an
automatic, looked at it, weighed it in his hands and then put it
away. He did not look at Palfrey, but Palfrey took it for
a warning. He touched his pocket; but the gun he had taken
from the Hall was not there. He was wearing the same Norfolk
jacket and trousers, the same dark brown shoes.

They began to lose height.

He glanced out again as the land seemed to come nearer.
There was a house at one end of a large, dark field. The light
was still good enough for him to see the grassland about the
field, which was surrounded by water, although they had passed
the irrigated area. From a greater height he would have thought
this field ploughed, but now he saw that the soil was almost
black. It puzzled him because of the contrast of the bright
green all about it, and the riotous flowers which grew near the
house.

Not far from that building was a scattered collection of huts
and a small hangar.

The aircraft circled to land. Two or three people came out
of the house and stood watching. Two of them waved, then all
three turned and went back into the house.

54

They touched down, and the man said: 'Get a move on, Palfrey.'

FIVE

BLACK EARTH

THE aircraft had landed on a concrete strip which shone white against the dark earth on either side. The soil was caked, as if it had been heavily watered and then baked by the sun. It gave way under their feet, and as the girl walked ahead she raised tiny clouds of dust at her heels.

A tiny stream separated this dark earth from the flower garden. They walked across a small stone bridge, the girl still in front, the man walking behind Palfrey. None of them had spoken since they had left the aircraft, and two mechanics who had been waiting near the landing strip had greeted the man and the girl but ignored Palfrey. He had learned one more thing, however: the girl's name was Löis.

Small, bright lawns, bordered with flower-beds, made an even sharper contrast with the black earth. Palfrey wished he could get the thought of that out of his mind. It reminded him of the ashy-grey soil of parts of the Scottish Highlands and of Dorset—of land where fir trees grew, and gorse and fern; but out of that dark field nothing grew, not even grass.

Light streamed from the hall, but there was no one waiting to meet them.

Palfrey heard the hum of machinery, and thought it was an electric generating plant. There was a small brick building at the back of the bungalow; it was probably housed there. Then he glanced to the right, at one wing of the bungalow, and saw several white-smocked figures inside a brightly-lit room, and the paraphernalia of a laboratory. He caught just a glimpse as glass and metal glittered, of huge retorts on a long bench.

Outside the porch, they waited, as if they must have permission before they went in. Palfrey turned to look at the darkening earth. They had flown in from the north-east, and it was darker over the field than beyond the bungalow. He could see one white-smocked figure close to a window, a thin-faced man, wearing glasses, peering intently at something in his hand.

The man turned and moved away.

'Okay,' he said, and went inside again.

The girl now walked by Palfrey's side and the man behind him. It was as normal a walk as Palfrey could have expected anywhere—no hint of danger, no suggestion of a threat, except the remembered one of the gun in the man's pocket.

The door was open.

Palfrey paused on the porch. 'After you,' he murmured.

The girl laughed and preceded him. Since she had talked to the man, she had been much more composed, although Palfrey remembered how his talk had affected her. If he could talk to her when she was on her own, she might begin to worry—and a worried woman was likely to give information away.

The passages, which ran right and left, were wide and cool.

'Isn't the pilot coming?' asked Palfrey.

'Later,' said the man behind him. 'Come along.' He took Palfrey's arm and led him to the left. The girl had gone.

'That door,' said the man, pointing to one on the right.

Palfrey opened it, and stepped into a pleasantly furnished bed-sitting room, with a divan beneath the window, several easy-chairs, a hand-basin in one corner.

'You ought to be comfortable here,' said the man, and laughed, as if it were a brilliant sally.

'Very, thanks,' murmured Palfrey.

'And don't forget—no tricks,' said the man.

He went out and closed the door. Palfrey heard the key turn in the lock.

He went slowly to the window and looked out. All he could see was meadowland, clear in the bright afterglow. Had he woken up in this room, he would have assumed that he was in England.

He inspected the glass more closely. Then he smiled ruefully. There was a faint yellowish tinge to it, not noticeable except when one looked at a certain angle, but it told him that it was toughened glass which would not be easy to break. He thought it was very thick. The window did not open, and was set in a metal frame.

He turned back and looked round the room, trying to remember what it was that had been strange about the outside of the house. It dawned on him suddenly ; there had been no chimneys! And there was no fireplace in this room ; of course there would be no fireplaces anywhere, as there was no vent for the smoke.

How many English houses were there without chimneys?

He began to look more closely about the room, opening the hanging cupboards and the drawers, turning on the water—one tap ran hot immediately—and making a thorough search. Nothing indicated where he was.

Without thinking, he took out a cigarette and lit it.

He had smoked it half-way, when he heard a scream.

It came so suddenly out of the silence that it sent a shiver up and down his spine. It was just one high-pitched scream; and it seemed unnatural.

He jumped up, his heart racing.

Someone was running along the passage!

They were quick, nervous footsteps, as of a woman in flight. They passed his door. He thought he could hear the woman gasping for breath—but, as suddenly as they had begun, they stopped.

Nothing happened for ten minutes.

He went to the window and looked out.

All he saw was a patch of dark green, and it was *not* the field beyond. There was a shutter in front of the window. He had not heard it slide into position, but the light was good enough to tell him that something had closed down outside. He was locked in; and even if he managed to break the glass he would not be able to get past that shutter.

He shivered uncontrollably. The silence was getting on his nerves. He wiped his forehead; it was cold and damp.

'This won't do,' he said, aloud.

'Won't it?' came a man's voice.

Palfrey jumped, but there was no one in sight; the room *was* empty. The voice seemed to have come from the passage; he realized then that he was being watched; unseen eyes could peer at him.

He must keep his nerve steady.

A thought flashed into his mind; he could give as good as he got for a while.

'No,' he said.

'You'll find out,' said the man.

It was not the passenger of the aircraft; it was a strange voice, but the English was good, and free from accent.

'We've all got a lot to learn,' said Palfrey, as cheerfully as he could. 'Things like this seldom succeed.'

'Don't they?'

Palfrey spoke again; always he was answered by a cryptic

question; the unseen speaker gave nothing away. Palfrey hardly realized the effort which it had cost him to maintain that eerie conversation, until he stopped and found he was sweating freely. His hand went to his cigarettes. He stared at the case, seeing just three, and he had no idea how long they would have to last him. He shut the case with a snap and looked round again. If there were something to read it would'help.

'Bored?' asked the man.

'Well,' said Palfrey, with an effort, 'you aren't particularly entertaining, you know.'

'Try some music,' said the man.

Palfrey stared at the door——

Suddenly music filled the room. It was a symphony orchestra playing a melancholy piece. Palfrey did not recognize it, but classified it as Wagnerian. It grew louder, too loud. He looked about the room to find out where it was coming from, and for the first time he saw a small hole in the wall, not unlike a microphone. It was so well disguised that he had missed it first time, for it looked like part of the mottled wallpaper. The music was coming from there; as he pressed his ear close to it, it was deafening.

He backed away.

It was deafening wherever he sat, and continually grew louder. His head began to sing. This was a trick to unnerve him; so was the scream and the running footsteps. He was being hoist with his own petard with a vengeance; he had started to try to shake the freckled girl's poise, and now they were working on his.

He lay down, making himself move in leisurely fashion. As his head touched the pillow, he realized what was happening. Two gramophones or radiograms were playing, and each a different piece of music, one against the other; it *must* be part of a deliberate attempt to break his nerve. He must not forget that.

The music grew louder and louder.

'I must lie here,' thought Palfrey, desperately. 'I must lie here. I——'

The noise stopped.

His head seemed to lift from his shoulders. The intense silence was worse than the noise, for what seemed a long time.

What would they do next?

He sat up and began to whistle.

He stopped whistling; *but the whistling went on.*

58

Without realizing it, he had been whistling *The Londonderry Air*. Someone else had taken it up, and did not stop for a long time.

Music, real music, soft at first, floated into the room; it was *The Londonderry Air* on a gramophone record. It grew louder. Louder still; they were going to put him through that ordeal again..They were going to keep at him until he could stand it no longer; they were going to break his will-power; they were not going to just try, they were going to do it. He knew that he would not be able to hold out if they went on like this.

Why, why shouldn't he give them what they wanted?

The thought was hardly in his mind before it obsessed him. Their scheme was straightforward enough, and he was helpless; so it would be better to pretend that they had succeeded, so that at least he would know what next they had in their repertoire. They probably wanted to interrogate him, and this was to induce him in the proper frame of mind.

He shouted: 'Stop it! Stop that row! *Stop it!*'

The tune went on and on.

He stood staring at the wall with his hands raised and clenched. He shouted again, and then suddenly bent down and picked up a chair, raised it above his head and flung it at the wall. Nothing stopped the tune. He had started to feign frenzy —now it was perilously close to the real thing.

'Stop it! Stop it! Stop it!'

The music stopped.

He dropped what was left of the chair and wiped his forehead with the back of his hand. He was hot; he felt suffocated. He was trembling, too, but he had saved himself from being completely subjugated by the frenzy that had seized him, and stood away from the wall.

Then he jumped! The door was open, and the girl of the aeroplane stood there, smiling.

'So you couldn't take it,' she said.

Palfrey licked his lips.

'You'd better come with me.'

She was alone, but quite unafraid; it was strange that they let her be with him alone so much. He took a step towards her as she stood aside to let him pass.

As he entered the passage there was another ear-splitting scream.

Even the girl jumped.

Palfrey gasped: 'What—what was that?'

'You'll find out,' she said. She looked at the door of the room opposite, and Palfrey thought he could hear someone muttering or groaning; it made a gibberish which no one could have understood.

She led him to a room at the end of the other passage. It was in exactly the same position as 'his' room. She tapped on the door, and a man called: 'Come in.'

She opened the door.

'I've brought him,' she said, and stood aside for Palfrey to enter.

Palfrey steeled himself to face any shock as he went in, but his effort availed him nothing. He felt sure of one thing: that a man would be in the room, but it was empty. He swung round on the girl, but she pulled the door to, he saw her smile and fancied that he heard her laugh. That was all.

He began to tremble.

A man *had* said come in.

An invisible man——

Palfrey turned and flung himself against the door, beating at it with clenched fists and calling out; and there was a hysterical note in his voice. One half of his mind was warning him that he was being watched—if he showed any signs of recovering his self-control, the situation would only get worse; the other half was warning him that he must keep himself mentally calm and alert.

He continued to beat at the door, until suddenly he realized with a shock that he was making no noise. He was striking hard rubber. He drew back, gasping for breath, staring at the door and feeling his heart thumping. The only sound was his breathing.

He shivered uncontrollably.

One of the worst things about this place was the uncanny quiet between storms of noise. He pushed his hand through his hair and stood quite still, but soon he began to shiver again and he could not stop himself. Vaguely, he realized why: the room was bitterly cold.

He started to beat his hands across his chest. He walked round quickly, because there was no room to run, beating his arms but unable to keep the cold out. It closed about him, and his forehead and neck became clammy-cold. It began to hurt to breathe. The temperature must be far below zero.

Soon he began to gasp for breath; he could not breathe if he kept moving; and unless he did move he would freeze.

60

The need to breathe won the day. He stood still. The cold gripped his legs and arms and he began to shiver uncontrollably. These people could make him do what they wanted; they were sapping his will-power and now his physical strength. He had thought he could outwit them, but they were ready for all the tricks he could try to play.

This was a cold-room—a refrigerator—not intended for this, but cunningly adapted.

His teeth were chattering and when he raised his hand it was shaking violently.

He lost count of time.

He did not notice a door open.

It was opposite the one through which he had come in; he had not known that it existed, although had he looked closely he would have seen it. The first he knew of the opening door was a man standing by his side, gripping his elbow. He knew the man was doing that, but could not feel the pressure of his fingers. He was led towards the door, walking stiffly. The man did not speak. They entered a smaller room, with pipes running about the plain grey walls a little above Palfrey's head, but he did not notice the colour of the walls or the pipes. The man released him, and went out of another doorway. Both doors closed.

It was as cold in here as it had been in the other room; perhaps it was even colder. Palfrey moved, saw the pipes and the walls vaguely, but gave them no thought. He heard a hissing noise; and then water began to spray over him from the pipes; of course, it reminded him of the showers in any club dressing-room. Jets were coming in all directions so that no matter where he moved he could not get away from it. In a few seconds he was soaked to the skin; and he was colder even than before.

He tried to move, but could not; his clothes were stiff, he heard his trousers cracking as he moved his knees. So his clothes were freezing on him.

His mind began to wander.

His thoughts were of other days. . . .

He had been cold like this, lying in the open in the wild mountains of Yugoslavia in mid-winter. He had spent nights in the Alps hiding from the Germans. He had known what it was to fight the awful encroachment of weariness, to feel the cold dragging at his eyelids, to force himself to keep awake but fail . . .

He had known what it was like to plunge into an ice-covered

lake and swim for his life, with men on the banks firing at him, and a tiny motor-boat rushing towards him to pick him up.

He did not know that the water stopped and that two men came into the chamber wearing oilskins. They lifted him between them and took him into another chamber like this one, but without any pipes and with one chair. They sat him down and went out and left him.

His clothes were frozen stiff when he sat down; he did not notice that gradually they were thawing, and the water ran on to the chair and the floor. But at last he realized that he was waking up. He blinked and stirred. He sat still, shivering again, watching the pools of water gathering at his feet.

Soon he was warm. He sat up. He could move freely enough now. Water was dripping from his hair, but it seemed like sweat; it was as warm as sweat. He ran his hand across his forehead and tried to get up. He staggered, gripped the back of the chair, and stood quite still.

It *was* warm.

It was getting hotter!

He looked about the blank walls wildly. Nothing came from them, although he remembered the water hissing out of the pipes in the other room; no, there were no pipes here, nothing at all that he could see to explain the warmth. But when he looked down he saw that the water on the floor was steaming; his clothes were steaming, too, as if he were standing in front of a great open fire. This was no accident; they were deliberately baking him. First the cold chamber, then the steam heat.

He took off his coat. It hung limp and steaming in his hand. He draped it over the back of the chair. His shirt was much drier now; so were his trousers. He took off his tie. The neck of his shirt lay limp. Breathing in the heat became as difficult as it had been in the cold. The heat seemed worse than the cold. It was as if he were standing in front of roaring furnaces, blast furnaces which sent out a white-hot glow, as if his skin were being shrivelled up. He could feel the heat in his eyes like burning sand. He felt a great weariness again; he must close his eyes, close his eyes, close his eyes . . .

A door opened, men came in, and he was carried out.

Palfrey lay on a settee in a room like that into which he had first been shown. There were two men in the room, neither of whom Palfrey had ever seen. One sat at a writing-table, well-dressed, good-looking, in a thin, aquiline fashion; a man with keen grey eyes, a man with a sense of command. The other stood in front of him, short and thickset.

'He shouldn't give any trouble now,' said the man, who was standing up.

'How did he behave?'

'He began to crack with the music.'

'Music,' murmured the other, with a faint smile. 'That wasn't very long for Dr. Palfrey, was it?'

'You can never tell.'

'Yet I expected him to last longer than that.' He picked up a cigarette and lit it. 'Did you put him through the hot and cold chambers?'

'Yes, and I'm glad they're free now,' said the short man. 'We've plenty of stuff ready for processing.'

'He probably thought the rooms for his special benefit. All right, leave him to me.' The short man went out and closed the door.

The man at the table picked up a pen, and began to make entries in a loose-leaf book. There was little sound in the room. He smoked all the time, and lit three cigarettes from the butts of others before Palfrey stirred. Palfrey looked about him. He did not see the man at first; when he did, he riveted his gaze upon him. Memory began to come back.

The bungalow, the quiet room, the sudden noises, the cacophony of music, the girl, the cold, the heat; it all came back. Palfrey closed his eyes. He was suddenly aware of hunger and thirst; they began to obsess him. He forced himself to think of other things. They had put him through his worst ordeal and now they would expect him to talk freely, but—he did not know what they would want him to talk about. He opened his eyes again, and saw that the man was looking at him.

'Good evening, Dr. Palfrey.'

Palfrey opened his lips. 'Who—are you?'

'Dr. Mallory,' said the man at the desk.

Palfrey lifted his head; it was painful and difficult.

'I don't think—we've met.'

'We hadn't, until tonight,' said the man who called himself Mallory. 'Sit up.'

Palfrey tried. His arms and legs were like water; he had no control over them. Three times his fingers slipped on the edge of the settee, and he tried again. Then he got a grip. He eased himself upwards.

'Dr. Palfrey,' said Mallory, 'you are a very sick man. We

have been trying to help you, but you are an extremely difficult patient.'

Palfrey looked at him blankly; what was he talking about?

'I—I'm sorry,' he said.

Mallory smiled. 'You were brought here two weeks ago,' he said, 'and since then you have been violent—extremely violent. You have been screaming and raving, as if you were having most unpleasant nightmares.'

Palfrey gulped. 'Yes,' he said. 'I was.'

'I have handled other cases similar to yours,' said Mallory, 'some with fair success, some without any success at all. The failures, I am afraid, are most disappointing. It appears that these hallucinations of nightmares return, and get much worse. What form did yours take?'

Palfrey tried to think clearly; this man was telling him that he *had* been dreaming, that nothing had really happened to him. He looked down at his trousers——

He started.

The creases were razor-edges. He remembered how they had hung wet about his legs and then frozen stiff and then been melted, and they should be looking like misshapen barrels, but they had been pressed and were just as he had worn them that morning—or the morning when he had left Brett House. He fingered his coat. What he could see and feel of it was normal enough. He glanced down. He had taken off his tie, but it was knotted about his neck neatly enough now.

'You *have* been dreaming,' Mallory assured him. 'I think it all started when a man named Lannigan came to see you at Brett Hall,' Mallory said, casually, and he glanced at his nails. 'Do you remember Lannigan?'

Palfrey did not answer.

How could he deal with the situation? He had made grandiose plans in the room with the music; he must outwit these people by *pretending* that they had achieved the results they wanted.

'Palfrey!'

'I remember Lannigan vaguely,' Palfrey said, and closed his eyes and ran his hand across his forehead. 'I'm so tired, and thirsty, I—I can't think.'

'Tell me what you remember of Lannigan,' said Mallory, 'then I will get you something to eat and drink, and afterwards you can rest for as long as you like.'

'I—I remember him running with a girl in his arms,' Palfrey

said. He closed his eyes again, as if with the effort of remembering. He wondered for a wild moment whether it were possible that Mallory really thought he had lost his memory—as Diana had done. No, that was nonsense! It was half-way to admitting that he might have dreamed his ordeal.

'Go on,' said Mallory.

'Someone had hurt the girl,' Palfrey said. 'She—she was the Bretts' granddaughter. Brett!' He opened his eyes and gazed wildly at Mallory, burning to impress the man. *'Brett!'* he repeated, 'he——'

'Let me help you a little,' said Mallory, softly. 'You were playing cricket at Brett Hall when Lannigan came, and he told you a story about a girl who had lost her memory——'

'No, that's not right,' objected Palfrey. 'She had been kidnapped. It wasn't until I saw her that I knew she had lost her memory.'

'So she told you,' murmured Mallory.

Palfrey said: 'Yes, she told me——'

'About Karen?' The name was uttered softly.

'Yes,' said Palfrey. 'But if you know——'

'I know a little,' said Mallory. 'Go on, Palfrey.' When Palfrey did not answer at once, he shrugged his shoulders. 'You are only making it worse for yourself,' he said impatiently. 'What are you frightened of? Do you think——' he broke off abruptly, and laughed. 'You think you're still in the bungalow, don't you—where you were found. That was a long time ago, Palfrey; you were rescued. Brett sent men after you, he traced the aeroplane. You *are* ill, you know.'

'I suppose I am,' said Palfrey.

'But you doubt it. What will convince you?'

'If—if I could see Brett,' said Palfrey, hesitantly.

'He was here this morning, and he will be here again this evening,' said Mallory, glibly, 'but it is much better for you to tell me what you remember now. If you waited for Brett, I am afraid you will have another relapse. One of my patients was so possessed by his dreams that he broke out of his room, went downstairs to the furnace and was severely burnt. So severely that he did not recover. Apparently he had been dreaming that he had been thrust into a furnace——' he shrugged his shoulders. 'Do you want anything like that to happen to you?'

'You seem very sure that it might.'

'I am sure,' Mallory told him.

So the man was going to insist on the story of lost memory; his threats were all going to be by implication.

The telephone on the table rang sharply.

'Excuse me,' said Mallory. He picked up the receiver. 'Dr. Mallory speaking,' he said. 'Who . . . Yes, yes, send him in !' he exclaimed, and for the first time he showed some signs of excitement. He replaced the receiver and jumped up. 'This is really good news, Palfrey! Brett has called again. When you've seen him you may find that your mind will clear and you will be rid of the trouble.' Palfrey stared at him, a sickening suspicion in his mind.

He *had* forgotten——

There ·was a tap at the door, and Mallory hurried to it, opened it and said heartily: 'Come in, my lord! You've timed this visit nicely!'

SIX

END OF A NIGHTMARE

HAD Palfrey seen the man who came into the room in the street, he would have taken him for Brett without hesitation. He was of Brett's height, looked remarkably like him, and had the same white hair, brushed back in waves from his high forehead. He smiled like Brett, and came forward, with his hand outstretched.

'Sap, my dear fellow, how are you?'

'Er—getting along,' said Palfrey.

'We've been really worried about you,' said 'Brett'. 'You must have had a rough time for it to have affected you like this.'

Mallory interrupted.

'He seems to think that I have sinister motives!'

'Sinister?' echoed 'Brett'. He patted Palfrey's shoulder. 'I assure you that you needn't worry about Mallory,' he said, 'he's the only man who's been able to help us. But for him, I think Drusilla would have drooped until she died. Adamson wasn't able to help at all.'

'Oh,' said Palfrey.

'Sit down,' said Mallory, and offered cigarettes. 'Perhaps if I go on with the discussion now, Palfrey will be less hostile. Unless my patient is in sympathy with me, it is extremely difficult to work.' He smiled as he offered the man who looked like Brett a cigarette. 'Brett' sat down. He did so without first hitching up his trousers at the knees. It was a trivial thing, but it settled Palfrey's mind once and for all: he was not the Marquis. Palfrey could see traces of careful make-up. This man had been near him only for a moment, then had gone to the chair some yards away so that he could not be too closely inspected.

'Now, Palfrey,' said Mallory, 'you remembered Lannigan and Diana Leeming, didn't you? And Lannigan told you a story. If you will concentrate on trying to remember what he told you——'

Palfrey said sharply: 'I can't think of anything until I've had something to eat and drink. Starvation isn't part of the cure, is it?'

'Brett' and Mallory exchanged glances; that move had taken them by surprise. Mallory looked impatient, but lifted the telephone and ordered some coffee and sandwiches. Palfrey thought it better not to be too obstinate, and 'remembered' Lannigan's story; nothing Lannigan had told him could be unknown to these men.

A girl brought in a laden tray.

Palfrey ate the sandwiches with relish; the coffee eased his throat and seemed to pour new strength into him. He could think more clearly. He was not surprised when 'Brett' glanced at his watch and said that he would have to go.

'I hoped you could stay longer,' said Mallory.

'I'm sure Palfrey understands,' smiled 'Brett', and came across and shook hands. 'Place every confidence in Mallory,' he said, 'you needn't worry after that.' He turned, as if he were anxious to avoid close scrutiny, and hurried out of the room.

'Now, Palfrey,' said Mallory.

Palfrey had decided that he could safely tell practically the whole story—Lannigan's, Kennedy Lee's and Diana's. There was surely little about it that this man did not know. Mallory sat back, with his eyes narrowed, occasionally made notes and, after Palfrey had been talking for the better part of an hour, he rubbed his hands together with satisfaction.

'This is very good indeed,' he said. 'We'll soon have you right, Palfrey. Now, there's one reticence, I think—you haven't been really frank about what Kennedy Lee told you.'

'I've told you all I remember,' Palfrey said.

'I'm sure there's something else,' said Mallory, 'something

which will come back if you concentrate enough.' He waited, and Palfrey looked at him blankly, for he knew nothing more about Kennedy Lee. Did the man seriously think he had withheld something?

'Well?' asked Mallory.

Palfrey shook his head.

'Then we'd better leave it for now,' said Mallory. 'Listen to me, Palfrey. You're very tired. You've been through a severe ordeal, and you've been unconscious for a long time. You'll probably feel strange for a few days, and you may have absurd dreams, but they shouldn't be serious now. Just concentrate on trying to remember everything that Kennedy Lee told you. Once you get that out of your mind, I feel sure you'll be really well again. Do you understand?'

What would they do to try to make him 'remember' what Kennedy Lee had never told him?

Palfrey dreamed many dreams.

They were not nightmares; they had the breath-taking beauty and mock-reality of hallucinations; they elated and exhilarated him. Pipe-dreams! Of beautiful women in a fair garden, women who were all Drusilla and yet were nothing like Drusilla; wild, Rabelaisian fantasies which seemed quite real.

He woke when it was daylight.

The dreams faded and yet he remembered them and he wanted more of them. He felt a curious sense of depression. There was something for which his mind and body craved, and all he could think of were those phantoms of his sleep.

Suddenly the sense of depression was lifted; he realized the truth. It flashed into his mind so vividly that it almost blinded him. *Hashish* made a man dream like that; he had been drugged. Mallory had told him that he would dream, knowing full well that he would.

They were trying to take his senses away from him.

He had drunk coffee and eaten sandwiches; he remembered swallowing nothing else, there had been no injection; so it was not safe to eat—he could never be sure when his food would be drugged.

He looked for his clothes.

The coat and trousers had gone. In their place was a neatly folded suit of white linen and a pair of summer shoes.

He pushed back the bedclothes and swayed when his feet

touched the floor, then walked to the window. He was glad to lean against a chair.

He looked at a brick wall. Leaning forward, he saw that there was a garden between this building and the next; so he was not in the bungalow, they had taken him away from there. He was in a town! A town where there were telephones, policemen, normal people. He could hear the hum of traffic not far away. There was one thing like the bungalow; the window was not made to open. He examined it closely; looked at from one angle, it had a yellowish tinge; so it was toughened glass.

The door opened, and Mallory came in.

'Good morning, Palfrey!'

Palfrey started and turned round. 'Oh, hallo,' he said, weakly.

'You shouldn't walk about without getting dressed,' Mallory told him. 'How are you feeling this morning? Did you have nightmares?'

'No—just dreams.'

'I thought you were on the mend,' said Mallory. 'You're looking much better, too. Do you remember anything more clearly?'

'I'm—I'm afraid not,' said Palfrey.

'Nothing more about Kennedy Lee?'

Palfrey drew in his breath.

'I am quite sure that I have told you all that Kennedy Lee told me,' he said.

'Good!' exclaimed Mallory, unexpectedly. 'Another week here and you'll be all right. Have they brought in your breakfast yet?'

'No.'

'I'll have it sent in,' promised Mallory. 'I think I'd have breakfast in bed, if I were you.'

He helped Palfrey back into bed and went out.

Palfrey immediately got out again and went to the door. It was locked, although he had not heard the key turn. He went back and pulled the bedclothes about him.

The door opened, and a nurse, a girl, came in, carrying a tray.

'Good morning, sir.'

She put the tray down on the bedside table. There were boiled eggs, toast, butter and marmalade, in ample quantities. Palfrey hesitated, and the girl went out; a chance to speak to her was lost.

Was he wise to eat? Were they trying to drug him again

now? Wasn't it more probable that they would give him a rest until the day was over? He was ravenous; he took the top off an egg and the creamy yellow yolk welled up and spilled over, running down the egg-cup. The bread-and-butter was delicious. He forgot his qualms, poured out a cup of tea, sipped, and then took the top off the other egg.

The shell broke as if it were hollow. The egg-cup fell and the shell toppled out, rolled against the tea-pot, and stopped. Something fell out of it: a tiny piece of folded paper.

He looked about him. The room was empty, he did not think that anyone could be watching him. He remembered that he had been watched at the bungalow; they might have peep-holes here. He scanned the ceiling and the walls; there seemed nothing amiss.

He unfolded the paper and smoothed it out. It was thin tissue. With quickening pulse he read:

They will inject you soon after you have had breakfast. The injection should induce heavy sleep and afterwards a lapse of memory. When you wake up they will give you more food, then another injection. That process will go on for several days. At the end of the treatment, your memory should be gone completely. You must pretend that it has. Don't be violent, don't be stubborn, do what they tell you, answer all their questions frankly. They do not know that I am helping you and they do not know that all they will inject will be water—I will see to that.

Put this message into the tea-pot when you have finished. It will dissolve before they empty the pot. Remember, you must convince them that they are succeeding.

Palfrey re-read the letter, then poured himself out another cup of tea and put the paper into the tea-pot. It floated on the dark tea that was in the bottom. He put on the lid, then closed his eyes. He could remember every word of the message, as if it were written in front of him.

It was a breath of air from outside, the touch he had needed to give him courage and confidence.

The girl came again, soon afterwards, and took away the tray. Then Mallory came in, was a little too hearty and reassuring, and gave him an injection.

Ten days after Palfrey had disappeared from Reading

70

Station, the Marquis of Brett—the real marquis—entered the big study at his London home and saw Drusilla Palfrey sitting in an easy chair by the window.

'Is there any news?' Drusilla asked, quickly.

'Yes and no,' said Brett. He held her hands and smiled reassuringly. 'My dear, you have as cool a head as any of us, and you know that there was no point in taking Sap away if they wanted him dead.'

Drusilla said dryly: 'You remind me of that every morning.'

'There is no news of Sap, but there is other news—and it's cheering. Washington and Moscow are both going to work with us,' said Brett. 'Bruton and Stefan will be coming in the next few days. Renaud has already arrived from Paris. If Sap knew, he would be as pleased as I am.'

There was a brighter glow in Drusilla's eyes.

'Yes,' she said. 'And if anyone can find him——'

'They will,' Brett finished for her. 'I can't help feeling, 'Silla, that they will get through to him, you know.'

'Has anyone *any* idea where Sap might be?'

'Not really,' Brett admitted, 'but there is a curious report from Washington. A man looking very much like me was seen in New York three days ago. It might lead to something: they are looking for him again in New York.'

'I don't see how it will help,' said Drusilla.

'We never do see how these things will help at first,' Brett reminded her. 'There's one thing we can be sure of, 'Silla.'

'What's that?'

'Whatever happens, Sap was right to pay so much attention to Lannigan and to get the story from Kennedy Lee. If we hadn't heard that, if Lannigan hadn't come to see Sap——' he shrugged his shoulders. 'We might never have known that trouble was afoot, it would have burst upon us without warning.'

'The papers were stolen,' Drusilla reminded him.

Brett said slowly: 'We've just heard from Washington,' he said. 'The papers have been found in a desk in Lee's room at the Embassy. The popular theory there seems to be that they were never lost, but tucked behind the desk. If Sap hadn't forced Lee to tell us what he did, Lee would have been cleared of any charge and there would have been nothing to worry us. Now at least we do know something of what's afoot. The papers were taken away and, after being copied, replaced—that's evident enough.'

'When are you expecting Corney Bruton and Stefan?'

'Within a few days,' Brett told her. ''Silla, wouldn't you be happier at the Hall for a few weeks? London is unbearably hot, and——'

'I'd much rather stay in town.'

'Then move in here, and shut the flat up for a while,' urged Brett. 'I'm not happy about you living on your own.'

'Do you mean you think there might be danger?'

'No, only that you might get depressed.'

'I'd much rather stay at the flat,' said Drusilla, and gave a quick, bright smile.

She went downstairs to a waiting car.

As they turned into Piccadilly and reached the Circus, Drusilla looked towards the Criterion outside which Palfrey usually met her; it had been their first rendezvous in London, and it had retained a sentimental association for her. Her smile was strained as they drove past.

The lights were against them. They were at the front of the line of traffic and they stayed there for some time. A taxi was just behind, and the fare leaned out, without Drusilla seeing him, and beckoned to a newsboy, who hurried to him, shouting his 'headlines'. It was the first time Drusilla had heard him clearly.

'*New Palfrey Sensation,*' he intoned. *''Frey sensation, piper!'*

Drusilla's heart seemed to stop.

It was in the *Stop Press.*

Body of Dr. Palfrey believed found hanging to floating wreckage of two-engined aircraft found off the southern coast of Iceland—Reuter.

Drusilla tapped at the glass with a sudden frenzy, and Sanders started and turned his head.

'Brierly Place, quickly,' said Drusilla.

Sanders had driven the Marquis and his friends on all manner of strange missions, but, even had he not been used to such sudden changes of instructions, Drusilla's expression then would have impressed him.

Christian opened the door.

'Mrs. Palfrey!'

'Where is he?' Drusilla gasped, and pushed past the butler. 'Where is he, Christian?'

'He's just gone into the study,' said Christian, 'but——'

She reached the study door and burst in, and Brett jumped

72

up from his desk. She did not realize that he had been speaking into the telephone.

''Silla!'

'Look!' she gasped, waving the paper in his face. 'Look, they —they've found his body.' She closed her eyes, and Christian came hurrying in and helped Brett to take her to a chair.

'Some tea, Christian,' said Brett, and glanced at the paper. He thought that Drusilla had fainted, but her eyes opened.

'Have you—seen it?'

'I'd just heard by telephone,' Brett said. ' 'Silla, you're letting yourself down, you know.'

The words acted like a blow. She sat up, and her expression grew cold.

'You mustn't let yourself go,' insisted Brett, taking her hands. 'This is a newspaper report. The aeroplane was sighted by a trawler off the Iceland coast, someone on board "thought" it was Sap, because the man looked something like him, but there's no evidence at all.'

'You're—just fending off the facts,' she said.

'*You're* asking for trouble,' said Brett. 'How is it going to help Sap or anyone else if you make yourself ill.'

'I'm sorry,' she said, flushing. 'I heard them crying it out in the street. Marquis, I must see him—I must see it, I must be sure.'

'This body's been taken to Reykjavik,' Brett said, 'and it will be a day or two before it is brought here. But Stefan will be here in the morning, and I'll send him and Brian by air to Iceland. They will telephone as soon as they've looked at the body. They won't make any mistake,' Brett added, 'they'll be able to judge as well as you.'

Christian came in, and Brett poured a splash of whisky into Drusilla's tea.

SEVEN

Z.5

STEFAN ANDROMOVITCH towered above the other men in Brett's study, the only man who seemed big enough for that great room. Brian and Charles Lumsden were there, with a short, dark, curly-haired man whose clothes were American cut.

73

He was Cornelius Bruton, who had arrived an hour before by air from New York. Renaud, from Paris, was a tall, thin, melancholy-looking man; none of the others had worked with him before.

'How much of the story do you know, Corney?' asked Brian, who was leaning back in an easy chair and smoking a cigarette.

'Everything, I hope,' said Bruton. 'The Marquis has just told me that Sap wasn't picked up on that aircraft.'

Everyone looked towards Brett. He was sitting behind the large, intricately carved, mahogany desk. He smiled.

'What I haven't told any of you is that he was wearing the clothes which Sap had on when he left England,' he said, 'and that it's evident, from the papers in his pocket, that someone hoped we would think it was Sap.'

Brian looked at Stefan. 'The body had been in the water for two or three days,' he said, slowly. 'Stefan, is it——'

'No, it isn't Sap,' said Brett, quickly. 'The insteps are much higher, for one thing, there is slight malformation of the left foot, the shoulders are squarer, and this man has a burn mark on his chest—one of long standing.'

'What do you make of it?' Bruton asked.

'I'm more concerned with what you're going to make of it,' said Brett. He picked up a silver pen from a Georgian inkstand, the only thing on the desk, and rolled it between his fingers. 'All of you now know the developments leading up to this. You also know'—he paused and smiled faintly—'that for the first time for twelve months you are all working together for a common cause. You are the first active agents of *Uno's* Secret Intelligence Bureau!'

Brian's eyes lit up, Renaud exclaimed: *'Nom d'un nom!'* Lumsden whistled, and Bruton snapped: 'Is that official?'

'Yes.'

'I guess *that's* worth waiting for,' said Bruton.

Only Stefan showed no sign of excitement, unless it were in the gleam in his eyes and the set of his full lips.

Brett said slowly: 'If you succeed in this task, there will be others.' It seemed almost as if he were speaking to himself, his voice was so soft. 'You succeeded during the war, you can succeed now. I doubt if anyone has a greater responsibility. On your goodwill, on your sincerity and trustworthiness depends the future of much more than Z.5. Your reports will go before a special committee, what you learn will be passed on to all

74

your countries. One might call you the Secret Police of the World!' He smiled again. 'Does my expansiveness amuse you?'

'Amuse!' exclaimed Bruton.

'There is a development in a different sphere which will probably help us,' said Brett. 'Have any of you seen a copy of *World Citizen*?'

Bruton said: 'All the copies.'

'I haven't heard of it,' said Brian.

'I believe the English edition is to begin publication next week,' Brett told him, and explained, as Lannigan had done to Palfrey, the policy of the newspaper. He was able to go further. Plans were well in hand for publication in every country of the world, an edition was to appear soon in the U.S.S.R. 'It's likely to be a big power for good,' said Brett, 'and——'

Bruton chuckled. 'Are you behind it?'

Brett looked startled.

'No, I'm not. Nor is anyone officially connected with any Government, as far as I know. If it were even suspected that it was another Government-sponsored propaganda sheet, its value would be lost. Much of its value lies in its independence. Watch it. If at any time you think you've a story that would appeal to the editor, send it through one of the accredited news channels.'

'It sounds excellent,' Renaud said. 'Is there to be a French edition soon?'

'I understand so,' said Brett. 'For the rest—it will support us.'

'But what has achieved the miracle?' asked Stefan. He leaned forward. 'I have not been happy for a long time,' he declared, 'so much that we did during the war seemed wasted, I was afraid that there was too much suspicion for us to break down the barriers, but now—it *is* a miracle. Has common danger united us again?'

Brett said: 'Yes.'

'When are we going to hear what the danger is?' asked Bruton.

'Now,' said Brett. 'Perhaps I should first tell you what I have often told you before. Secrecy even about the most trivial things is vital. You are on duty now and you will always be on duty.' He paused, looked at each one, and then went on: 'The papers which were taken from the Embassy and afterwards replaced gave full details of a chemical discovery made in this country during the war, but never used. As a means of destructive warfare, it is probably more terrible, in its way, than the atom or hydrogen bomb. I know that sounds far-fetched,' Brett added, quietly, 'but I think you will agree with me. The chemicals were found accidentally when experiments were being made with artificial fertilizers, so that we could increase the yield per acre in all our crops. One particular experiment not only failed to increase the yield, but totally destroyed the fertility of the soil. It was used on a small farm in the West Country ; the farm is derelict today. Three fields were used ; the soil disease, something hitherto unknown in this country, spread to adjoining fields, and in one season the farm was useless. Urgent steps to prevent a further spread were taken. It was found that the disease, the blight, call it what you will, was stopped only by water. The farm was therefore cut off from neighbouring land by irrigation canals, and there has been no further trouble. Smaller experiments, carried out on different kinds of soil, have all had the same effect. Once the soil has been treated with that particular preparation, it becomes barren.'

Brett stopped speaking.

Every man was looking at him ; no one spoke, no one stirred.

'Experiments continued for a while, and as the war went on, there was a proposition that it should be dropped from the air over part of Germany. The suggestion had one good effect. Experimental work on it was stopped immediately, contemplation of the irremediable damage which might be done forced the Government to act. The succeeding Government fully agreed that experiments must cease, but—as in all branches of science—a similar discovery appears to have been made in America.'

Bruton drew in a sharp breath.

'American agricultural observers noticed, last year, that certain tracts of land in Alabama and others in California seemed to become barren,' Brett told them. 'The farmers had no explanation. The trouble spread, covering fairly wide areas—areas which stopped only in the direction where the land was intersected by water. Immediate steps were taken in both States to cut off the affected areas by artificial streams, and the trouble did not spread. The American Government informed the British and Soviet Governments, through the usual diplomatic channels—chiefly because it was extremely puzzled and wanted to find out whether any other country knew a similar phenomenon. As far as we knew, it had only occurred in England, where it was so rigidly controlled.

'Soil from the affected districts in America was sent to England for comparison, and the appearance and chemical structure of the barren soil coincided in every respect with that in Devon. A further exchange of samples took place and the formula, from which the defertilizing matter had been made, was sent to Washington. A copy was passed on to the White House, the other was retained—and it is that which was stolen.'

Again Brett paused; and again none of the others spoke.

'It now appears obvious that someone outside the Governments of the two countries has possession of the formula or a similar one,' said Brett. 'That is why I tell you that, in some ways, the effects of this material might be worse than that of the atom. It is not particularly difficult to manufacture, no special manufacturing plant is required. Some comparatively rare chemicals are needed, but they are obtainable in several parts of the world, and undoubtedly there are many other unknown and undiscovered deposits. The chief raw mineral for the chemical is *bitua,* which is found usually—as far as is known, invariably—in regions ice-bound or snow-bound for several months in the year. The only deposits known in the British Isles are in the north-west of Scotland, high up on the mountains. It is found fairly freely in arctic, antarctic and regions in the extreme north and south. So far, it seems, only the greater Powers know of its existence, and your task is to find who is using it in America and whether it has been used elsewhere.'

After a long pause, Brian said: 'Why should anyone want to use it?'

Renaud raised his hands. 'It becomes clear, I think, that if the harvest in one country, or a part of one country, were affected, shortages in certain crops would create famine conditions, and so, high prices. Is that not so, M. le Marquis?'

'Obviously,' said Brett.

Brian threw up his hands. 'I'd almost forgotten that people might try such a racket.'

Bruton asked: 'Is there any way all this ties up with what's happened to Sap, apart from the Embassy trouble?'

'Not clearly,' said Brett, 'but some curious things have come to light. This man Karen, who was mentioned, did live in New York, but left a fortnight ago, and there is no trace of him or his wife. There's another reasonably interesting fact. Valerie Grayson, whom we think is Diana Leeming, spent a lot of time with one of America's biggest fertilizer experts and a fairly large landowner—Edward Hoffner, of Austin, Texas. She was with Hoffner on the night she disappeared. He is one of the first men you will approach,' added Brett. 'There is another thing: Grayson himself is thinking of retiring and is going south ; he planned to buy a fruit farm in California. Part of the affected land is on that farm.'

'He's been a mighty long time coming to see whether Diana's his daughter,' Bruton commented.

'His ship's due to berth at Southampton to-morrow,' Brett told him. 'I've seen photographs of Valerie Grayson, and I must admit that they show little likeness to Diana Leeming, except the birthmark and the other characteristics which Lannigan told Sap about. Still I think it possible that Diana Leeming's loss of memory was induced, that is medically possible, to make her forget——'

'This?' asked Brian, sharply.

'Yes,' said the Marquis. 'I think she probably learned too much about it.'

'They'd have been wiser to put her right out.'

'They have shown little mercy to others,' Renaud murmured.

'We must face the facts, my friends,' said Stefan, putting a hand on Brian's shoulder. 'She was spared, they preferred her to forget rather than to die. That is another of the facts which might help us as we proceed. Marquis'—he looked at Brett—'this man who is like you and was in New York. Do you yet know more about him?'

'He hasn't been seen again,' said Brett.

'This Hoffner—what is his reputation?'

'Good,' said Brett.

'Is it on reliable information?' Stefan asked.

'The Federal Bureau of Investigation,' answered Brett.

Bruton stirred. 'I've known F.B.I. make that kind of mistake,' he declared. 'Are you planning for all of us to go to the States?'

'There's no need for you all to stay together,' said Brett, 'but I would like you to go with one party and Stefan with the other, if you do decide to break up. What are you thinking about, Bruton?'

'Chiefly, Lannigan,' said Bruton. 'I see it this way. Lannigan did a lot of work. He was good, we all know that. He didn't have time to tell Sap everything, but he did tell him that he had a girl operative working with him on the other side. Have you checked on her?'

'Yes,' said Brett, and Stefan nodded and smiled, as if it could be taken for granted that Brett would leave nothing undone. 'When Lannigan left for England, she was working in a New York nursing home, and she's still there.'

'You told us you hadn't a line!' exclaimed Bruton. 'She must have been working both ways in that place—and Diana came round in a nursing home. The quicker we contact that girl the quicker we'll get results!' His eyes were shining with excitement. 'I'll fly over,' he declared. 'Who's to come with me?'

'I should wait for Grayson,' Brett temporized. 'And when you do go to see Lannigan's girl, you'll need to be careful. If she has managed to get work inside this organization, we might do more harm than good if we approach her.'

'I'll be careful,' promised Bruton. He looked impatient and dissatisfied, but did not argue.

With Brian and Renaud, Bruton was at Southampton when the s.s. *Adua Star* berthed on the following day, and he was first aboard, after the port officials, eager to see Grayson. They hurried to the purser's office and, by some miracle, Bruton managed to push to the front of a crowd of eager inquirers.

'This way,' he said, and hurried towards the 'A' deck. 'Twenty-two,' he added, brusquely, and they turned a corner, jostling passengers and stewards, and saw three or four men standing outside Grayson's cabin.

Bruton pulled up.

'Reporters,' he said. 'I can smell them a mile off. They've connected Grayson with Palfrey, you can bet your life,' said Bruton. They stood watching, and suddenly one of the newspapermen pushed at the cabin door. They heard him say:

''Morning, Mr. Grayson——' and then break off abruptly.

'Come on!' snapped Bruton.

He hurried forward, not knowing what to expect but half afraid that something had happened to Grayson. Renaud stood one side of the door and Brian the other as Bruton went in.

The cabin was empty.

There were no signs of a struggle, nothing at all to indicate what had happened to Valerie Grayson's father.

'After this,' Bruton said determinedly, 'I'm going to New York.'

EIGHT

DAY NURSE

THE nursing home was on Long Island, in the old district, where solid, rambling houses still resisted the onslaught of the sky-scraper and office block. Bruton walked past it.

He had left England on the afternoon of the search on board the s.s. *Adua Star*, with Brian and Renaud. Stefan, and possibly Lumsden, were to follow. They had been one night in New York, and had talked to the British agent who had traced Lannigan's girl. He had been able to tell them little about the nursing home, except that it had a good reputation and had a resident doctor—Dr. Patrick Mallory. The man who looked like Brett had been seen in this district; Bruton did not think that was a coincidence.

He strolled past, seeing Renaud at the other end of the street. Brian was at their hotel, held in reserve.

Stella Dale, who had been Lannigan's secretary, and who was known at the nursing home as Stella Day, was a day nurse. She had come on duty at nine o'clock and would not be off again until early evening. That much they knew.

Mallory had left the house soon after nine o'clock, and had not come back.

Bruton made a complete round of the nearby thoroughfares and then stood near the end of the street, from where he could see the house. Renaud had gone. A taxi was waiting several blocks along, and stayed there for some time, until a mail-carrier turned into the street. The taxi moved towards Bruton, and it waited for him after it had turned the corner.

'Mallory's inside the house,' the driver said.

'What's he like?' asked Bruton.

'Ordinary and dark,' said the taxi-driver. He patted his pocket and grinned. 'In one hour, you can have a print of him.' He drove on, dropping Bruton at Fifth Avenue. Bruton strolled along to his hotel, satisfied that nothing would be neglected.

Brian was sitting in front of an open window at the top of the high building, coat off, collar and tie unfastened. There was a jug of iced water by his side, and he looked flushed with the heat.

'Where's Renaud?'

'He telephoned that he would be late,' said Brian. He took a cigarette case from the table in front of him, and opened it.

'No thanks,' said Bruton, and lit a small cigar.

'Corney——' said Brian, and broke off.

'Something's on your mind,' said Bruton, and laughed. 'I mean more than there is on all our minds. What's worrying you?'

Brian hesitated, then said: 'What do you think of Renaud?'

'Brett's okayed him, hasn't he?' asked Bruton, with a lift of his eyebrows.

'Yes, of course, but—oh, I'm probably crazy,' Brian exclaimed.

'You don't like him,' Bruton murmured.

'It isn't exactly dislike. He seems to be watching me wherever I am, whatever I'm doing. Not openly, but covertly. And his eyes——'

'Shadowed eyes,' Bruton said, soberly. 'Do you know his history? Five years in German hands, one and a half of them in solitary. Brett should have told you. Think about it, and then forget what's on your mind. Brett wouldn't pass a man unless he were sure of him.'

'He was deceived once in the early days,' Brian said.

The telephone bell rang.

Bruton crossed the room with quick, nervous footsteps and lifted the receiver. 'Yes,' he said, and waited, looking at Brian.

'You'd better listen-in,' he said.

Theirs was a two-roomed suite, and there was an extension telephone in the next room. Brian hurried into it and picked up the receiver as Bruton said in his clipped voice: 'That's right.'

'This is Renaud,' came a soft voice, as if the Frenchman were whispering to prevent himself from being overheard.

'What's the time?' asked Bruton, promptly.

'It is eleven minutes past twelve,' said Renaud, in the same hushed voice.

It was a quarter to twelve; question and answer were part of the simple code by which they identified one another.

'Where are you?' Bruton asked.

'I am in the negro quarter,' said Renaud. 'I think I have seen Casado. I am waiting near the house into which he has gone. I would like you to send someone else, not you or Debenham,

81

you have other work, but someone, so that I am not alone. Will you?'

'Sure,' said Bruton. 'Just where will they find you?'

'Near the church of St. Saviour,' Renaud said.

'Right,' said Bruton, 'you won't have long to wait.'

Brian hurried into the main room to join him.

'Harlem's a tough spot if there's going to be trouble,' Bruton said. 'I guess I'll go along to the City Hall and arrange for the right men to go.'

'Has Renaud ever seen Casado?' asked Brian.

'He's working on Sap's description,' said Bruton.

'Aren't there hundreds of such types?'

'You mean that he's making a guess,' Bruton said. 'I don't know about that. Renaud's no fool.' He snapped his fingers irritably. 'He didn't say that he was sure, anyway, he said he thought he'd seen him. I won't be long.'

He was back in half an hour.

'That's arranged,' he said, briefly. 'Any news here?'

'No.'

'What time did I say Stella Dale's off duty?'

'Six-thirty.'

'It's a hell of a time,' said Bruton, and lay down on a bed.

They had been busy since they had reached New York. Brian was already fitted out with two suits of clothes of American cut, and, for out-of-doors, he wore square, rimless glasses and succeeded in losing the characteristic appearance of an Englishman; those who knew him in England would have thought it impossible. Now he sat, sweating freely, feeling as impatient as Bruton and yet glad that there was no prospect of immediate action. It would be cooler towards evening.

He thought of Renaud again. What had made the man say that he thought he had seen Casado? None of them had a photograph, they had only Palfrey's description to go on, and it might apply to a dozen, to a hundred, men. Had Renaud any other reason?

Was it wise, even if the man were Casado, to follow him? Their objective was Stella Dale. He——

The telephone bell rang again.

Brian started, but Bruton was off the bed and at the instrument before Brian was out of his chair.

'Yes,' said Bruton. 'Yes . . . You sure? . . . Okay, that's fine,' he added, and banged down the receiver. Tiredness and nerviness seemed to have disappeared at the prospect of action, and Brian jumped to his feet. 'The girl's left the nursing home,' he said, 'she's gone to a small joint nearby for some food. Come on.'

Bruton went into the restaurant first. A long-jawed man sitting in his shirt-sleeves at a table near the door raised his left hand and snapped his fingers. 'Coming,' said a harassed waiter, but Bruton knew it was a signal, and sat opposite him.

'The red-haired dame in the corner,' said the long-jawed man.

'Thanks.'

'Gimme my check,' said the long-jawed man, as the waiter came up. He was out of his seat and at the pay-desk before Brian came in. Brian looked round, and then went to a table near Bruton.

Both he and Bruton ordered one course only, and received their checks before the girl had finished.

The girl got up.

Bruton reached the pay-desk in front of her, Brian behind her. Bruton turned left towards Longton Street where the nursing home was situated. Stella Dale followed him. Brian stood outside the door, on the sidewalk, looking as if he had nowhere to go and did not greatly care. Stella walked briskly, and Bruton kept ahead of her. Brian turned in their wake at last, but not until he had seen a short, very swarthy man, in spruce white linen, walking not far behind Stella. The man's spruceness made Brian wary; the fact that he *might* be covered by the description of Casado made him more watchful.

Bruton crossed the road.

Stella Dale went on for a hundred yards, then waited at a crossing.

The dark man stood a little way from her, and crossed at the same time.

Longton Street was two blocks along.

Bruton reached the end of it, and an important-looking official, carrying a black bag and a note book, approached him. He was one of the men watching the house. Stella passed them and turned the corner. So did the man, who followed her into the nursing home.

Brian reached the hotel first. Bruton came in a few minutes afterwards.

'So she's being followed wherever she goes,' said Brian.

'Sure.'

'That might mean they suspect her,' Brian remarked.

Bruton nodded.

'Or it might be a precaution they take with all of the staff,' said Brian.

'That's so,' agreed Bruton. 'I've asked the other boys to find out what happens when nurses leave. Bry, it's going to be difficult to contact that girl.'

'What chance is there of getting a room in one of the houses opposite? If we could do that and watch all the time, we might get an early break.'

'The City Hall is trying to fix that for us,' Bruton said. 'We'll hear soon if they can. Bry, that chap got under my skin. I'm wondering if he's the man whom Renaud saw.'

'Saying it was Casado would be sheer guess-work,' Brian said, reasoningly. 'He'd want something better to go on than that, surely?'

They waited for half an hour, Brian drinking iced water, Bruton looking through the notes which he had made of the case. They were written in code, but he could read without difficulty.

'How long are we going to be finding Hoffner?' asked Brian.

'The girl's the first job,' Bruton said. 'Bry, I think we ought to have Stefan and Charles over here soon. We can't wait indefinitely for Hoffner. I reckon——'

The telephone-bell rang and he moved towards it in his quick, nervous manner and said, laconically: 'Yes.' He listened intently. Brian saw that his grip on the telephone tightened, and then relaxed. It was impossible to judge from his expression what was being said. Brian got up. Bruton said sharply: 'Yes, I heard you.' He listened again, but now he was looking at Brian, who turned belatedly towards the other room for the extension telephone. Before he reached the door, Bruton said: 'Okay, thanks.'

Brian turned.

Bruton wiped the perspiration from his upper lip, and said very slowly: 'You won't need to worry any more about Renaud.'

Brian caught his breath.

'He was run down by a car twenty minutes ago,' Bruton said.

Brian shivered.

'Sure, it gets me that way, too,' said Bruton, and added, after a long pause: 'It makes it look as if he did see Casado.'

After a long pause, Brian said: 'Yes. What worries me is how

84

he knew.' He lit a cigarette mechanically. 'What a difference it would make if Sap were here!'

'There's only one Palfrey,' Bruton admitted. 'The quicker we let Brett know what's happened, the better,' he added. 'I guess I'll——'

He broke off again, for the telephone-bell rang.

Bruton beat Brian to the instrument, and answered as brusquely as he had before. 'Yes.' This time Brian went into the other room immediately, and picked up the receiver. He heard a man saying: 'I guess that's all I can tell you. The ambulance left ten minutes ago, and the girl was inside it. The patient was covered up, we couldn't get a peek at him.'

Bruton said: 'It's being followed, I guess.'

'We're getting reports on its movements,' the man assured him.

Bruton replaced the receiver. 'It looks as if they've taken her away from us,' he said. 'With a patient! *Could* that patient be Palfrey?'

Brian did not speak.

'I'm going to send for Stefan,' Bruton said, and lifted the telephone. He put in a call by radio-telephone and was told that he would have to wait for an hour. He replaced the receiver and went to the open window, through which the sounds of traffic were coming softly.

Suddenly the door opened.

They had heard no one approach, and as the door swung inwards they jumped up—but their alarm faded quickly, for the newcomer was a huge man who had to duck beneath the lintel, and then straightened up and grinned at them.

Brian cried: 'Stefan!'

'Someone's been reading my thoughts,' Bruton said, and went forward, smiling broadly. He was little higher than the Russian's chest. 'What's brought you?' he demanded.

'I would not tell everyone this,' said Stefan, as Bruton gripped his hand, 'but you—I will make an exception.' There was a gleam in his eyes as he went on. 'I think the Marquis was worried in case you were not being looked after, and sent me to see that you were!'

'And then some,' jeered Bruton.

'What has brought you?' Brian demanded.

Stefan laughed. 'Something quite simple. Casado was traced in England, but a little too late for us to get him there. He flew to New York yesterday and I flew on the next aircraft. Charles is still in England; the Marquis thought we could get what help we needed here.' He frowned. 'What's the matter, Brian?'

Brian told him about Renaud, and the Russian's face grew bleak.

NINE

DOWN SOUTH

PALFREY found the strain of acting a part greater than he had thought possible. He had been 'introduced' to Mallory again. Since then, life seemed to be a series of injections, of interviews with Mallory, of a desperate struggle to pretend that he had lost his memory. Mallory seemed to think it possible that the drug would not work effectively. Trick questions were freely mixed with others, and during those interviews Palfrey had to be constantly on the alert. He did not know whether he was winning or losing.

He had received no more messages.

The only person he saw, except Mallory, was his 'nurse'. She reminded him of 'Löis', although she was not the same girl. She had auburn hair and a snub nose, and he liked her eyes, clear grey and flecked with brown and green. She had little to say, and she was expert at her task. Twice a day he was allowed to get up and dress in the borrowed clothes, which fitted him perfectly. He was allowed as many cigarettes as he wanted, but no alcohol.

The room was always cool, although he could guess from the brazen sky that it was very hot outside. The nurse always seemed cool and fresh. He came to look forward to her visits, just as he hated Mallory's.

He had been there for three days when he heard footsteps in the passage, and frowned; Mallory's footsteps, deliberate and firm, were unmistakable. Palfrey sat up, and forced a smile.

'Well, my friend, how are you today?' Mallory asked cheerfully. He picked up the temperature chart, studied it, and then smiled. 'You are making real progress,' he said, heartily. 'How do you feel?'

'I am all right in myself. But I can't think!' Palfrey burst out. 'I can't remember anything but these four walls. Can't you tell me who I am? It's—it's driving me crazy!'

'You mustn't upset yourself,' Mallory said, soothingly. 'You will remember, in time. You need a change.' Mallory smiled; there was nothing pleasant about the smile. 'You need open air, my friend, and a complete rest. I am going to send you away this afternoon.'

Palfrey stared at him.

'You will enjoy it where you are going,' Mallory assured him. 'I am sending your nurse with you; she will look after you all right. You like her, don't you?'

'She's—not bad,' muttered Palfrey.

'How does she compare with other nurses?' Mallory asked, casually.

'I—I don't remember being ill before,' said Palfrey, and closed his eyes.

That was how the trick questions came; an indirect association with the past, and the suggestion that, as a doctor, he should have a good knowledge of the qualifications of nurses. It was the kind of question which, unless he were on the alert all the time, he would answer truthfully—and so betray himself.

'Where am I going?' he asked.

'South,' said Mallory.

Palfrey clenched his hands. 'What does that mean? South of where? Where am I now? Why won't you let me see someone else? Why do you keep me in ignorance of where I am?' He began to tremble, and Mallory watched him with evident satisfaction.

'You mustn't upset yourself,' Mallory said, soothingly. 'I did not realize that you had forgotten that as well! You're in New York. Now, roll up your sleeve, my friend.'

Palfrey drew back.

'Now don't be foolish,' said Mallory, sharply. 'These injections have never hurt you, have they? You aren't well enough to make a long journey unless I give you a sedative. This will make you sleep, and when you wake up you will find yourself farther south. I think you will begin to recover when you find yourself able to go in the open air. Roll up your sleeve.'

Slowly, Palfrey did so.

'Now rest for half an hour,' Mallory said.

He went out, and closed the door.

Palfrey lay for what seemed a long time. For the first ten minutes he was as alert as ever, but gradually he began to feel drowsy. So this injection had not been prepared by his unknown friend. One worry had gone for good; he no longer feared that they would kill him. They wanted complete control over him; the control Karen had obtained over Diana Leeming.

He knew nothing of the journey.

He was taken to a great house, built partly of wood, in a strange district in a strange land; but he did not see the house or the great hall and the white-painted staircase up which they took him.

Stella Dale was left in the room alone with him for ten minutes after he had been put to bed.

She sat on a chair, looking at him steadily.

Lannigan had told her a great deal about this man. If there were a hope of avenging Lannigan, it lay through Palfrey.

Palfrey stirred.

She stood up abruptly, and opened a small bag in which was a letter of instructions from Mallory. He had ordered her not to open it until she had reached this quiet backwater of Alabama.

The instructions were simple. She was to leave Palfrey alone most of the day. He was to be allowed to go into the grounds each morning and afternoon, for an hour at a time at the most. He was to be well-fed and reassured that she—and Mallory— were trying to nurse him back to full health. The last paragraph brought a smile to her lips; she was to question him frequently and make sure that he had completely forgotten what had happened until he had come round in the nursing home.

There was a postscript.

'Leave a copy of the *New York Daily Mirror* dated July 17th at the side of Palfrey's bed, so that he finds it when he comes round, and observe his reactions from the next room.'

There was a copy of the *Mirror* in the case.

She left it on the chair and went out, as Palfrey stirred again.

The next room was her bedroom—a large, pleasant room overlooking sunswept fields where a gentle wind made what looked like millions of pieces of cotton-wool dance gently close to the ground. Farther away, there was a tiny stream, and beyond that a patch of dark earth; she had never seen anything quite so dark as that barren patch before, and, as Palfrey had done at the bungalow, she wondered why it had turned like that.

There was a spy-hole in the wall, and she could see Palfrey lying in bed.

For all she knew, she herself was being watched from the next room.

The only man who had travelled on the private aircraft from New York with her was somewhere in the house, a short, thick-set dark man whose name she did not know. He moved softly, said very little, and always seemed to be watching her.

Palfrey gave up trying to get out of bed, and looked about the room. Nothing more different from the nursing home could be imagined. That room had been small, this was huge. The ceiling was elaborately plastered, the walls were painted with landscapes, the furniture was heavy and old-fashioned.

He saw the newspaper by his side.

It was the first he had seen since he had left England, and he snatched it up. As he read, he realized that his tension was too great ; he was probably being furtively watched. There was nothing surprising about snatching up the newspaper, but he must be careful not to betray his emotions at anything he read. So he had schooled himself by the time he reached page three, and saw a single column headline:

FRENCH VICTIM OF HARLEM ACCIDENT

A Frenchman carrying papers which identified him as Anton Renaud, of Paris, was killed in a car crash . . .

Palfrey stopped reading.

The shock was so great that for a moment he could not think. Then his caution returned ; he must show no exceptional interest in that page. He turned over, a little too quickly.

So he had been followed to New York, but all the experience of the Z.5 agent had not saved him from being killed. He discounted the probability of an 'accident'. Here was another murder, committed with the same ruthlessness and cold-bloodedness as Lannigan's.

Why had he been spared?

He reached the back page, and saw another headline:

ENGLISH SECRET AGENT
DROWNED

FAMOUS WAR ACE

Clinging to the wreckage of a twin-engined aircraft off Southern Iceland, the body of Dr. Stanislaus Alexander Palfrey, famed British Secret Service agent, was found a week ago. Inquest findings gave an open verdict. See early edition.

Palfrey put the paper down.

His thoughts flew to Drusilla and what she would be thinking. He must get word to her, must somehow let her know——

He clenched his teeth.

He was behaving like a fool. There was no chance of getting word to England, and if there were he could not take it yet. He had enough experience of the people whom he was fighting to be sure that Drusilla would be watched, and she might give the truth away without thinking. He had to see this ordeal through.

As darkness fell, the nurse came in with a laden tray.

She switched on the light.

'Sit up,' she said, and arranged his pillows. As she leaned forward, she whispered, 'Keep it up.' Then she straightened up, as if she were as frightened as he of being overheard.

Though he had slept so long, it was easy to doze off again when he had finished a good meal. He had given up worrying whether his food was drugged; he had to stop worrying about small things; and there was little point, he reasoned, in drugging his food when he was injected so often.

It was broad daylight when he woke up after a fitful sleep. He was feeling much better, tired but rested. He got out of bed and put on a patchwork dressing gown which was draped over the foot-panel, but it was so warm that he hardly needed it. He looked out of the window and saw the 'cotton-wool'. He stared; and then he realized that it *was* cotton. In the distance he could see people dotted against the white, and after a while he could see black faces beneath huge white hats. So Mallory had meant 'South'.

Far off, he could see the broad white streak of a river; beyond it, a mass of forest land. Cotton seemed to be everywhere except in one direction, where corn was growing fairly near the house. He saw several tiny rivers, intersecting—and, just within sight, a patch of dark earth surrounded by narrow streams. It reminded him vividly of the soil over which he had walked from the aeroplane. He stared towards it.

An hour later, for the first time since had had left England, he went out of doors, free to walk about the spacious grounds. The girl walked by his side.

'Do you feel steady?' she asked.

'Not too bad,' said Palfrey. He did not smile, but he always wore that strained, anxious look when he knew that he was being watched—and he had seen a man in the grounds, standing by a patch of juniper. The man's white linen suit was perfectly cut, but his face was hidden. Palfrey glanced towards him once or twice, and then saw him move. *It was Casado.* Palfrey stiffened.

'What's the matter?' asked Stella Dale.

'Nothing,' Palfrey muttered. 'Nothing.'

He must not show any sign of recognition. If he had been confronted by the man without warning, he would have betrayed himself.

Casado walked towards him, a faint, mocking smile on his flat face.

'Good morning,' said Stella, and Casado nodded. He looked at Palfrey, and asked: 'Haven't I seen you before somewhere?'

Palfrey started. 'You mean—before *this*?' He jumped up, and his hands gripped Stella's shoulders tightly. He stared at the man intently; then suddenly he relaxed, turning his head away. 'I don't remember you,' he said. 'If only I could remember something!' He buried his face in his hands.

Casado said: 'Maybe I'll call it to mind.'

Between his fingers, Palfrey watched him walk off.

Stella said: 'You're incredibly convincing!'

'It's a devil of a strain,' said Palfrey. He did not look up, he knew that Casado might not be alone; it was wise to remain there, a picture of utter dejection. 'Can you get messages outside?'

'Not yet.'

'Do they suspect you?'

'I don't think so.' The sun was pouring down on them, but she shivered. 'We won't talk too much.'

'No,' said Palfrey. He straightened up, took out a cigarette and lit it.

A man walked past, beyond a white fence which was only two feet high. He wore an old white jacket which drooped shapelessly from his huge shoulders. His hair was falling over his eyes, and he brushed it away. In one hand he carried a canvas hold-all. Palfrey did not see his face clearly, the man was too tall, and one of the branches half-concealed him, but —it was Stefan.

He passed out of sight.

'What is it?' asked Stella Dale.

It was on the tip of Palfrey's tongue to tell her. He stopped himself. It was better that no one but he should know ; he must not show his fierce surge of elation at the knowledge that he had been traced.

He heard a telephone ringing.

He saw Casado walk quickly into the hall, through the open doorway, and disappear. The bell stopped. Palfrey watched the house closely, and the girl said: 'There's someone else in the garden.'

'Thanks,' said Palfrey. 'Let's walk again.'

He strolled towards the house. He could not get the thought of Stefan out of his mind. Were others here. Bruton would surely be in America, Brian and Charles might have come. By now, Brett must know that he was alive——

He could hear Casado speaking.

'I didn't think there was a man that big,' Casado said, and Palfrey started. 'Sure, I will see to it.' He listened for what seemed a long time, but Palfrey walked very slowly, intent on catching his next words. 'Sure,' Casado said, and Palfrey heard the ring of the telephone as he replaced the receiver.

'*I didn't think there was a man that big.*' Could he have been talking about anyone but Stefan? Someone had traced Stefan——

'You're looking tired,' the girl said. 'You'd better come in.' She touched his arm as Casado appeared on the porch, which was hung with a creeper, a mass of delicate blue flower.

'That's enough for today,' Casado said.

As they passed him, he looked at Palfrey narrowly. Palfrey went wearily towards the stairs, thinking desperately. He must get a warning to Stefan ; it might seem impossible, but it must be done. The girl was the only likely messenger.

In the bedroom, he gripped her arm. 'You must——' he began.

'*We're being watched,*' she whispered, and led him to the

92

easy-chair by the window. 'Sit down and rest,' she said, in her normal voice. 'It was the sun, I expect.'

'A big man, who passed, you must——'

'*Don't talk!*' She went towards the door. 'I'll get you a drink,' she said, and went out.

Palfrey stood up and looked out of the window. Casado came in sight. Two or three other men appeared in the garden; they had left the house from different places, but were converging on an oak tree, a great, gnarled giant with branches which almost swept the ground.

Casado stood a little way away from it.

Palfrey saw his lips move.

The branches of the tree seemed to tremble. Casado spoke again. Leaves began to fall from the tree, and one of the branches was swaying up and down. Someone jumped into the garden.

For the first time, Palfrey saw that three of the men had guns in their hands; they kept their hands close to their pockets, as if anxious that they should not be seen except in emergency, but Palfrey thought little of that, and was aware only of a terrible disappointment; for the man who had been hiding in the tree was Stefan. He dwarfed the others, but stood with his head hanging, the hold-all dropping from one hand.

Casado jerked his fingers towards the house.

With a man behind him and one on either side, Stefan shambled towards the house. His face was yellowish; at a quick glance he might have appeared a mulatto.

Why had he let himself be caught so easily?

Palfrey drew in his breath.

Of course, Stefan had climbed that tree deliberately, and could have only one reason: to get into the house.

There were footsteps on the stairs.

Palfrey went back to his chair and lit a cigarette. He had been standing too far from the window for any silent watcher to have seen his expression. Now he schooled himself to show that weary, haunted look.

Men walked along the passage. One, a little ahead of the others, opened the door. It was Casado, who beckoned to whoever was outside in the passage.

Stefan came in.

Palfrey looked up, blankly.

He saw the eager look which sprang to Stefan's eyes, but showed no sign of recognition. The eagerness vanished. Stefan took a quick step forward, his hand outstretched. Casado pulled at his arm. Stefan brushed him aside, as if he were of no account. Another man by the door snatched out his gun. Casado, his face set in a scowl, waved the man back.

Stefan reached Palfrey.

'Sap, my friend——'

Palfrey stared at him.

Except for the colouring of his face, everything about Stefan was familiar ; precious and familiar.

But Palfrey continued to stare blankly.

'Who is this?' he asked.

'He says he knows you,' Casado said.

Palfrey gripped the arms of his chair.

'Do you?' he snapped. 'Do you?' He half rose, and the look of strain increased. His voice became a squeak. 'Do you know me? Answer, man, answer!' He gripped Stefan's coat, while Casado stood watching, and horror sprang into Stefan's eyes.

The girl came into the room, and waited by the door.

Stefan said: 'Sap, you remember me, surely. Stefan—Stefan Andromovitch.'

Palfrey said slowly: 'Stefan?'

'Sap, you must remember——'

'That's enough,' said Casado again, and gripped Stefan's arm. 'I'll see you downstairs,' he added, 'and——'

Stefan swung his right arm round.

His forearm caught Casado on the chest, and swept the man off his feet. Casado hit against the bed, and fell headlong on to it. Stella exclaimed, one of the men jumped forward, gun in hand, but he hesitated just too long—just long enough for Stefan, with his enormous reach, to stretch out and snatch the gun from his hand.

The other man fired.

Palfrey dared not act ; he must keep up appearances, he must not show fight.

The bullet hummed past Stefan's head, and next moment the man was reeling from a resounding blow. Downstairs, someone shouted an alarm.

In Stefan's huge hand the stolen automatic was lost ; but it covered Casado, who had picked himself up from the bed and was standing with his hands by his side, with a dazed look.

94

Once he put up his hand, to rub his chest where the Colossus had hit him.

'Go into that corner,' Stefan said. Casado and the others obeyed.

The shouting below grew louder, and there were footsteps on the stairs. Palfrey glanced out of the window, for men were running in the garden. It was alive with men ; among them he saw Bruton, and fancied he caught sight of Brian's fair hair. Wild relief mixed oddly with alarm ; if they took him away now, he might lose every chance of learning the truth, the motives behind the attack on him and the remorseless effort to sap his memory and his will-power.

'And you,' said Stefan to Stella.

She opened her lips ; then closed them again and went obediently into the corner. There was no shouting downstairs now, only a sound of scuffling and one single sharp report. Silence fell, but was quickly broken by footsteps on the stairs.

Bruton came rushing in, saw Palfrey, and stopped in his tracks.

'Thank the Lord for this,' he exclaimed. 'Hallo, Sap !'

Palfrey stared at him, blankly.

Brian came in, breathing heavily, but elated.

'Hallo, Sap.'

Palfrey took a step forward. 'I—I don't understand this,' he said. 'Who are you? What are you doing here? Where is Dr. Mallory?'

Brian blanched.

'They have made him lose his memory,' Stefan said, gently, 'but he will recover.' He turned and laid a hand on Palfrey's shoulder. 'You are among friends,' he said, and had Palfrey really forgotten, he would have been comforted and re-assured by the tone of the Russian's voice. It was odd to find such gentleness in the man who had acted with such terrifying violence.

Casado and his men still seemed dazed. Bruton, with an automatic in his hand, kept them covered.

'I just don't understand it,' Palfrey said, and glanced at the nurse, who was behind Casado, free from observation except by Stefan. She nodded, approvingly. It was a gesture no one else could have noticed, but Palfrey was waiting for some such sign. It satisfied him that he was wise to keep up the pretence in front of Casado, but he had to have time, had to think clearly. They must decide quickly upon a course of action, and he must give Stefan and the others some idea of what he was doing.

'Let's get a move on,' Bruton said. 'Downstairs, you.' He motioned to Casado, and the girl went with them towards the door, where another man was standing, gun in hand. Palfrey thought that Stefan must have brought all the police from the district. Once they had found him, they had taken no chance of failure.

Bruton thrust out his hand and gripped the girl's wrist.

'Not you,' he said. 'Take the others downstairs,' he ordered the man outside, and Brian followed the little party.

'Is it the girl who worked for Lannigan?' Stefan asked.

Stella looked at the door and then at Palfrey, and then glanced round the room. The others stood puzzled but Palfrey knew what was in her mind ; she could not rid herself of the fear that she was being watched, that everything said was overheard.

They must get some order into confusion.

Brian came back. 'They're safe,' he said, 'five of them in all.' He looked at Palfrey as if he did not know what to do or say. 'Sap, surely you remember——'

Stella said, in a hoarse whisper: ' The next room—see if there is anyone in the next room.'

Brian looked at her in astonishment. Stefan turned suddenly out of the room, and they heard him fling open a door. He gave an exclamation which took Bruton in his wake and made Brian stand with his gun in his hand by the door.

Palfrey signalled to Stella.

'That's one way,' Bruton said, in a low-pitched voice. 'A recording unit.' They heard him walk across the room, as Stefan observed:

'She told us, Corney.'

'Sap——' began Brian, in a taut voice.

'It's all right,' said Palfrey, and Stefan, in the doorway of the next room, swung round. 'Not too much noise,' Palfrey added, and Stefan followed him with Bruton into his own room. He felt suddenly weak, and sat on the edge of the bed ; when he looked up, it was to smile at Stella Dale.

'What *is* this?' demanded Bruton.

'I'll make it short,' Palfrey said. 'They thought they were drugging me with a drug to cause amnesia. Stella substituted water. I've been putting up an act. It will help if they think they've had their way. It'll be better for Casado and the others not to know until we've sorted the situation out.' He got up

96

and went to Stella and took her hands. 'My dear,' he said, 'one day I hope to be able to say thanks.'

She said quickly: 'We haven't done anything yet; we don't know anything like enough.' She swung round on Stefan. 'Why did you have to come *now*?'

Bruton grinned. 'There's gratitude!' he said, ironically.

Brian said: 'I'm just beginning to understand.'

'We've got to make up our minds what to do,' insisted Stella. 'We've got to make Mallory believe that Dr. Palfrey doesn't remember anything of his past life, but—how can we take advantage of that now? If you'd sent a message, if you'd warned us——'

'Hold hard,' said Brian. 'We believed Sap was in a fix.'

'Oh, I suppose it can't be helped,' said Stella, 'you meant so well, but—you've undone everything we've been trying to do for ten days, and we were getting so near to success; I hoped we would find out—everything.'

Palfrey put his hand on her shoulder.

'We'll see it through,' he said. 'Who are the men who've helped you, Stefan?'

'American agents,' Stefan said.

'Not police?'

'Not official police.'

'The shots would have been heard outside,' said Palfrey, frowning. He looked at Stefan.

'I do not think that anyone took much notice of the shooting,' Stefan said. 'I understand that there is a great deal of shooting in the copse nearby. No alarm has been raised—had there been, we should have heard from the police by now.'

Bruton said: 'There'll only be a marshal here.'

'Where are we?' asked Palfrey.

'Randall City, Alabama,' Bruton said. 'It's a one-horse town, Sap, if you can call it a town. It's off main roads, more dead than alive. There's cotton and corn, but the land's playing out. It's a centre of trouble, too. The Civil War passed this place over, and the whites have given the negroes a raw deal for a hundred years. Now there's been trouble between the two races, and of late someone has been selling illicit whisky in the Quarters. That's liable to cause more trouble.' He paused, and then grinned crookedly. 'The city's got enough troubles of its own without worrying about us; that's what I'm trying to tell you. We're safe from interference, I guess. No one who matters knows we're here, and if they did, a word with the marshal would put that right.'

'What is on your mind?' asked Stefan, slowly.

Palfrey smiled vaguely; it was a smile they had often seen on his lips, and did more than anything else to cheer them up, for this was the *real* Palfrey, who looked hesitant and uncertain and diffident because his mind was working at high pressure.

'It's like this,' Palfrey said. 'Mallory's been working on me with some purpose in mind, and we want to find out what it is. If Casado and the others turned the tables and got us back, Casado would report that I didn't know you from Adam. So——'

Brian interrupted sharply: 'You're not going back to them!'

'I may have to,' said Palfrey. He hesitated. 'Do you know anything more than you did when I left England?'

Stefan said slowly: 'A little more, Sap, and it is not good. Briefly, it——'

'We'll have details later,' said Palfrey. 'Is it really of primary importance?'

'Yes.'

'Then I'll have to go back,' said Palfrey. He smiled more freely. 'It won't be so bad as it has been! And you can get word to 'Silla and tell her——' he broke off. 'Now who's wasting time?'

'We can't just walk out and leave you,' said Brian, stubbornly.

'No, we'll all have to leave. We'll have to let Casado or some of his men follow us. There isn't any other way. Where are you staying?'

Bruton chuckled. 'Not at the best hotel! We've picked up a shack by the little river—the one you can see out of the window.'

'We'll go there,' Palfrey said. 'We'll take Casado with us, and we'll work something out when we get there.' He looked at Stella. 'You'll have to be treated as a prisoner, I'm afraid.'

'That's all right,' Stella said, 'but when we're at this shack, what are we going to do?'

'Well—roughly something like this: I've been hurt and I am too ill to move. One of these three will stay with me and you will stay as a nurse. The others leave, to make a report. Then Casado escapes—he doesn't strike me as being a man without courage. And it wouldn't surprise me if there aren't plenty of his men nearby, waiting to be called on in an emergency. We

98

can work all that out,' he said. 'The first thing to do is get out of here.'

'The first thing to do is to get to the airfield and leave the district,' Brian said, hotly. 'Haven't you taken enough risks?'

Palfrey smiled. 'We've got to play out this hand, Bry; don't be awkward. What transport have you got?'

'An old Ford and a Chevrolet truck,' Bruton said. 'We came as a working party from Montgomery.'

'Then let's go,' said Palfrey.

TEN

THE RIVER

PALFREY slept for an hour, after a lunch of small trout cooked over an open fire in another room of the shack, with new maize bread and coffee as good as that at the house. When he woke up, he felt much more himself.

Stefan told him of the black dirt . . .

As the Russians talked, Palfrey remembered the black soil near the bungalow and the patches he had seen from the window of the house nearby. When he had seen it, he had felt uneasy, as if the dark earth were sinister, holding an unknown threat; now he understood the feeling which had come over him.

Would men use such a discovery to force artificial food shortages and put up prices, even risking yet another world famine?

Stefan brought him out of his dark reverie.

'Now, Sap, we have to decide what to do—quickly.'

'Oh, yes,' said Palfrey. 'Any advance on what I've suggested? We could let Casado get away on his own and keep the others. Or send them somewhere safe. How many men did you have with you altogether?'

'Seven,' said Bruton.

'There are only two outside.'

'We can call on the others if we want them,' Bruton said; 'they're in Randall City. It's time we told you just what happened.'

After the ambulance had left the nursing home, patrol cars had reported its arrival at the New York airport, where the invalid had been put into a private four-seater plane which had immediately taken off. A small aircraft had set off immediately after it, and its flight had been charted as far as the airfield at Montgomery, which was thirty miles south of Randall City. Another ambulance had been waiting to take Palfrey off. Airport officials had shown no great curiosity about it; but for the watching aircraft, the four-seater's arrival and departure would have been logged and then forgotten. Within an hour of its arrival, however, Stefan, Bruton and Brian had left for Montgomery in a specially chartered aircraft, and the Federal Bureau had detailed the seven men to assist them.

There had been no difficulty in finding the house where the ambulance had finished its journey.

Even then, none had been sure that Palfrey was the passenger, but the house had been watched throughout the night, and a little after nine o'clock they had seen Palfrey standing at the window. Thereafter it had been decided quickly that Stefan should be 'caught' and the others raid the house while the attention of Casado and his men was distracted.

'Are you still thinking of letting Casado go?' asked Brian, who was sitting fanning himself by an open window. He felt the heat more than any of them, and that may have accounted for his stubborn opposition to the original suggestion.

Palfrey said: 'There just isn't anything to do. Only by letting Mallory recapture me can I find out what he wants me for. It's as simple as that.'

The two men keeping guard left in the early evening, taking with them all the prisoners except Casado. Palfrey watched them leave in the Chevrolet, and then strolled along the river bank.

Bruton joined him.

'I wonder who's behind this ramp,' Bruton murmured. 'This man Mallory——'

'Isn't the leader,' said Palfrey.

'Karen we don't know. Grayson—I wouldn't rate Grayson high, but I wish he hadn't disappeared. Then there's Hoffner. Have any of those names been mentioned to you?'

'No,' said Palfrey.

Bruton told him all he could about Grayson and Hoffner as they strolled back to the shack. Stefan was bringing Stella from the other building.

Darkness had fallen, and the lights were on, dim lamp-lights.

100

There were muslin screens at the window, to keep out the mosquitoes, for the window was wide open.

In the distance, men were shouting and singing.

'They're lit up in the Quarters,' Bruton said. He went to the door and listened. 'I guess Randall City is getting worried,' he said, with a grin which was a little anxious. 'They've had trouble with the negroes, I'm told.'

All of them soon heard a car approaching along the river bank. Bruton opened the door again, and the noise of singing and shouting seemed much nearer. Brian joined him on the veranda. They all felt uneasy, and it was clear that Stella Dale was affected. She kept staring at the white figures of the two men who were standing outside.

Suddenly a single rifle-shot sounded above every other sound. A bullet smacked against the wall of the shack. In a flash, Brian was inside the room, and Bruton jumped forward and knelt behind one of the posts of the veranda.

There were two more shots. A bullet hummed through the open door and buried itself in the wall opposite.

'Look here,' Stefan whispered.

They could see dark figures moving about the undergrowth at the back of the shack. Several men reached the hut where Casado was imprisoned. Someone shone a powerful torch. It flashed on white faces, and on an axe, which crashed against the door and shattered its age-rotted timbers at the first blow. Other men were coming warily towards the house, carrying all kinds of weapons.

Bruton called out from the front: 'What are the odds?'

'Too heavy,' Stefan called back.

'Come on,' said Bruton.

Stefan said: 'Go on, Sap, I will follow.' He was standing by an open window, with a gun in his hand. As Palfrey went into the main room, Stefan fired four times. The shots seemed very loud. Much nearer, too, was the rumbling of a van or car along the river bank, and the drunken bellowing of the men in it. Dark figures were about the shack, but the movements towards it had been stopped by Stefan's shots.

Brian and Stella were standing just behind the door ; Bruton was still outside.

'They fired from across the river to distract us,' he said. 'The main raid's coming from the back. Look there.' He pointed towards the river, and in the dark, shimmering surfaces, they could see men wading, waist high. 'They're coming to lend a

101

hand,' said Bruton. 'You can see the game a mile off. They've poured whisky into the negroes; they'll blame the poor beggars for this. I'm beginning to see why they chose that house and Randall City,' he added, with a savage note in his voice.

'What are we going to do?' asked Brian.

Bruton said: 'They'll expect us to fight it out here. We won't oblige—that boat's near enough for us. Where's Stefan?'

'Holding them off at the back,' said Palfrey.

Bruton said: 'Fetch him, Bry.'

They stepped down from the veranda, imagining stealthy figures in every direction, but the shack was between them and their near assailants. Only the singing could be heard now. Palfrey wondered whether the attack would be made from the rear only, whether there was not a chance that men were waiting on the opposite bank. But the last of the men who had crossed the river was now climbing up near the truck.

Bruton slipped down the sticky bank. Palfrey plunged after him. The water was cold, but not icy. The river bed made him slither to and fro; once he nearly lost his footing, but he regained it and went on. He kept looking over his shoulder at Stella. Could she make it? He saw Brian join her, and take her by the waist. Next moment Brian lifted her to his shoulder and floundered across. That was bad; Stefan should have carried her, but Stefan always liked to bring up the rear in such a journey as this.

Bruton had reached the far bank, and Palfrey stood immediately beneath it. He pulled himself up by the help of a branch of a tree, and stood on the side, gasping for breath. Stefan drew level with Brian and took the girl. Effortlessly he lifted her and stood her on the bank.

'Hurry!' Bruton urged. 'They're breaking in.'

Under the cover of the fusillade and the shouting, men had rushed the shack. They were smashing the windows and battering down the doors with wild, pointless frenzy. In a few seconds they would know that their quarries had escaped, and they would know there was only one way for them to go.

The headlights of the truck blazed out.

The darkness faded on the opposite bank, engulfed by a great glow of light. It shone on the surface of the river, on the trees growing from the bank, on *their* side of the river! Men were calling out on the other side; someone was giving orders, thought Palfrey. The singing and shouting continued, and he heard the smashing of wood as if the shack were being broken down.

Suddenly he saw a flash of light.

He looked round. Flames were rising from the shack, and he could see that one side of it was alight; it was just possible that Casado thought someone was inside, perhaps in the loft, and he was trying to smoke them out.

'They're following,' Bruton said.

They were standing on a small mound, and could see both banks of the river near the shack. Half a dozen men were jumping into the water. The wind carried the sound of the splashes clearly. The men waded across, and Stella, leaning against Palfrey, shivered uncontrollably.

Bruton said: 'We'll have to get back to the other side. Keep close to me.'

They were in a hollow now, and the bank was lower. They stepped into the water—and Palfrey promptly went knee deep. Stefan carried Stella, and they went straight towards the other side. The current seemed stronger here, and the river bed was stony. There was less danger of slipping, but when they reached the middle, the water rose sharply to Palfrey's chest and almost to Bruton's shoulders. Bruton forced his way onwards, and the river grew shallower.

They found the track on the bank much wider, and progress was easier.

Bruton said: 'Steady, now.'

They passed another shack, which looked half-finished but was really half-rotted. Opposite it was a small landing-stage, and a flat-bottomed boat was moored alongside. The jetty creaked under Bruton's weight.

Stefan put Stella down.

'I had better not tread there,' he said, and stepped into the water again, reaching the skiff almost as soon as Bruton. In the yellow-red glow from the fire, Palfrey could see the outlines of the fragile-looking craft. But something else cheered him: there was a motor in the stern.

'Will it take us all?' asked Stefan.

'And more,' said Bruton, confidently. 'Get on board.'

He did not start the engine immediately. They waited, looking towards the far bank, and they could hear the rustle of movement, a noise like they had been making. It was between them and the shack, so the men had not yet drawn level. The tumult near the shack seemed wilder, but, being nearly half a mile away, they heard less of it. The flames were still leaping high, but the boat was outside the range of its light.

'Now,' said Bruton.

He swung a handle.

Stefan stretched out his long arm and pushed them away from the landing-stage. The boat swung into midstream, but seemed to be travelling very slowly.

A shot rang out.

'Miles wide,' said Bruton. There was an elated note in his voice, as if he knew that they would get away now. 'We'll give them shooting!'

Brian said: 'Do you know where we're going?'

'We'll hit the big river eight or nine miles down,' said Bruton. 'We'll be all right. Don't——'

Suddenly shots ran out from the other side, almost immediately opposite them.

Bruton said: 'That's bad.' None of the others spoke.

It was clear that someone had come along the bank, that Casado had not sent all his men across the river; and the party now threatening danger was only a few yards away from them.

The engine roared; the boat trembled, but gathered a little speed.

'If we could get another knot or two——' Bruton muttered. Stefan leaned forward and touched Palfrey's knee.

'Come this side, Sap,' he said, and Palfrey stared at the pale blur of his face.

'Come on,' Stefan said.

Palfrey crouched low as he crossed to the other side. Only then did he realize what Stefan was going to do.

'Hold it steady,' said Stefan. 'I'll find you later, Sap—in Montgomery, if I do not catch up with you farther along.'

'Stop rocking the damned boat!' snapped Bruton.

'Steady, now,' said Stefan, 'I'm going over the side.'

How he managed it without upsetting them, Palfrey did not know. One moment Stefan was standing up, the next he had plunged into the river, and the splash smacked at the side of the boat so that it heeled over, shipping some water. Then it swung back and righted itself. For a moment the craft was quite out of control, but gradually it steadied.

Palfrey could see Stefan's head as he began to swim *away* from the boat, back to the shack.

Brian shouted: 'Stefan!'

Only the wind and the splashing water answered him; then came another fusillade of shots in front of the bows. Bruton made no comment, and settled in the middle of the boat to give full attention to the engine. They were making much greater speed without the Russian.

Palfrey felt cold dread at the thought of what might happen if the Russian were caught. There would be no mercy from Casado, and whatever happened on that dark night would be blamed on to drunken men, men probably deliberately driven mad with liquor.

The forest closed about them.

They could not see the trees or the banks, only the water close by the sides of the boat. A crash as they hit an obstruction. Brian lurched forward, grabbed the side and saved himself from falling. Stella fell into Palfrey's lap, and Palfrey jammed his back against the side of the boat; it was so painful that it seemed to cut him in two.

The boat swung round wildly, out of control.

Bruton picked himself up as the engine spluttered and stopped.

'We can't do a thing here,' he said, after a pause, 'we'll have to get to the bank. Where are the paddles?'

'Here,' said Brian.

Bruton and Palfrey took the oars. They cleared the obstruction without much difficulty, but there was an ominous rending sound.

'Propeller's caught it,' Bruton said, laconically.

The stern bumped against the bank and an overhanging tree brushed their heads, sweeping Palfrey's hat into the water. Stella said, *'Oh!'*, and they could hear her teeth chattering. Palfrey straightened up, his back aching, as Bruton and Brian climbed over the side. Palfrey got out and joined them, telling Stella to stay where she was. She disobeyed, and climbed over. The water came up to her knees. Between them they tugged at the boat. There was one piece of good fortune: they had struck a fairly clear stretch of bank, and were able to get the bows out of water.

'We'll be all right,' Bruton said.

'All right's one word,' Palfrey said, and there was an echo of a laugh in his words. 'How far are we from Casado?'

'Eight or nine miles.'

'Will it be safe to light a fire?'

'No,' said Bruton, 'but we'll have to. We want some light.'

He took a small torch from his pocket, but it was water-logged and did not work. Brian also had one, which gave off a dim glow. Bruton sniffed.

'It's a good thing the boat was stocked,' he said, and, taking Brian's torch, stepped precariously on board and opened the locker. He passed out some tinned foods, cigarettes and matches. Next he produced a sheet of water-proofing, and when he rejoined them on the bank he said:

'We can rig this up to hide the fire from anyone who's coming after us. There's a chance that they won't trouble.' There was no confidence in the words.

The forest held no terrors by day.

It was not as thick as Palfrey had thought, and the fresh green of young trees made a welcome brightness against the dark branches of pines. The little river was crystal clear up here. The shrubs growing in the banks, which were darker than in the backwater stretch, seemed to sway gently, but it was an illusion created by the rippling water.

Stella said: 'I could enjoy it out here.'

'Well, start enjoying it,' said Palfrey.

She laughed. 'You know what I mean.'

It was not until half an hour later, when Brian had gone to explore on his own, that she told him about her work with Lannigan.

Lannigan himself had discovered that Dr. Mallory was Karen's medical adviser, and that he owned the nursing home. There was some evidence that Diana Leeming had been at that nursing home after the 'accident'. On that slender clue, Stella had taken the nursing job at the home. She had once been a trained nurse.

Palfrey glanced at the fire as he mulled this over. 'That's smoking a lot,' he remarked.

Stella laughed. 'You're dreaming.'

The fire was burning red, with the dry wood giving off little smoke; but there was a smell of smoke in the air.

Brian appeared. 'Can you smell burning?' he asked, as he sat down beside them. 'I thought you were playing the fool with the fire.'

'There's burning all right,' said Palfrey.

They became aware of other unexpected things.

Birds began to fly overhead, skimming the trees or coming through the branches, many more of them than there had been earlier in the morning. Suddenly a colony of rats appeared—a thick, grey carpet. Stella sprang up, gasping.

It's all right,' said Brian, grabbing her.

She clutched at him as the rats sped along the river bank, coming with a few feet of them in a seemingly endless phalanx ; then rabbits seemed to fill the clearing, scuttling through the undergrowth ; and squirrels came springing from tree to tree, and the air was suddenly filled with squawking and cackling, as flocks of birds flew past—quail and wild-fowl, and birds Palfrey had never seen before, their bright plumage caught in the sun. On the other side of the river they saw small brown deer loping along between the trees ; the forest and the air seemed alive.

Stella said unsteadily:

'What is it?'

The smell of smoke was stronger now, but Palfrey did not put the fear which had sprung to his mind into words.

'Get into that boat!' None of them moved as Bruton ran to the bank, waving wildly to the boat. 'Get in!' he cried.

'So it's a forest fire,' said Brian, slowly.

The smell of burning was too strong for them to be in any doubt ; and they thought they heard the distant roar of the flames. They rushed to the boat, and unshipped the oars. Brian exclaimed suddenly: 'We want the stores,' and jumped back on the bank. He tossed back the few tins they had unloaded, and soon they were pushing into midstream.

It had been so warm in the clearing that they had not been able to tell the difference between fire-heat and the warmth of the day, but they felt it now. They were pulling gently at their oars, and watching the sky. It seemed darker, as if the smoke had risen above the wind and was coming towards them. They could hear the distant crackling of the flames as they swept along the ground.

Palfrey and Bruton pulled with long, seemingly casual, strokes, while Brian sat in the bows and Stella the stern, looking with awed fascination at the scene on either side of the river. The fact that the alarm among the wild creatures was on both sides worried Palfrey, for it suggested that the flames had leapt the river farther down.

It was not surprising.

Among the frightened birds over their heads were fiery specks from the burning trees, for the fire had drawn level with them now, some distance from the water, driving the creatures of the earth into the river.

They reached a bend in the river as trees on either side caught alight. Behind them a great tree crashed into the river, and Palfrey caught a glimpse of it as it fell, blazing, a torch of red against the dark forest beyond. Cypress trees and bamboo canes were burning close to the water's edge. The fire devoured the grass where there were clear patches; he had not believed that fire could move so fast. They were almost completely surrounded now, and he found rowing in that suffocating air almost impossible.

Bruton rested on his oars.

'I'm near finished,' he gasped.

'I'll take a turn,' Stella said.

Bruton did not try to stop her. They changed places, and Brian shouldered Palfrey aside.

Then they turned a bend in the river; and the water stretched out on either side, the banks receded; unexpectedly, they had come upon a lake.

ELEVEN

AFTER THE FIRE

STELLA stopped rowing, and stared at the distant banks, then redoubled her efforts until they were well into the middle of the lake, and the banks were a quarter of a mile away on either side. There was a break in the forest immediately in front of them. The sky, even there, was filled with smoke; but they knew that they had reached the end of the trees and the worst danger was gone.

Dead creatures floated past them.

Bruton said: 'Well, they didn't win that round.'

'If you're trying to say that Casado started that lot, you're crazy,' said Brian. 'That fire came in from three directions and was started both sides of the river. It came the same speed on both sides, which means that it began about the same time, and if the fire on one side had started from a fire on the other it would have been much later starting and wouldn't have caught up. Is that clear?'

Palfrey nodded.

108

'I saw the smoke from three directions at once,' Bruton said, 'south, west, and north-west. It's tinder-dry. It wouldn't need much starting. One tin of petrol or kerosene at every point, and that would be enough. They wanted to smoke us out, Sap —or roast us.'

After a short silence, Stella said: 'What about your friend?'

'Stefan,' said Brian, and left it at that.

'There's a chance that he went past the shack and into Randall City,' Bruton said. 'They wouldn't be looking for anyone going in that direction; that's a thing we forgot when we saw him go off. And the fire wouldn't spread that way. We don't have to worry too much about Stefan.'

'I wish I could feel sure,' said Stella.

'Where did he arrange to meet us?' Brian put the question as if it were a simple matter of making an appointment and keeping it. Stella looked at him sharply.

'In Montgomery,' Palfrey said.

'How far away is that?' asked Brian.

'Forty south from here,' said Bruton. 'It won't take us long to get there.' He sat brooding. 'Rather than let you go, Sap, Casado wanted you dead. So he didn't want you alive all that much.'

'They haven't properly trained me yet,' said Palfrey.

They rowed in turns for an hour before they neared the far end of the lake. Beyond, the country was hilly, and on the hills were orchards; nearer the shore, corn was growing, already golden. The sun was forcing its way through the thinning smoke clouds. They could see people on the banks, pointing towards them. They pulled towards the shore, and saw black men and white standing, and heard them shouting. Between the lake and the big river beyond, there was another narrow stretch of water, with the familiar red clay, and the trees growing close to the water's edge. It reminded Palfrey vividly of his first sight of the shack; Casado had fired the shack, as an earnest of what was to come.

He and Bruton rowed the last few yards, and men splashed into the water to pull them ashore. There was a cottage close to the water's edge, and farther away, a few newly-painted shacks; they had come upon a village.

Palfrey climbed out and looked at his blistered hands, and a man carried Stella to the shore.

Only then did he remember that even here he must 'forget' who he was.

A tall man, his face burned brown by the sun, an old, wide-brimmed linen hat on the back of his head, his long, yellow moustaches giving him a false impression of fierceness, came into the room.

'Well, gentlemen,' he said, 'I trust you are feeling better.'

'We're fine,' said Bruton.

'I'm glad of that,' said their host, hooking his thumbs into his waist-band. 'I'll admit I did not consider there was any hope for anyone in the forest during the fire.'

'Was anyone else there, do you know?' asked Palfrey.

'No,' said their host, frowning, 'I know of none from here, which does not mean that the forest was empty. But most people would be in the fields today, there would be little hunting. How far have you come?'

'From Randall City,' said Bruton.

'There was trouble there last night,' said their host, and his face took on a hard, bleak look.

Palfrey, huddled in blankets and sitting near a small fire, studied him. Palfrey was still acting 'ill' and had uttered hardly a word since he had reached the house. It did not seem likely, but it was possible that Casado had an agent in this village; it was near enough to Randall City for that. He did not yet know the man's name; but he knew that this man had authority which stretched beyond the confines of his small house.

'There has been trouble in Randall City since Arnold Grayson bought most of the land,' the southerner went on. He did not appear to notice the way Brian and Palfrey started, nor the sudden narrowing of Bruton's eyes.

'Grayson?' echoed Bruton.

'Yes, sir.' Their host went to the mantelpiece and took down a curved pipe and began to fill it. 'I must apologize to you, gentlemen, because I have not introduced myself. My name is Farraday. I come from Randall City.' He paused between each sentence, and went on filling his pipe, as if it helped him to concentrate on what he was saying. 'I once owned plantations in Randall City. Today, Grayson owns most of it, and most of the real estate. From the day he first came there was trouble with the workers.'

Bruton said, 'Grayson's got a good reputation in the north. Do you remember when his daughter was kidnapped?'

'I do, sir.'

'Had she ever been to Randall City?'

'Once,' said Farraday, 'and she was not wanted again, the

110

painted Jezebel. She——' he broke off abruptly, and Palfrey had some idea of the strong emotions conflicting within him. 'I wish harm to no one ; I was sorry for Grayson when I heard that his daughter had been taken away from him, but it was a fate which the young woman invited, by her looseness, and which the man, by his acts here, had brought upon himself—a justice executed by stronger powers than ours.' He seemed to have forgotten the card which Bruton had shown him. He fell into a reverie, again giving the impression that he was hardly conscious of time. Then he asked abruptly: 'How well do you know Grayson?'

'We're looking for him, among other things,' said Bruton, who had introduced himself by producing his F.B.I. identity card. 'He sailed for England, but didn't arrive.'

'When was that?'

'Most of a week ago,' Bruton said.

Farraday shook his head. 'Grayson did not sail from the United States ten days ago,' he said. 'I saw him myself only four days back, when he was visiting a house recently bought by a Dr. Mallory. That is how Grayson behaves,' he went on, slowly. 'He should not have allowed that property to be sold to a Yankee. Everything he does is liable to cause trouble.'

There was a long silence as they brooded over that. Then:

'When Grayson comes to Randall, where does he stay?' asked Bruton.

'At the Great House,' said Farraday, 'the largest house in the city, and the first he bought.'

The door from the kitchen opened and Stella came in.

'You are very welcome, ma'am,' said Farraday, and glanced at an old grandfather clock in a dark corner of the room. 'And I have been talking too freely ; all of you must bath and have dinner.'

Palfrey would have enjoyed every moment of the meal but for the thought of Stefan.

They were drinking coffee and smoking cigars when Farraday told them casually about 'black soil' which had appeared in parts of the land near Randall City. Even Stefan was forgotten then.

A black footman in a blue coat and knee-breeches opened the door of the Great House in Randall City and started when he saw the gigantic figure in the porch. He backed away in alarm when Stefan stepped over the threshold, and stared up at his set face.

'I wish to see Mr. Grayson,' Stefan said.

'De massa is in bed, sah!'

'He can get out of bed,' said Stefan. 'It isn't late.'

'Yo'—yo' hab an appointment, sah?'

Stefan looked at him, and smiled faintly.

'Tell him I have news of his daughter,' he said.

'Ob—ob his daughter! Yassah, Ah go tell him.' The footman turned and hurried off.

Stefan went to a high-backed, wooden chair and sat down.

The 'Great House' was rightly named. This hall was vast. Heavy oil paintings hung on the white walls, with one of ex-President Eisenhower holding pride of place. The furniture was old-fashioned but of fine quality. A huge Indian carpet covered the floor, and in each doorway was a skin rug.

Stefan, still damp from the river, shivered as he sat back, glad of a respite. The chance of seeing Grayson while Casado and the others were by the river could not be missed. He wondered what kind of reception he would get, whether mention of his daughter would make Grayson receive a stranger. Stefan smiled, thinking of the description which the footman would give of him. Then he stopped smiling, and he thought of the story which the local doctor, chance-met in his wanderings, had told him of the effect of Grayson's 'improvement' campaign.

A door opened at the top of the stairs, and the footman came hurrying down.

'Mis' Grayson will see you, sah, in two-three minutes.'

'Thank you,' said Stefan.

'Yo'—yo' close, sah,' said the footman, and goggled. 'Yo'se so wet.'

'I haven't any others,' said Stefan, gravely.

'Yo' will catch yo' death,' said the footman, nervously. 'Yo' should have dem close dried, sah, the massa say yo' hab dem dried.' He spoke so quickly that he nearly swallowed his words. 'Yo' come wid me, sah.'

Stefan let the big man lead him along the passage by the staircase, through other passages into a big, stone-floored kitchen which struck warm. No one else was there. The man hurried out of the room, and Stefan caught a glimpse of a narrow staircase and heard him pattering up. In a few minutes the man was back with a white coat and trousers, and Stefan stared in astonishment.

112

'Dese are nearly big 'nuff,' said the footman. 'Take off dat coat, sah.' Stefan obeyed. The coat was big enough, except in the length of the arms; the sleeve ended half-way down his forearms. 'Dey's a bit short,' admitted the footman, 'but dey will serve for a while.'

Ten minutes later, dry and washed, Stefan was led back. Grayson stood up from behind a small desk—a short, wiry man with a goatee beard. He was the image of the photographs which Stefan had seen of him, of the man for whom Bruton and the others had searched at Southampton. His head was bald at the front, but bushy grey hair stood out at the sides and the back.

Stefan dwarfed him.

Blue, gimlet eyes peered at the Russian.

'I hope you've not lied about my daughter,' Grayson said. He did not smile; nothing about Stefan's appearance seemed to strike him as funny.

'I have not,' said Stefan.

'Who are you?'

Stefan gave the name Stevens, and added: 'I am a friend of Dr. Palfrey.'

'Indeed,' said Grayson. 'Who is Dr. Palfrey.'

Did he mean the question seriously? wondered Stefan. Or was his blank face just a mask covering his thoughts?

'Dr. Palfrey knew Lannigan well,' said Stefan.

For the first time, Grayson showed animation.

'Did you know Lannigan?'

'No. He went to see Palfrey, thinking that Palfrey could help him. Later Palfrey found his body. Lannigan told Palfrey all that you had told him.'

'I—see,' said Grayson. 'Had Lannigan found my daughter?'

'He thought so.'

'Did he tell Palfrey why he thought so?'

'Yes,' said Stefan.

The man continued to puzzle him. There had been messages to and fro across the Atlantic. Grayson himself was supposed to have sent word that he was catching the s.s. *Adua Star*, yet now he behaved as if this were all news to him.

'What have you to tell me?' asked Grayson.

Stefan said: 'When were you last at your house in Seattle, Mr. Grayson?'

'Three weeks back.'

'Palfrey corresponded with you there.'

'Now, what's this?' asked Grayson, sharply. 'Palfrey didn't do anything of the kind. I've recalled the name now. Wasn't he a secret service ace, who died a few days back?'

'That's the man,' said Stefan.

'He didn't get in touch with me.'

Stefan said: 'Someone who said he was you spoke to Palfrey's agent and travelled from New York to Southampton, but disappeared half an hour before the ship berthed. That is the truth, Mr. Grayson.'

'I don't believe it,' said Grayson.

Stefan leaned forward and picked up the telephone. He was answered promptly. 'Get me Police Department, New York City, please,' he said.

'There will be a delay of one hour,' said the operator.

'No,' said Stefan. 'I said the Police Department.'

'Okay, I'll make it quicker, if I can.'

Stefan replaced the receiver.

Grayson said: 'I'm beginning to believe you.'

'A girl we think is your daughter is in England today,' Stefan said. 'She goes under the name of Diana Leeming. She has lost memory of all that happened before she came round in a nursing-home, and does not recall the name Grayson. You were to have gone to England to identify her—or otherwise.'

'Or otherwise,' said Grayson, and he laughed harshly. 'I have seen a hundred women—corpses included. A great many people would like to be my daughter.'

'This one doesn't care whether she is your daughter or not,' Stefan argued. 'All she wishes to do is to find out who she is. Will you fly to England to see her?'

Palfrey, Stella, Bruton and Brian reached Montgomery late on the night after the forest fire. They had been driven in an open car by Farraday, who saw them to the Alabama Hotel and left them, with his good wishes echoing in their ears. Palfrey was still treated as a sick man ; if Casado's agents were watching, they would be completely deceived.

The telephone rang.

'I'll answer it,' said Brian, and went quickly to the side of the room. 'Room 35,' he said. 'Yes, I'll hold on.' He waited, smiling at Stella, and then suddenly he stiffened, his face was creased in a wide grin. '*Stefan!*' he announced.

Stella jumped up.

114

'I told you not to worry about that big ham,' said Bruton. 'He's too big to meet trouble.'

Brian was saying: 'Yes . . . Yes . . . *What?*' He snapped his fingers excitedly. 'Where . . . Yes, this is as good as anywhere else.' He finished speaking, replaced the receiver, and turned round, his smile broader than ever. 'He's got Grayson,' he said, and there was a laugh in his voice. 'The old boy was in Randall City. Stefan contacted Long-jaw and the others, who hadn't left, and they held up Grayson's car. He says he's got quite a story.'

TWELVE

KAREN

PALFREY was feeling much more himself.

For one thing, he had spoken to Drusilla by telephone, and she had reassured him ; she had never felt better, she had said ; Palfrey had not disbelieved her. She had been staying at the flat, but now that she knew that he was all right she was going to Brett Hall until he returned.

Palfrey had not gone out a great deal.

To build up the impression on the minds of any who might be watching that Mallory's 'treatment' had been successful, he received a call every day from New York's leading specialist on loss of memory. The specialist was puzzled and intensely sorry for Palfrey, whose reputation he knew well. Palfrey found deceiving him easy enough ; the worst part of the business was convincing himself that it would be worth while.

Grayson, too, had been held in a small house in Far Rockaway. He had been questioned time and time again, but remained sullen and uncommunicative. He still gave the impression of being frightened. Now and again he protested against being held, and Washington officials were worried, since there was only suspicion against him. Eventually he would have to be released.

The police had intercepted a letter telling Casado that Mallory would go to Randall City, but the man had not arrived and there was no trace of him. Bruton had suggested dosing him with scropofaline, the truth drug.

Palfrey had advised against it, and Grayson was now flying

115

to England. Palfrey was waiting anxiously for the report of the results of the man's interview with Diana.

Brian had gone back to England on the same aircraft as Grayson. Bruton and Palfrey were staying in an hotel in the centre of the city. Stella Dale, although watched all the time by Federal agents, had gone to a hotel near Stefan. No one had molested her, no one appeared to be interested in her. That was one of the things which puzzled Palfrey.

Reports from Brett were sombre.

There were fresh discoveries of 'black earth' in the United States and in England. One had been reported from Russia and another from France. But for Grayson's stubbornness, Palfrey thought, they might now be on the way to learning who was behind the devilry. No one liked contemplating the possible consequences.

A widespread search in North America, on both sides of the Canadian-United States border, was being made for the bungalow with the laboratory, the airfield and the black earth. No news had yet come in.

Bruton was checking results, or the lack of them, with Government agents. One of his latest worries was that Hoffner had left the United States and was reported to be in India, but there was no official news of him. Brett had been informed and had been in touch with New Delhi. There was an uneasy feeling everywhere that Hoffner had been left too long.

On one of his frequent visits, Stefan was sitting in a large armchair overlooking the sea at Palfrey's temporary home. Palfrey was stretched out on a long-chair, smoking and twiddling his hair.

'Grayson and Hoffner,' he said, suddenly. 'The only two names we've got, except Karen, and Karen hardly counts until we've seen him.'

'You mean that he and Hoffner might be one and the same man?'

'It's possible,' said Palfrey. 'As far as I can gather, their descriptions tally. What a situation! Grayson being driven hither and thither because, he says, he's afraid for his daughter. Dark earth cropping up everywhere, and likely to lead to a dark harvest.' He laughed mirthlessly. 'And I am living in style!'

'It is as well you've had some rest,' said Stefan.

'I've had too much of it. I once thought they would be sure

116

to make another effort to get me, but I doubt it now. I over-rated my importance. A bad habit. We've lain low. We've the fullest possible co-operation from Washington and from the State police everywhere. We've deliberately "lost" Casado and Karen, who are probably continuing their little game and laughing up their sleeves. It might have been better to have kept Casado when we had him. We're not likely to have a second chance.'

'I see no need for this gloom,' said Stefan.

'I'm afraid I do,' said Palfrey. 'If only I knew what they were playing at with me! Why did they put me through those crazy tests. What were they driving at?'

'It is so obvious,' protested Stefan. 'They wanted to make sure that you told them all that you knew, and you convinced them that you had done so——'

'And I had,' said Palfrey.

'So, naturally, they were convinced,' smiled Stefan. 'And then they took your memory away from you, and they did not do that for nothing. That is what you have often said and what remains so obvious. They are bound to try to make capital out of it.'

Palfrey said: 'I hope you're right.' He glanced at his watch. 'It's time for my constitutional,' he added. 'I've never had an experience quite like this before. I take a daily walk on my own in the hope that the enemy will pick me up.' He shrugged his shoulders as he got up from the long-chair. 'If today's the day,' he pleaded, 'don't lose me altogether.'

'We shall know where you are taken,' said Stefan.

Palfrey put on a Panama hat and strolled towards the door. Stefan, properly clad again, watched him out of the window. The long garden stretched down to the beach. It was a lonely spot, neglected by most pleasure-seekers, with a dangerous current just off shore. As Palfrey walked towards the beach, a small motor-boat came into view, cruising slowly less than a hundred yards out.

Stefan went quickly upstairs, where he had a better view of the bay. Despite the precautions which he knew had been taken, he watched Palfrey anxiously. An aeroplane circled over-head, very high up, and then disappeared, but the engine's drone was out of earshot only for a few seconds. It was a reconnaissance machine, equipped with powerful cameras, and one of its kind was always circling over the house, night and day.

Stefan heard the roar of another aircraft.

Palfrey was strolling along the beach, and stooped to pick up stones. He stood clearly outlined against the sea, tossing the stones and trying to make them ricochet across the water. The motor-boat turned slowly towards the beach. The second aircraft was much nearer and lower than the spotting plane. It swooped into sight and Stefan saw that it had floats.

He stood tense and expectant.

Three men appeared from grounds nearby, one clad in trunks, with the sun shining on his tanned body, one in a swimsuit, the other fully dressed. They seemed to be taking an aimless stroll, but to Stefan the combination of motor-boat, flying-boat and men had a sinister implication.

Palfrey stopped his idle throwing.

The three men turned towards him.

Stefan watched what followed with reluctant admiration.

The assailants took action when they were only a few yards behind Palfrey. They rushed forward. The man who was fully-dressed raised his arm and struck Palfrey on the head. The others caught him as he fell, and rushed with him towards the sea.

Stefan flung the window open. Some people further along the beach shouted, and he heard the sound clearly. Palfrey splashed into the water, on his back. The others started to swim, supporting him between them, and the motor-boat drew nearer, its engine beginning to roar.

The flying-boat touched water, skimming towards the motor-boat and some hundred yards away from it.

Stefan turned and hurried downstairs, reaching the front of the house as the man who had struck Palfrey started to run. Stefan gave chase, rapidly overhauling him and glancing at the scene on the water as he did so. The shouts were still echoing in his ears. A man plunged into the sea and started to swim powerfully towards the party. Stefan wished he had not done that ; he might get seriously hurt.

The two swimmers reached the motor-boat, and pushed Palfrey into it, then clambered over the side to join him. The would-be rescuer was soon left behind.

By the time Stefan had caught his man, the flying-boat was skimming over the water again, with Palfrey on board.

Stefan and Bruton reached Montreal by air soon after dark when the first reports from the watching agents had been received. There, for the first time, they saw the reconnaissance report. They sent word of what had happened to Brett immediately by radio, for transmission wherever he thought necessary. When that was done, Bruton smoothed his hair, and said with a crooked smile:

'So Sap's back at the bungalow. He didn't have a good time there before.'

'He is not likely to receive the same treatment again,' said Stefan.

'He's going to have his work cut out to put up his act,' said Bruton, brusquely. 'And if they catch him out——' he broke off, and lit a cigar. 'When are we going to move in on the bungalow?'

'Not yet,' said Stefan. 'Perhaps not for a long time.'

The journey seemed unending, but Palfrey thought they were losing height, and looked out of the window. A great river stretched out below them, glittering in the sun and fading into the distance. He could see the dark mass of a large town on the river banks. They had been flying north-east; the river was probably the St. Lawrence Seaway, the town might be Montreal.

They flew over the river.

The landing on the lake, the transfer to the car, and comparatively short journey by road, all passed quickly, and he made no attempt to get away. The first time he was really forced to exert himself to retain his composure was when he saw the dark earth and the bungalow. There were white-clad men working in the laboratory. He kept his face expressionless, but the temptation to look up when an aircraft flew fairly low overhead was almost overwhelming. That would be one of the patrol planes; the bungalow had been located at last.

He was taken to a different room, one much larger and more comfortably furnished than that to which he had been taken on his first visit; it had the look of being lived in. Dr. Mallory was standing by a chair, and another man was sitting down and looking at the door.

Palfrey felt quite sure that he was at last face to face with Karen.

Palfrey looked at him closely.

He saw a thin-faced, good-looking man, with chestnut hair, thin at the front, wavy and thick at the back. The man had a curious pallor, not greyish-white, but dead-white—almost as if his cheeks had been thoroughly bleached to take every vestige of colour away. His nose and chin were pointed; he had deep-set eyes, fine grey eyes with a greenish tinge. His high forehead denoted a man of great intelligence, Palfrey thought; he was probably an intellectual.

'Well?' the man asked, sharply. His voice had an unusual timbre, not metallic but curiously harsh. 'Did you expect to come here again?'

Palfrey started. 'Again?'

Mallory and the stranger exchanged glances, pleased glances, Palfrey thought. Then 'Karen' spoke again, and his well-shaped lips were twisted in an ugly smile; there was mockery in his expression, and it was easy to understand how this man had frightened Diana Leeming—and Little Whitey—and——

He must not allow himself to remember too clearly.

'I am Karen,' the man said.

Palfrey raised his hands sharply, and stared afresh. Ought he .o recognize the name? Yes, of course, this was the danger—he could remember what Stefan and the others had told him; his mind was blank only from the moment he had come from in the nursing-home.

'I—see,' he said.

'You appear to have heard of me,' said Karen.

'My—friends—mentioned you.'

'Which friends?'

Palfrey said: 'You know whom I mean.'

'The Russian?'

'Yes.' Palfrey sat back in his chair, and the others watched him narrowly. He put his hands on the arms of the chair and gripped them tightly as he stared at Karen. 'Haven't you done enough to me?' he asked, in a low-pitched voice.

Karen laughed.

Yes, it was easy to understand how frightening he could be.

He leaned forward. 'Palfrey, listen to me. I have no desire to hurt you for the sake of hurting. I have sent for you because I want information. You can give it to me. If you are amenable'—he shrugged his square shoulders—'then you will have nothing to worry about. You remember the hot and cold chambers, don't you?'

Thought of those had already passed through Palfrey's mind. again it was on the tip of his tongue to say 'Yes'; and then he remembered that the injections had come after his visits to the chambers; he did not remember them.

120

'I don't understand you,' he said.

Mallory laughed. 'It's all right,' he said.

'Palfrey,' said Karen, 'we are going to give you a pencil and paper, and you are going to write down everything your friends told you. Understand me? *Everything*. You will write down what they told you about yourself, your wife, your friends, what has happened since you first became involved in my affairs —everything. And you will particularly remember all that they told you of the arrangements they are making to fight me. Do you understand?'

Palfrey said: 'I don't intend to——'

Karen strode forward and struck him on the side of the head; the blow dazed him. There was a mist in front of his eyes when he straightened up. The mist cleared; Karen was standing in front of him, with a hand upraised; and he looked a different man. There was a glow in his eyes which reminded Palfrey of the red glow beneath the billowing smoke of the forest fire.

'Don't make difficulties,' said Karen.

Palfrey sat white-faced and speechless, and it was not all pretence.

Karen went out.

Mallory coughed, and Palfrey looked at him. Compared with Karen, the man was insignificant, although in the nursing-home he had seemed formidable enough.

'I don't advise you to any mock-heroics, Palfrey,' he said. 'You think you've been badly treated. Karen can do much worse if he sets his mind to it.'

Palfrey did not answer.

'The memory is part of the mind,' Mallory said, as if he were repeating a lesson, 'but you might lose your sanity if he really gets angry with you.'

Still Palfrey did not answer; nor did the threat seem in vain.

Mallory went to a writing-desk and took out a writing-pad and a pencil.

'Don't lose any time,' he said.

Palfrey got up and went to the desk when Mallory had gone out. He had expected something like this, and had planned his story carefully; he intended to tell as much of the truth as he could, without giving anything away. The most difficult thing was to explain the secrecy and effectiveness with which his friends had worked. Karen must not be allowed to suspect that

121

Z.5 was working against him. If there were a weakness in the story he had to tell, that was it. He began to write.

When he had finished, he went to the window. He was not surprised to see the green shutter. The room seemed smaller than when he had first entered it.

He had been sitting doing nothing for a quarter of an hour when the door opened and Mallory came in.

'Have you finished?'

'Yes.'

'Good,' said Mallory. 'I hope you took my advice, Palfrey.' He picked up the closely written sheets, did not look at them, but folded them and pushed them into his pocket. 'We're going to have dinner in half an hour,' he said.

A footman was standing behind Karen, who was sitting at the head of the table. Löis was sitting on his right, Mallory on his left. There were three empty places, one at the end of the table.

'As our guest,' murmured Karen, 'you will sit opposite me, Dr. Palfrey.'

Palfrey said: 'Thanks.' The footman pulled the chair back for him.

It was fantastic!

Löis wore an evening gown of dark green, cut low. A single diamond glittered in her corsage. Her hair had been dressed, and shone beneath the bright light. Powder helped to hide her freckles. She seemed intent on enjoying herself. Karen and Mallory wore dinner-jackets; only the pilot and Palfrey were in lounge suits.

They were half-way through the meal when the door opened. A woman came in. She was tall and stately, a lovely creature; but Palfrey, who looked round at her, saw the dread in her eyes when she looked at Karen. He glanced at his 'host'. The man's lips were set tightly, he looked the personification of cruelty. It was a fact; he could frighten by his very expression.

Karen pushed his chair back and stood up. Palfrey rose, but the others remained sitting.

'You are late, my dear,' Karen said.

'I—I am sorry,' the woman murmured.

She had a low-pitched, humble voice, sounding as if she had been cowed into submission. Her beauty was like a mask, quite spoiled by the expression in her eyes. She sat down beside Palfrey and he saw that she was trembling.

'Dr. Palfrey,' said Karen, 'allow me to introduce my wife.'
Palfrey bowed.

Karen's wife smiled ; a pitiful little smile which did not lessen
the terror in her eyes. She ate mechanically and did not touch
wine. The others talked as if she were not present, although
towards the end of the meal she spoke a little. Karen lost no
opportunity to make her look ridiculous. Usually she smiled, as
if she did not understand what he was doing, but once Palfrey
saw her flinch ; and there was something akin to hatred in her
expression as she glanced at her husband.

This was the woman whom Diana Leeming had so pitied.

Karen said: 'Talk to Dr. Palfrey, my dear.' He was looking
at his wife. She started.

'Don't ask *too* much,' mocked Löis.

It was the first time she had made Palfrey dislike her ; and
the fierce rush of emotion he felt was stronger than dislike.
She looked disparagingly at the older woman, who flushed pitifully but made no retort.

They finished at last.

'We will join you later, my dear. And you, Löis,' said Karen,
and the women went out, Löis casting a languishing look on
Karen, who followed her with his eyes.

'I ought to be busy, sir,' said the pilot.

'All right, Monsell,' said Karen. He looked round at the footman. 'Liqueurs,' he said, 'and then you may go.'

Palfrey leaned on the table with a tiny glass of Benedictine
in front of him. Karen was sipping a glass of what looked like
absinthe, but might have been green chartreuse. Mallory was
inhaling the bouquet of an old brandy. The air of unreality
remained.

Karen offered cigars, and Palfrey accepted one.

'I have read your report,' said Karen, 'and it appears to be
quite satisfactory, Palfrey. Unless I find that you have lied to
me, I shall cause you no more harm. After we have finished
here, you will have another course of treatment. You will be
well cared-for during your convalescence and afterwards you
will be quite free. Doesn't that attract you?'

Palfrey licked his lips. 'Why—why give me further treatment?'

'I shall not want you to remember what has happened here,'
said Karen. He laughed. 'You see, Palfrey, I think you deserve
to know what I am doing. You have worked so well in this and
other cases. There is little you have done of which I have

123

not heard. And I think it only just that you should know.' But for the smile on his lips, he would have sounded sincere; but there was something in his expression which made mockery of the words. 'You will have the satisfaction of being in possession of all the facts. And when, afterwards, you forget them—can it be helped?'

'I would rather not know,' said Palfrey.

'It is a case of my wish against yours,' murmured Karen.

Mallory sipped his brandy.

Palfrey thought it would be better to pretend that he wanted to know nothing; it was likely to increase Karen's determination to tell him. Once he knew, he must try to get away.

'Now,' said Karen, 'from your report I see that you have been told about the mysterious appearance of black earth in different parts of the world. You have been told that it was first discovered by a British scientist. He was careless enough to tell a friend of mine what he had discovered and, under pressure, he disclosed the method by which the material was made. I was extremely interested. I employed experts to test and then to develop the material. It is now much more effective than it was a few years ago. The concentration is greater. A handful can turn a thousand acres black in a few hours. The only counter, as you have also been told, is water.' He laughed softly. 'I should say it *was* water. I have been experimenting with a form of the defertilizer which will cross water-barriers, and the first tests were made two days ago. It works! The effect across the water-barrier is not yet so quick as that across dry land, but I shall correct that. No man has ever been able to rot the very *earth*, Palfrey.'

Palfrey said: 'No sane man would want to.'

Karen chuckled, as if the retort pleased him.

'Oh, I am quite sane. And I don't want this destructive agent generally used yet. But imagine some of the effects of it. For example, if an aeroplane were to fly for an hour across fertile land, spraying this powder, think how vast a track of land could be made barren almost overnight.'

Palfrey said: 'You've boasted of what you can do. You have not said why you intend to do it.'

'There is an excellent reason,' Karen assured him. 'Black earth can be used to subjugate individuals, races, *and* nations. The threat of starvation is probably greater than the threat of being blown to pieces by atomic disruption. If a people knew what was likely to happen to them'—he shrugged his shoulders

124

—'would they be prepared to fight, or would they not give way to this unusual pressure?'

'I hope you won't try to find out,' said Palfrey.

'But I shall, Palfrey! And there are other motives. There are powerful landowners in America, in the British dominions, in parts of Europe, in China and India—men whose wealth gives them a great influence. How pleasant it would be to let those men see the source of their wealth fade before their eyes!'

'And create world famine,' Palfrey murmured.

'No, not *world* famine. Shortages of food in various parts of the world, shortages which will force the affected countries to beg for the help that the unaffected nations can give them. A hungry man has no will of his own; a hungry nation will have no will of its own.'

Palfrey stirred restlessly. 'I don't think Washington would take kindly to the notion,' he said.

'I am quite sure that Washington won't—and I understand that the use of the defertilizer was rejected even during the war. One of the troubles with the leaders of the democracies, Palfrey, is weakness masquerading under the guise of human kindness. I have little time for democracy. I would much prefer a country governed by a benevolent autocracy.'

'All power corrupts,' murmured Palfrey.

'And absolute power corrupts absolutely! I have read Acton!' Karen still seemed pleased with himself. 'Properly equipped, I can spread a dark harvest over all parts of the world, and I have put plans in hand for that. I have airplanes at tactical and strategic places on the American continent, in Asia and in Europe. For many years, you see, I have been an executive of a large company of exporters in America. My agents have permits to fly wherever they like. Shipments of the defertilizer can be sent out to them by air. One or two journeys will be enough, once the water-barrier is really broken down. There will be no stopping it, Palfrey, except at the great river barriers and at the coast. Salt water has still proved an insuperable barrier.' He was smirking with satisfaction, and rubbing his long, white hands together. 'Certain countries are making difficulties even today, Palfrey, and I shall deal with them when I have completed my initial step, which is to dispossess a number of American competitors. Grayson is one of them. There are others. My syndicates will control most of the good soil in the great wheat- and fruit-growing districts. Kill wheat and fruit, and the rest doesn't matter. I have control over vast areas of wheat-producing land in many countries. When the demand for corn comes from abroad—it will hardly work to my disadvantage, will it?'

Palfrey said: 'No.'

'As for Washington,' said Karen, 'they will be faced with *faits accomplis*. They will take no part in the preparations, I shall look after that. Washington will have to take steps to help the rest of the world. True, it may be said by some that Washington or other governments have helped to create the famine; but once the thing is done, the will of the bigger nations will be undermined.'

He walked to the side of the room. There were no pictures in it, just panelled walls. He pressed a button in one of the panels and immediately what had looked like heavy carving at the top, beneath the picture rail, showed a gap. Something white, stretching across the whole length of the wall, began to unroll. Soon Palfrey saw that it was a map; two maps, one of each hemisphere. Only the main towns were marked, and the maps were in outline.

Palfrey's lips set as he studied it.

There were several tiny black patches; one was in the west of England, another in Alabama, a third in California. A quick glance showed that every place where outbreaks of black earth had been reported were marked in black. They concerned him less than other patches, where there were great grey stretches. Southern India, part of South Africa, Australia and Canada were shaded. So were parts of France and Italy, Central Europe and the Far East. Before Karen spoke again, Palfrey guessed what the shaded patches indicated.

Karen said softly: 'The grey will soon be black, Palfrey.'

'Black harvest, black death,' Palfrey said. His voice did not sound like his own.

'Now you see at what I am really aiming,' said Karen. 'For fifty years we tried to keep out of the quarrels of the Old World. Twice we have been dragged into them. It shall not happen again.

'I will prevent another crime,' Karen went on. 'I come from the South, Palfrey, and I have lived to see great tracts of land covered by the squirming, squalling black race. The fair face of America has been defiled, and I will crush the niggers; I will crush them to a condition where slavery would be a heaven for their black minds and their black bodies! I have been working

126

for years to inflame the people of the South against them, and I am getting results.'

The man's eyes were glowing; it was a dangerous moment, the more dangerous because Palfrey felt an almost irresistible urge to attack him. If he could get his hands about that white throat and squeeze, if he could choke the life out of the man as he stood there, there might be some chance.

He said: 'Are you supreme commander, Karen?'

'I am one of a syndicate,' said Karen. 'The project is too great to allow an accident to one man to spoil it.' He stood there as if inviting Palfrey to lose his self-control.

Palfrey turned away.

Karen laughed. 'In the morning you shall see the first airspray, and after that you will forget, so that you need not torment yourself. For tonight—perhaps I can help you to forget in rapture, Palfrey, in a woman's arms.'

He laughed again.

THIRTEEN

RAPTURE?

PALFREY remembered the exaltation of the dreams he had once known here. As he went to his chair and sat down, he believed that the man intended to drug him so that he should dream again; and in the sickness of his heart he wished that it could be so. He buried his head in his hands. His heart was beating slowly yet heavily, threatening to choke him.

Dreams——

There was no time for dreams, he must get away! Would Mallory countenance this thing? Would Löis? Would Monsell? If they knew what was to happen, would they allow it to be done? Wouldn't they help him to escape? Surely they could not know what was in Karen's mind.

'Come along, Palfrey,' said Mallory, and Palfrey felt the doctor's hand on his arm.

He went out, as if in a daze. He did not look at Karen, but could imagine the man's expression. He walked blindly along the passage, until Mallory opened the door of a bedroom.

Palfrey said: 'Mallory, did you know about this—before?'

'All about it,' said Mallory.

Palfrey turned from him abruptly.

The room was empty.

He must do something before they drugged him . . .

Löis—Monsell—how could he get to them? How could he tell them what he had been told? They had been sent out of the room ; they couldn't *know*. But he had been sent here alone, and was locked in. But—rapture, in a woman's arms. What had Karen meant? Surely he was not simply talking of drugs which would give him fantasy for a bed-mate?

Being alone was the worst thing ; it would almost be better if he could talk to Karen again ; or Mallory.

The door opened, and Löis came in.

Her creamy shoulders and arms, her flawless throat and the gentle swell beneath, showed vividly against her dark dress. She tossed her hair back as she entered, and Palfrey heard a man's voice in the passage. That was Monsell. Again it flashed into his mind that they might be working as Stella had done.

The door closed.

Palfrey drew a sharp breath. 'Löis, *do* you know?'

'What?'

'What Karen plans.'

'I helped to shade the maps,' she said.

'And—you'll let it happen.'

'I want it to happen.'

'*Get out!*' cried Palfrey. If she stood there for a moment longer, he would fling himself at her. He shouted again: '*Get out, get out!*' Afterwards, when the spasm was over, he had at least the satisfaction of knowing that he frightened her.

She went out of the room.

She wanted it to happen.

All hope of help from her or from Monsell had gone.

If he could only get into the laboratory and wreck it, that would be something gained. But contact with the outside world was what he needed most ; he must summon all his wit and cunning to get outside.

Overhead, probably at that very moment, a spotter aircraft was flying, keeping the bungalow under constant surveillance, using a night-photography unit. There would be other men within a few miles: Stefan and Bruton would not have lost this chance. But he had arranged that they should not raid the rendezvous immediately. He had expected that it would take time before he learned the truth.

'*Doctor—Palfrey.*'

128

A woman spoke from behind him. He swung round. Karen's wife stood there.

She had changed into a long, cream-coloured robe which fitted her waist closely and flowed round her feet, making her so beautiful; the harassed expression in her eyes had gone, and in its place there was a strange calmness.

Palfrey said: 'How did you get here?'

'From the dressing-room,' she said, and pointed behind her. Palfrey could see the outline of a door in the wall. She smiled. 'You look so miserable,' she murmured.

Palfrey did not speak.

'Has he—told you?'

'Yes.'

'He told me,' she said, but the calmness remained in her eyes and she smiled again. 'He has promised to make me forget. He will make you forget, too; it will soon be over.'

Palfrey could find nothing to say, but he seemed to hear the echo of Karen's voice: *In a woman's arms!*

'I can help you,' she said.

They lay side by side.

She was limp and relaxed, and her hand strayed to his hair and played with it, gently. There was a subtle perfume from her hair. Her eyes were close to his, and had a lambent loveliness. She was quite calm.

'Pretend,' she said. The word was no more than a whisper. 'Pretend.'

He touched her cheek, but he was rigid with a fierce excitement.

'Relax,' she said. 'Even here they are watching us.'

She took his hand and rested it against her robe.

Do your friends know you are here? she murmured.

Yes.

Are they near?

Her voice was so low that, even close to her, he could hardly hear it.

'They are watching,' he said.

'How many are there?'

He did not answer at once, and his fingers stiffened. Then he said abruptly: 'Why does Karen want to know?'

'No,' she said, shaking her head gently, 'don't think that of me. I hate him more—yes, much more—than you do. He has done so much to make me hate him. Even—this.'

Would Karen so besmirch his wife? The sudden anger on the man's face when he had struck him loomed up in front of Palfrey's mind; and he did not doubt that Karen would sink to any depths. He remembered, too, Diana's story. How much did Karen's wife know?

'They watch all the time,' she said, 'and they listen all the time, and the windows are unbreakable and are shuttered outside. But one door is always kept open or unlocked. It would be possible——' she broke off. 'Can you hear me?'

'Yes.'

'It would be possible for me to switch off the electric current,' she said. 'I have often wondered what I could do to hurt him. That has been the weakness. The spy-holes through which they watch, the listening machines, the lighting, are all operated by electricity, and if that were to break down it would take some minutes before they could switch over to the emergency supply.'

'Can you do it?'

'Yes.' She smiled again, dreamily. 'Karen thinks I am almost mad; that he has completely subdued me. I am allowed to wander as I please, although never allowed to go outside. Before they realize what I am going to do, it will be done. The lights will be out, the whole place in darkness. Once you reach the passage——'

'How can I do that?'

'In the pocket of your dressing-gown there is a key,' she said. 'Will you try to escape?'

'Of course.'

'Don't come back for me. Don't lose a moment for me. It might prevent you from escaping.'

He was silent.

'I shall not help you unless you promise,' she insisted.

'All right,' said Palfrey, slowly. Whatever promise she had asked him to make, whatever risk there was for her, he must get away if the chance did come; he dared not risk failure on her account. But her words had reminded him of what Karen would probably do. Diana Leeming had said . . .

He shut his mind to the past.

She smoothed his cheek with her soft hand.

'Don't think of me.'

Palfrey gripped her shoulder tightly.

'No,' he said, and then, with an effort: 'How long have you known what he was trying to do?'

'Only a few days.'

130

'How much did you know before?'

'Not very much,' she said, 'except that I was always frightened, always forced to help him in dreadful things. There was that girl——'

'Valerie Grayson?' asked Palfrey.

'He called her Diana—Diana Leeming. She was at the nursing home for a while. I know—I have been there.' She shivered uncontrollably, and edged a little nearer to him. 'That was the worst time of all,' she said.

Palfrey whispered: 'Do you remember who went to see Karen in New York, about the time when you saw Diana Leeming?'

'Many people.'

'Do you remember their names?'

'Not—well,' she said.

'Was Arnold Grayson one of them?'

'I don't recall the name.' That was after a long pause.

'Or Hoffner, Edward Hoffner?'

Her eyes lit up. 'Yes, he was there. I remember him because he was so kind. And Karen was—courteous to him. Yes, Hoffner. But—need we talk now? Why don't we rest? They will fetch me away before long. You will know when to act, because the light will go out.'

'You must try to remember a little more,' said Palfrey, urgently, and his voice rose.

'Hush!' She placed a hand on his lips.

'A little,' he insisted. 'There was the apartment, the nursing-home and this bungalow. Where else does Karen work?'

'He has houses everywhere.'

'There is a laboratory here. Where else is there one?'

'A laboratory,' she said, and closed her eyes. 'I have not seen another, but I have heard talk of "the factory". This is only—experimental, that is the word. There is a factory.'

Palfrey was rigid with suspense.

'Where?'

'I think—yes, it is in Alaska,' she said. 'It is supposed to be a salmon cannery; there are underground rooms and workshops. I have heard them talking about it. I believe they intend to use Alaska as a base——'

They would, for Russia.

He said: 'One thing more. What is Karen's real name?'

'That *is* his name.'

'He isn't well known, but such a man——'

'He has never sought publicity,' she said. 'His influence is always underground. Please,' she pleaded, 'I will do what I have promised, I will give you your chance, but let me rest now. Let me rest. It has been so—hard. It isn't easy to realize that it is—over.'

'Over?' echoed Palfrey.

She looked radiant. 'Yes, the strain is over,' she said. 'I can do something to hurt him now.'

She meant more than that.

Suddenly she pulled him close and kissed him.

The light was still on.

Palfrey did not know what time it was, and sat in an easy chair, with a book in his hand, hoping that by staying up so long he would not arouse suspicions. Karen's wife had gone; he had been alone for at least an hour.

Would she succeed in her task?

Now and again he heard footsteps. There were little noises, like the opening and shutting of tiny doors. He wondered whether the listening apparatus at the bungalow was so perfect that their whispered conversation had been heard. If she were going to do as she had promised, surely——

The light went out.

He had been waiting for it, with strained eyes, for a time that seemed unending; now that it had happened, he was taken by surprise. He stood blinking in the darkness, his heart beginning to thump, and took the key out of his pocket.

He fumbled for the keyhole.

It seemed an age before he touched it with one hand and pushed the key in. The lock turned. He opened the door cautiously, and as he did so he heard a man crossing along the passage, and saw the glow of a torch. He pressed closely against the wall. The torch shone on to the open door and into the room, and he heard the man exclaim. If a warning shout came now, his chance might be gone.

The man entered.

Palfrey saw a gun in his hand, just visible in the ray of the torch. He kicked out savagely and caught the man in the groin. A sound that was half-shout, half-groan came from the man's lips, and he dropped the torch. Palfrey snatched it as it fell. He did not save it, but broke its fall, and the light remained on. He plucked the gun from nerveless fingers and shone the torch on the man's head. His victim was drawing his knees into his stomach and trying to shout.

Palfrey struck him with the butt of the gun so hard that he thought he heard the skull crack. Then he slipped the torch into his pocket and hurried towards the front door. Men were calling out, others were running along the farther passage. Another torch shone towards Palfrey; the light fell on his waist and also showed him the front door and the open door opposite.

He fired from his pocket.

The man with the torch fell, and the torch hit the ground and went out. The echo of the shot, although muffled by his coat, seemed terribly loud. He heard someone call out: 'Who was that?'

He reached the front door and found it open. A bright beam of light shone on to garden, flowers and running figures. The headlamps of a car were on. He saw Karen's wife running and men following her. He heard shots, but did not see her fall.

He heard the drone of an aeroplane overhead—a Z.5 patrol? What else could it be?

He turned towards the open door. Other men appeared in the bright beam of light outside. Most of the strength at the house was concentrated on the woman; they had sent only two men to see that he was safe.

Another door, opposite the front, opened suddenly.

In the reflected light he saw Mallory.

Mallory exclaimed: 'Pal——'

Palfrey struck at his face and felt Mallory sag from the blow. He heard other sounds in the room; a man spoke, and it sounded like Karen's voice. One shot, and Karen would not live to——

'Get out the back way,' Karen was saying. 'I will stay here. Warn the men at the front.' He sounded as calm as if he were talking in the dining-room.

Palfrey slammed the door and turned towards the front. He stumbled down the steps leading from the porch, recovered and raced towards the car. The men were still running farther away, and he caught a glimpse of white; so Karen's wife was still free. If he could help her——

He thrust the thought aside.

He heard Monsell's voice, near the bungalow, raised in a warning shout; the pilot had seen Palfrey, but the pursuing men did not appear to understand what he meant. Palfrey turned towards the car. He could only just see the outlines of the car itself, the beam of white light from the headlamps shone out over the flowers and to the black earth. He heard footsteps on the gravel of a path. He reached the car and peered across it through the two windows. A man was coming round the corner with a torch in his hand, flashing it to and fro. Once it shone on a gun in his hand.

Palfrey pulled at the self-starter, and the engine turned at once. He let in the clutch in a sweat of anxiety. If he failed to get the car away he would be worse off than if he had tried to escape by foot. He felt the gentle throb of the engine and turned the wheel towards the drive. The headlights shone on Monsell. He heard the crack of a shot. A hole was drilled in a side window; the car was suddenly peppered with shots. He swung the wheel desperately as Monsell leapt forward as if hoping to get on to the running board.

The car crashed into the man and Monsell disappeared beneath one wheel.

The car lurched. Shots were coming more frequently from the house now, and Palfrey saw lights in the distance. He thought that the men who were chasing Karen's wife had heard the shooting and had been diverted by it.

The drive gates loomed up; they were closed.

'That's that,' said Palfrey, aloud.

But he saw the frail wooden fencing at the side of the gates and swung off the drive. Flowers were crushed beneath the wheels: the same fate for Monsell—and flowers. The bumpers struck the fence; it sagged aside, the engine did not stall. Bullets were hitting the car like heavy rain. He felt a sharp pain in his shoulder as he turned into the road. The back wheels ran over something which sent the car up in the air then dropped it down on to the firm surface. He glanced right and left; all he could see were fields on one side and the wooden fence on the other. The bungalow and the grounds were hidden from him.

He heard another sound; it was the roar of a powerful engine. Suddenly a dazzling light appeared in front of his eyes, and for a moment he was bathed in white. He thought he saw a dark shape; only when the light had gone did he realize that an aeroplane had swooped low with its searchlight on.

Perhaps the aircraft had wirelessed the alarm and help might soon be coming. If he could only get a message to the men that he felt sure were watching——

He could!

He groped for and found the light-switch, and turned it off. He slowed down involuntarily as the blackness engulfed him. Then he switched on again and quickly spelt out the signal S.O.S.

The white streak of light was coming nearer to him, and it shone on the hangar. It had swung round as if to frighten the men below. He saw the little red and yellow flashes from the ground. So Karen's men were firing at it.

The light shone upon a grounded aircraft.

The speckles grew more frequent, coming one after another, as if a dozen men were shooting. Fools. They were using a machine-gun. He could hear the roar of the engine again now.

He heard an explosion.

There was a flash of flame, and then the roar; he turned and looked; there was fire falling from the heavens and the white light had gone out.

The patrol aircraft was gone.

The headlights of a following car shone in the driving mirror, brighter and closer. Palfrey trod on the accelerator harder—a futile gesture. The speedometer needle quivered towards the ninety mark; he doubted if he could get another atom of speed out of the car.

His engine spluttered. One moment it was going smoothly, the next it spluttered, picked up, then spluttered again. He looked at the petrol gauge; it was at zero. So a bullet had hit the petrol tank.

He felt the car trembling as the engine spluttered a third time. He pulled into the side as the engine stopped. He flung open the door and jumped down. The pursuing car was humming furiously along the road, but the range of its headlights had made it seem nearer than it was. There was a hedge at the side of the road, and he scrambled through it, still holding the gun. He crouched down on the other side. Another car was approaching.

He stood watching tensely. Neither car slowed down. Each driver seemed intent on a head-on crash.

Suddenly the car from the bungalow swung off the road towards the hedge, towards Palfrey. In the light from the other headlights he saw Löis at the wheel. There was a set expression on her face, and he knew that she was making a desperate effort to escape, not to pursue him. The car lurched into the hedge not a dozen yards from Palfrey.

It had been travelling too fast to take the hedge. The nose

went upwards, and then the car overturned. He caught a glimpse of Löis; she disappeared as the car crashed with a rending din. He stood quite still, trying to watch the smashed car as well as the one coming from the other direction. He heard the squeal of brakes; the rescue car was stopping. Others were much nearer now, and he knew that within ten minutes the bungalow would be in their possession. There would be a complete capture unless Karen had escaped by air.

He heard moaning from the smashed car.

He went towards it, and in the light of the torch he saw the girl trapped in the driving-seat, the steering wheel broken and driven into her chest, crushing her. There was a smear of blood on her lips.

Palfrey thought, bleakly: 'She wanted the horror to happen.'

He turned away as a man scrambled through the hedge and called sharply: 'Show your hands, you!'

Palfrey dropped the gun and the torch. 'It's all right,' he said, and he wanted to laugh; that was madness. 'I'm Palfrey. Don't lose any time, they——'

Then he broke off as a vivid white flash filled the country-side.

FOURTEEN

THE TASK REMAINING

PALFREY covered his ears with his hands. He felt the blast and the noise of the explosion almost simultaneously. The flash had died down, but a deep red glow followed immediately after-wards; the night seemed filled with fire. Flames were rising from the bungalow, as they had risen from the shack near the Little Randall River.

The man nearest Palfrey said:

'Well, what do you think of that?'

Palfrey licked his lips. 'It's as well we weren't any nearer,' he said.

'I guess so.' The man turned towards him, a heavily-built fellow, outlined against the headlights. Others were in the field now, and one of them went towards the car, but the moans had stopped. 'Did you say you were Palfrey?'

'Yes.'

'I'll have to make sure of that.'

'Yes,' said Palfrey. 'There's no hurry.' He stood watching the fire. Its glow was spreading everywhere, and the man's face was tinged with red.

'There's a woman here,' one of the other men said. 'She's dead, I think.'

'She got what she deserved,' said Palfrey. 'There's another woman nearer the house who deserves a better deal.' A note of urgency sprang into his voice. 'We can look for her,' he snapped. 'Let's get moving.'

Men fell in by his side as they walked along.

They found Karen's wife, with bullets in her head and back, near the runway of the aircraft, which had gone. Two mechanics were caught there, too—sullen, silent men. The heat prevented them from getting near the bungalow to look for Monsell and Mallory. Palfrey thought that Mallory had probably perished in the fire. He wondered what had happened to the other man; and then, as he shielded his face against the heat of the flames, he trod on something soft. A hand—— He shivered.

Gradually the true picture was formed as the fire died down and the agents, a dozen in all, were able to get nearer the red-hot mass. The men at the bungalow, including some of the scientists, thought Palfrey, had given chase to Karen's wife and then returned. Karen had escaped by air after setting the detonator which had blown building and workers into little pieces.

It was what one might have expected from Karen.

Now Palfrey had to face the task remaining.

He could not get one thing Mallory had implied out of his head: Karen had influence in high places. The difficulty was to decide whom to trust. That had always been a danger, but now it was of over-riding importance. A slight leakage might be enough to warn Karen what plans were being made: it would be suicidal to allow the man to suspect any detail of the great surge of activity against him.

'Who got away?' Palfrey asked the prisoners.

Neither of them answered.

Palfrey looked at Stefan. 'We've got to know,' he said.

Stefan towered over the two men; and as they looked at him they showed the first signs of cracking. They were remarkably like the men who had worked with Casado in Randall City. They wore dark overalls and their hands and faces were streaked with oil and grease—probably from their last-minute effort to save Karen.

'Who got away?' asked Stefan.

They did not answer.

He stretched out his hands and gripped their necks and banged their heads together. He pulled them apart, then banged them again, more gently. In his powerful grip there was nothing they could do to help themselves. It was less the pain of the blows than the fear of the giant, the promise in that beginning, which affected them. One was sweating freely, the other's lips were working.

'Who got away?' repeated Stefan.

The men began to talk . . .

Palfrey did not tell Stefan or Bruton of what he had learned as they drove to Montreal. They were discussing the story which the mechanics had told them. Karen and several of the scientists had escaped. The mechanics swore that they did not know where Karen had gone, except that he had headed north-west. That helped little, for he might have turned south when he was safely away from the bungalow. The aircraft had a range of 2,500 miles, and, according to the mechanics, a top speed of over three hundred miles an hour. There was just a chance that it had been followed by a spotting aircraft, but during the hours of darkness helicopters and slow machines had probably been used. Possibly the aircraft's flight was being plotted, but in the confusion and the crash of the reconnaissance aircraft it had been given a chance to escape unobserved.

'When can we find out?' Bruton asked, abruptly.

'There may be word waiting for us,' Palfrey said. 'I sent a request for information as soon as the ground patrols arrived.'

'Where will the message be waiting?'

Palfrey smiled. 'At your hotel—I was told where you were staying.'

When they reached it, Palfrey told his story.

'There's quite a job for the F.B.I., Corney,' he finished.

'They'll do it,' said Bruton.

'Probably,' conceded Palfrey. 'What matters is—will they do it soon enough?'

'You have probably delayed Karen a little,' Stefan said. 'He told you that he was going to make his first aerial experiment this morning, so he does not yet know for certain how well the work can be done by spraying from the air.' Stefan was hugging his knees as he sat in a large armchair, and his chin rested on his hands. 'Much of the work was done at the bungalow, and it is probable that he had some supplies there as well as the results of his latest experiments.'

'And presumably he took them away with him,' said Palfrey, stirring restlessly in his chair. 'I wonder if his wife was right when she talked of an Alaskan cannery?'

'It's a good time of the year to find out,' said Bruton.

'Yes. We know that *bitua* comes from the cold regions,' Palfrey went on, musingly. 'It may be that the chief factory is near a source of the mineral. That's another line we can take —known *bitua* deposits in or near Alaska. But it's a pretty grim outlook, and there's no point in pretending otherwise.'

'You want some rest, Sap,' Stefan declared.

Palfrey raised his eyebrows.

'I don't remember when I've rested and slept so much,' he said, and then stood up and laughed. 'But I feel tired out.'

'Stefan and I will sleep in here,' said Bruton. 'You go next door, Sap.'

Palfrey went into the next room. The others had brought him some spare clothes and all he needed. He undressed quickly and got into bed. His hand was at the light-switch when Stefan came in.

'Hallo,' said Palfrey. 'Come to tuck me up?'

'We forgot to give you this,' said Stefan, and handed Palfrey a letter. 'We don't think it will keep you awake.' He smiled as he went out, for Palfrey had taken once glance at the envelope and then completely forgotten Stefan, forgotten all he had heard that night.

It was from Drusilla.

A little later, when Stefan looked in, Palfrey was asleep, the letter was resting on the sheet which covered him, and there was a faint smile at his lips.

Stefan closed the door gently.

'How is he?' asked Bruton.

'He'll be all right,' said Stefan.

Palfrey woke up a little after nine o'clock, and within twenty minutes he knew that he had succeeded in shaking off the numbing shock of the encounter with Karen. Morcover, something had changed his outlook. It might be the fact that he now knew the worst they had to face, and that he had at least managed to peg Karen back by a few days. It might be that he kept remembering Drusilla's letter. It might be—and he thought it was, in fact, a combination of all three—that from now on it was a straight fight. He no longer had to submit himself to Karen or Mallory—all pretence was gone. Yes, he felt much better.

He bathed and shaved, and went downstairs to breakfast with the others.

A waiter came hurrying from the hall.

'A telephone call, messieurs, for M. le Docteur. It is long distance.'

'Probably it's Brett,' said Palfrey, dabbing his lips. The others followed him to the telephone booth in the hall. He picked up the receiver. 'Dr. Palfrey speaking.'

'Hold the line, please.' It was a girl's voice with a pronounced American accent. Then a man spoke very politely. 'Dr. Palfrey —please hold the line.' Palfrey waited, until another man's voice sounded in his ears, deep and authoritative. 'Dr. Palfrey? The President's private secretary wishes to speak to you.'

'Who is it?' whispered Bruton.

Palfrey grinned. 'Either a practical joke or the White House.'

'The President wished to speak to you himself, but has been called away,' said the private secretary, 'but he will regard it as a great courtesy if you will fly to Washington today and dine with him tonight. The President will expect you and your friends at seven-thirty, Doctor. Perhaps you will telephone your time of arrival as soon as you know when it is likely to be.'

'Oh, yes,' said Palfrey. 'Thanks.'

'Thank you. Good morning, Dr. Palfrey.'

Palfrey replaced the receiver. He looked absently at Bruton and then laughed.

'We've been asked out to dinner. What time is the first plane to Washington?'

'We don't have to catch the first plane,' said Bruton, 'we use one of our own. Did you say Washington?'

'I did,' said Palfrey.

They touched down on the airfield outside Washington a little after five o'clock and had time to go to an hotel to wash and dress in hired clothes. They had telegraphed their estimated time of arrival, and were met by officials who exerted themselves to be pleasant. The hotel had reserved rooms ; Bruton whispered in an aside that it was impossible to reserve rooms in any Washington hotel, and then laughed a little absurdly.

140

Palfrey was amused by the effect of the invitation on Bruton. Bruton was not a respecter of persons; but the prospect seemed to overawe him.

At seven o'clock they were ready.

There was a tap at the door and Bruton went to open it.

'That will be the car,' Stefan said, and then they heard Bruton exclaim in delight.

'Well, well, honey! What a picture you make!'

Palfrey and Stefan turned round abruptly.

Bruton stood aside and Stella came in.

She was dressed for dinner, and looked delightful. Her hair seemed to have captured the sun; there was a glow of excitement in her eyes. She came forward with hand outstretched, and Palfrey was surprised at the extent of his pleasure in seeing her; the coming occasion was momentarily forgotten.

'At least you remember *me*,' said Stella, and laughed. Her hand lingered in Palfrey's. 'I want to ask a thousand questions, but we haven't got time. Are you all ready? I'm coming too!'

Inside a large, high-ceilinged room, hung with portraits of past presidents, and with the flags of many nations with the Stars and Stripes in the middle, two men were waiting for them. One Palfrey recognized from the photographs of the new President which had spread round the world one day, which seemed an age ago, after tragedy had struck at the United States.

The other was the Marquis of Brett.

After a pleasant meal, during which talk and wine flowed easily, and the chief subject for discussion had hardly been broached, they went into a smaller room, and the President slipped from the almost idle talk into the matter which absorbed them, easily and quietly. Palfrey was surprised at the knowledge he showed of the situation. Now and again Brett interposed a word, but there was little that the President had not grasped.

Washington was, for the time being at least, the centre of interest, and the centre of Z.5 activities, and *every* country had pledged its immediate support. They would defeat the terror; failure was unthinkable. After that, his dream—and Brett's—stood more chance than ever of coming true. In twenty-four hours the secret services of the nations of the world had been put at the disposal of the United Nations; no country was unrepresented in that impressive list.

'I would like to know what you consider the primary facts now,' said the President.

Palfrey said: 'There are three. First, the location of the cannery or factory in Alaska. It's problematical, but I think it exists. Second, to find out what developments Karen's scientists have made on *bitua* products. The product first manufactured hadn't the same quick effect as that which he appears to be using now, and it was always stopped by fresh and salt water. If Karen's right, when he says that fresh water doesn't stop his, we've got to find what he's done and we've got to find a way of countering it. Because I feel sure of one thing.'

'And what is that?'

'Karen will use his preparation quickly,' Palfrey said. 'He may not be able to use it in big quantities yet; he may be limited as far as the regions where he drops it are concerned, but he'll use it as a warning to us that he means business. He got away with his skin, but he won't be pleased about what happened at the bungalow. Out of spite, probably, he'll show his strength—and in showing it, he might give himself away.'

'I don't quite follow you.'

'If the closest possible watch is kept on all aircraft, and a report comes in that one has dropped something from the air— it will be seen, the *bitua* product isn't invisible—that aeroplane must be followed to its base.' Palfrey rubbed his forehead. 'The only thing that went wrong last night was the loss of Karen's airplane. I've been hoping against hope that it would be traced.'

'There's no news of it,' the President told him. 'Things happened very quickly last night. The one airplane that might have followed crashed, and—but we won't go into details of what we already know, Doctor. You talked of a third primary factor.'

Palfrey smiled diffidently.

'Yes. Karen's boasted influence in high quarters. Presumably he means in America. He might mean in Washington. So precautions about the leakage of information from Headquarters is a vital responsibility.'

'I think the steps we have taken will ensure that,' said the President. Palfrey blinked. 'Don't you agree?' There was a sharper note in the President's voice.

Palfrey said. 'I'm sorry, no. I don't know what precautions you have taken, so I'm talking without the book, but one thing rather hits one between the eyes. Karen may really have influence in high places. He was able to get at Kennedy Lee. He may have got at some of your people. Are all your officials, all your leaders, free from the taint of racial hatred? You may be sure of your political leaders; you can't be sure of your

142

officials,' Palfrey went on. 'This tainted-blood fanaticism goes deep and blossoms in unexpected places.'

'I've got to agree with you there, but what do you suggest?'

Palfrey smiled. 'That nothing be put on paper here. That the few officials who know what is happening are immediately given leave. That the operational leaders of the co-operating forces—F.B.I., the Army and the Air Force--branches—are changed daily, so that there is continuity of action but no continuity of the men behind the action. And that the country is told there is a large-scale man-hunt but not told the reason for it. We must have a reason for all this activity. I think we can find one.' He smiled. 'A spy hunt.' He leaned forward, lost in the thoughts which flooded his mind. 'Supposing you make an announcement that you have discovered that secret service agents are making a nuisance of themselves? They can have stolen some details of industrial atomic processes or anything big enough to cause a stir in the public mind. Every minor official, everyone who doesn't know the real truth already, will be quite satisfied with that as a reason for emergency regulations and emergency actions.' He looked at Brett. 'Don't you agree, sir?'

The President frowned as Brett nodded.

'We don't want to exacerbate public feeling,' he said.

'When the thing's over and done with, you can tell the world the truth,' said Palfrey. 'But we want a big scare.'

'What do you think of it, Lord Brett?' asked the President.

'I see no objection to it,' said Brett, and added with a smile: 'Canada can be enraged by talk of enemy agents throughout the country. It's happened before.'

'We've got to have a reason for every branch of the secret service, every police force, every authority in both countries being on their toes, and we mustn't give the real reason,' Palfrey said. 'The worst danger will only come if we fail—and we mustn't fail. I——'

He broke off, for the door opened and a tall, grey-haired man came hurrying in. He recognized the American Minister of State, and he did not like the man's agitation, for the Minister had the reputation of never losing his self-control.

The door closed.

'What is it?' asked the President.

'There's a stretch of black earth for a hundred and fifty miles across the Texas corn belt,' said the Minister, in an unsteady voice, 'and it is spreading fast. It has leapt the water barriers; nothing seems able to stop it.'

FIFTEEN

THE SPREAD OF BLACK EARTH

A SINGLE aeroplane had flown high over the Texas corn belt at midday. Several civil airports reported having seen it, Defence Organizations also reported it, but it had been lost over the Gulf of Mexico, and there was now no trace of it. Farm workers and city dwellers reported exactly the same thing; a dark dust had fallen upon the land. It was as if a great storm had blown across the land, devastating everything in its path; or as if the river had overflown its banks and brought desolation.

There had been no wind, nor storm, no rain. The sun had shone out of a clear sky with the intense heat of a summer's day. The faint dust had come, with its coating of black over the plants and the earth. And then, during the afternoon, the flowers withering and plants dying and the earth crumbling.

Palfrey and the others walked through a silent city. The sun burned pitilessly down, itself enough to take the life out of the people, but there was something different here, for the city was in the centre of the ravaged belt. There were no living plants; and even the leaves of trees were withering, as if the sap were being drained out of them.

They got into their car and drove beyond the city.

Scriebner's face was pale, and his lips set grimly.

Before they had left Washington they had been told that Scriebner was to take over the superintending of the investigations within the United States. He was to remain at the head, although the other changes would take place as Palfrey had suggested.

They had learned more about Scriebner. He had been on the investigation from the beginning—one of those who had first been called when the loss of the documents had been discovered at the British Embassy. He agreed with Palfrey that there was no evidence that Kennedy Lee had stolen the papers; a stooge had been needed, and Lee, already on the edge of the

144

affair because of his infatuation for 'Diana Leeming', had been selected.

Scriebner was a tall, brown-haired man with a plain, homely face and expressive, steely grey eyes. Palfrey had liked him from the first. His laconic manner hid real feeling; he never seemed in a hurry, but he got things done quickly.

Dressed in a crumpled suit of cream linen, his face beaded with perspiration, a Panama hat pulled low over his eyes, he sat at the wheel of the car, glancing right and left at the desolation.

The glow of the radio receiver built into the car made him stretch out a hand and switch on. A hollow voice sounded clearly.

'Calling Captain Scriebner—calling Captain Scriebner. Over to you, over to you.'

'Scriebner talking—Scriebner talking—over to you.'

They listented intently as the hollow voice filled the interior of the car again.

'Small twin-engined aircraft crashed north of Dalhart, Northern Texas; immediate investigation advised.' The words were repeated, and then the man said again: 'Over to you.'

'Message received,' said Scriebner, 'proceeding Dalhart.' He repeated that, then switched off and glanced at Palfrey keenly.

'That's not far north,' he said, 'at the extreme end of the blight belt. You coming?'

'Yes,' said Palfrey.

The aircraft had caught fire before hitting the ground. Officials were gathered about it, already investigating the cause of the crash. There seemed no pointers, apart from the fire, and Scriebner looked dissatisfied and disappointed. Palfrey and Stefan were looking at a pitifully smashed figure not far from the wreckage. The pilot had jumped, but his parachute had not opened. He had been fairly close to the ground before he had left the machine, and, although his face was unrecognizable, his clothes were only scorched.

Palfrey went through his pockets and took out several papers.

'What have you found?' Scriebner asked, as he came up.

'A *World Citizen* reporter,' Palfrey said, and handed the detective a card. 'You might find out what he was doing here.'

'That won't take long.' said Scriebner.

He was speaking to the editor of the *World Citizen* within a quarter of an hour. Palfrey stood in the small office of the local sheriff, who had a heavy, rather lifeless face. Scriebner did not

145

like what he heard. He grunted several times into the telephone, and then replaced the receiver.

'Well?' asked Palfrey.

'It wouldn't surprise me if this fellow saw the other machine dropping the damned stuff,' said Scriebner. 'The *Citizen* had a flash from him, and then a report that he was in danger—the aircraft had caught fire.'

'Didn't he get a message through?'

'No,' said Scriebner, 'only said it was worth investigating.' He went moodily to the door and looked out into the sun-bleached street. 'The *Citizen* keeps its eyes open, Palfrey.'

'Yes. Did he come across the other machine by chance?'

'He was covering an oil fire story farther south,' said Scriebner, 'and saw that something was dropping from the other aircraft. I'll see Mangus when I get back, and find out more about it.'

'Who's Mangus?'

'Chief of the *Citizen*,' said Scriebner. 'Palfrey——'

'Yes?'

'The guys who call themselves experts think there *might* be a bullet hole in the wreckage,' he said. 'If this fellow was on the other's tail, maybe he was shot down.'

Scriebner pulled up at a bridge across a wide river.

The wheat on the other side had been unaffected the previous day; and there had been stretches along this side of the river hardly touched; but the blight had spread across the land during the night, and in the morning it had crossed the river. Now they could see the life being drawn from the corn as they watched.

Bruton said tensely: 'When's it going to stop?'

'They may have stopped it farther south,' Palfrey said.

One thing Karen had told Palfrey had given hope to the experts who were experimenting south of the city with layers of salt across the land. It was a temporary expedient, springing from Karen's admission that sea-water remained an insuperable barrier.

Half an hour later they were watching gangs of men bringing the salt from laden trucks and spreading it. Excavators and bull-dozers cut a shallow channel for the salt. Two hundred yards away the corn was wilting; the blight had travelled five miles from the river bank.

The salt itself would ruin the soil; but that was a minor danger.

'We shan't know for a couple of days,' said Bruton. He went to the side of one of the trucks and sat down in the shade while the men laboured. Stefan joined the men, working with them. Palfrey and Bruton sat watching; their aid would make little difference. 'Surely it will wear itself out in time, Sap.' Bruton's voice was harsh.

'I don't think it will spread indefinitely,' said Palfrey, but the words came slowly. There seemed nothing useful to say, nothing to do but wait until they knew the full results of the visitation.

On the second morning there were signs that the blight was stopping. Scriebner went to New York that day.

On the third it seemed that the results of that single visitation had spent themselves. Nothing was affected in new areas.

That third day, Palfrey and the others left Texas by air and arrived in Washington in the evening. The Marquis was still there, and they went straight to his hotel. He was standing by the window, looking out, and there was a slip of paper in his hand. He turned and smiled a greeting.

'Well?' he asked.

Palfrey told him what they had seen.

'Is there any news here?' asked Bruton.

'A little,' said Brett. 'It may help. The owner of the land mostly affected is Hoffner, and Hoffner's in Washington now.'

Edward Hoffner stood up from an easy chair, a tall, rangy man much younger than Palfrey had expected. He was nothing like Karen, although it was understandable that descriptions of the two men should tally, for Hoffner had a thin face, square shoulders, and piercing, deep-set eyes. He looked as if he had not slept for nights.

'You're Palfrey,' he greeted.

'Yes,' Palfrey smiled.

'You've been south?' demanded Hoffner.

'I left there this morning.'

'I left yesterday,' Hoffner said. 'I couldn't face it, Palfrey; I couldn't stay and see the land rotting under my eyes.' He tapped a sheaf of papers on the edge of his chair. 'I'm told it's stopped spreading.'

'It's over for the moment,' Palfrey said, and sat down. Hoff-

147

ner turned and poured out drinks. His movements were jerky: he was a badly-shaken man.

'I'm told you're investigating on behalf of the Government, and you've had some results.'

'Slender results,' Palfrey said.

'How can I help you?'

'I think your land was selected because someone wants to ruin you,' Palfrey said, slowly.

Hoffner jerked his head up. 'I've no enemies.'

'Yes, you have.' Palfrey lit a cigarette, and sat down on the arm of a chair. Hoffner was staring at him in some bewilderment, shaken out of his bitter reflections. 'That stretch of land wasn't chosen by accident, Hoffner. I think you might help us to find the organization backing it. More than one man is concerned, but the leader is—a mutual friend.'

'*What's* that?'

'Named Karen,' Palfrey said, and watched the man closely.

Hoffner put down his glass sharply, and shifted his position. Obviously the name shocked him. Palfrey remembered how Karen's wife had told him that she had liked Hoffner, and that Karen had shown him considerable respect. No one admitted knowing 'Karen'. Would Hoffner also declare that he did not know the man?

'Not *Karen*,' said Hoffner, and Palfrey's heart leapt.

'Yes, a man whom you knew in New York.'

'That's ridiculous,' said Hoffner, slowly. 'Karen wouldn't be behind a thing like this. And I knew him a long time before I met him in New York. He was once a manager for me in Texas, where he looked after my biggest farm. This doesn't make sense, Palfrey.'

'It's true,' said Palfrey. 'Did he always call himself Karen?'

'It's his christian name,' said Hoffner. 'He's Karen Jorgensenn. I went to see him and his wife when he was in New York. He——'

'The more I know about him the better,' Palfrey said. He felt a sudden wave of relief; so there was at last a chance of discovering the men with whom Karen worked; and the explanation of the name was simple. 'Before you go on, Hoffner, I want to tell you when I saw him, and what happened to his wife . . .'

'It doesn't make sense!' Hoffner burst out. 'I've known Karen all my life. He's older than I. I knew him when I was knee-high.

148

He left me to take up an executive post in United American Cereal Corporation——'

'Is that a big concern?'

'Probably the biggest in North America,' Hoffner said.

A glow of satisfaction began to spread through Palfrey. He said: 'That's fine. May I use your telephone?' He was at the instrument as Hoffner finished saying 'sure', and called the hotel. Bruton answered, and Palfrey said briefly:

'Check United American Cereals, Corney.'

'*That* outfit!' exclaimed Bruton, and then added crisply: 'Okay.'

Palfrey rang off to find Hoffner looking at him perplexedly.

'That's a precautionary measure,' said Palfrey, lightly. 'United American has a big overseas connexion, I suppose?'

'World wide,' Hoffner agreed.

'How long has Karen been with it?'

'Most of twelve years,' said Hoffner. 'But don't get ideas, Palfrey, he doesn't *own* United Americans. He's their chief foreign representative, as far as I know. I gathered he was doing fairly well for himself when he was in New York.' He frowned. 'I thought his wife looked on edge, but he told me she hadn't been well for some time. He was as friendly towards me as he'd ever been. There was a girl there——' Hoffner paused.

'Diana Leeming,' said Palfrey.

'That's so.' Hoffner looked at Palfrey narrowly. 'I had a feeling that I knew that girl,' he went on. 'It was her eyes, I guess. There was something about her that was strange, too, now you've told me I can imagine—but Karen!'

'About Diana Leeming,' Palfrey said. 'Did she seem to recognize you?'

'No. I knew her story. She'd crashed and lost both her parents. Karen was looking after her—it was the kind of thing I'd expect Karen to do. But the man you've described—that *is* Karen.'

'Did he have any prejudices?' Palfrey asked.

'He didn't like the negroes,' Hoffner said, hesitatingly. 'If there was one thing he wasn't sane on, it was colour.' He laughed, on a strained note. 'He would never employ coloured workers, even when labour was short. I didn't argue with him, he was so good in every other way. Palfrey, I can't understand why Karen should have this in for *me*.'

'Some time or other you crossed him,' Palfrey said. 'Did he know Grayson?'

'Not to my knowledge. Grayson doesn't come into this.'
Hoffner shook his head deliberately. 'I won't believe Grayson——'

'Grayson's suffered in a different way, as far as I can find out,' said Palfrey. 'You knew Valerie Grayson, didn't you?'

Hoffner's eyes were hard. 'I did.'

'I think——'

'I'd rather not talk about Valerie,' Hoffner said, abruptly.

'Karen was behind her disappearance,' Palfrey declared.

With the statement that Karen was behind Valerie Grayson's disappearance, Hoffner changed completely.

'What did he do to her?'

'She was hurt in one way, and one way only,' Palfrey said. 'She lost her memory. After that, Karen did some odd things. He took her to a nursing home. She wasn't conscious for much of the time. She didn't know what was happening to her. For one thing, her features were altered. Modern plastic surgery,' he added, with a wry smile. 'As far as I can gather, he gave her a different personality. He altered the shape of her eyes slightly, and the shape of her chin. He invented the story that she was Diana Leeming.'

Hoffner started. *'What?'*

'Grayson flew to England to see this Diana Leeming,' Palfrey told him, 'and the report from London came in just before I arrived here. Grayson has identified her. There was a birthmark few people would know about, and other indications. A scar on her right hand that Karen hadn't noticed, and a scar on her left thigh. Diana and Valerie are one and the same, Hoffner.'

The man seemed to be coming to life, but there was an incredulous note in his voice when he said:

'But Karen let me *see* her——'

'A refinement of torture, a joke which only he could see. The woman you loved sitting opposite you without you knowing who she was.'

'It's impossible!'

'It happened,' Palfrey said. 'The alteration in her appearance was easy enough. The memory's a different matter, but—well, it was done.'

'And she's in England now?'

'And staying there until this business is over,' said Palfrey.

'What happened to the real Diana Leeming?'

'I think she was killed with her parents,' Palfrey said, 'though

150

I'm not sure. But there's more that you can tell me yet, Hoffner. Don't misunderstand me.' He paused. 'Valerie Grayson had a reputation for liking the high-spots.'

'She had,' agreed Hoffner.

'She's changed in that way, too.'

Hoffner said slowly: 'She'd changed before she disappeared. Look here, Palfrey, I'm not a prig. I know my way about, and I've met a lot of people. But I never had any time for—for the people who lived like Valerie did when first I met her. I didn't like the way she behaved, but I guess I couldn't help my feelings. And'—he gave a rueful smile—'she didn't exactly take to me at first sight. You follow me?'

'Yes.'

'And then something happened to change her,' said Hoffner. 'I don't know what it was. I had the surprise of my life one day when I called at the house and Grayson wasn't in. She saw me. She looked—she looked as if the blood had been drained out of her. She'd had a shock. She asked me if I knew a man named Mallory——' he broke off. 'What does Mallory mean to you?'

'Enough, but don't worry about him now,' said Palfrey. 'Go on.'

'I didn't know the guy,' said Hoffner. 'I gathered Mallory was a doctor who was often with her father. She didn't trust him, but Grayson seemed to be impressed by the man. You know how it is—Grayson imagined he was ill, Mallory encouraged him, in order to draw fat fees. That was how it seemed to me. It sobered Valerie up a mighty lot. She agreed her father was ill, and she worried about him. She still went to parties and lived pretty fast, but her heart wasn't in it. I stuck around. I figured that the time would come when she would be really tired of the high-spots. It did. We got engaged. It was only a couple of weeks later that she disappeared.' Hoffner paused, and then asked slowly: 'Palfrey, why do you reckon they killed her memory?'

'That's what I want to find out. She learned something that Karen didn't want to get around. He didn't want to kill her, so he experimented with his drug—or Mallory's drug. It wouldn't surprise me if she learned that "something" from Mallory. It wouldn't surprise me, either, if Grayson knew a little about it and kept quiet because of his daughter. But Grayson told Stefan——'

'Told who?'

'A friend of mine,' amended Palfrey hastily. 'He told him

that he would talk freely when he made sure that Valerie was safe. That's why he's on his way back now.'

'Is he safe?' demanded Hoffner.

Palfrey said: 'Yes. He's coming over by special plane, and it's being escorted both sides of the Atlantic. We're not taking any chances with Grayson, you needn't worry about that.'

'I'd like to see him as soon as it can be arranged,' Hoffner said.

'I'll fix it,' Palfrey promised. 'There's one other thing, Hoffner.'

'Go ahead.'

'It's possible that I was seen coming here, and it's possible that you're in danger. You're one of the few men in the north who could tell us that Karen was really Jorgensenn and that he's with United American. I'd rather you lay low for a bit.'

'Well——' began Hoffner.

Palfrey smiled, diffidently. 'In fact, you must. You're a valuable witness. I'm going to arrange for your room to be watched and I'm going to ask you not to leave the hotel without first getting permission.'

One section of the isolationist American Press was working up anti-British feeling. On the street, Palfrey bought other papers; only the one named Britain, but others might take up the story. The *World Citizen* made a passionate appeal for uniting secret services, and Palfrey smiled wryly. That seemed a small drop in the ocean of national feeling.

Each paper gave a great deal of space to the GREAT CORN BLIGHT, and there was an article in the *Citizen* about the reporter whose dead body Palfrey had seen.

None of this made pleasant reading, but Palfrey tried to ignore it. The main problem remained—clear in itself and its implications, but otherwise obscure and baffling.

He got into the taxi and was driven three blocks to his own hotel, and walked thoughtfully upstairs. He had expected Karen to exert himself to the limit to trace the movements of his enemies, but Bruton and Stefan had not been followed, Stella had complete freedom of movement, and now apparently Karen was not interested in Hoffner.

Uneasily Palfrey wondered if Karen had withdrawn with all his key men to some inaccessible spot and was directing 'operations' from there. He himself had told Palfrey so much. He might even suspect that his connexion with United American would soon be discovered, and be acting as if that were now known.

If that were so, and if he could start operations on an extensive scale, the next few days might be disastrous.

Stella was coming out of her room opposite Palfrey's.

'Hallo,' she said. 'Seen a ghost?'

'Large masses of ghosts,' said Palfrey, half-seriously. He looked down on her.

'What dynamite have you got from Hoffner?'

'Didn't Stefan tell you?'

'As soon as you'd finished on the telephone, Stefan grabbed Corney by the scruff of the neck. They were in a cab before I realized they were out of the room!' Palfrey knew what Stefan was like when he acted like that. 'You certainly gave them dynamite, Sap.'

'Oh, a small stick,' said Palfrey.

She frowned. 'What——' she began.

He touched her arm lightly, a warning gesture, and she broke off. For no apparent reason his manner had changed. He was standing smiling at her rather vacantly, but was wary and watchful.

'A very small stick,' Palfrey said. 'Stella, hop downstairs and get me some English cigarettes, will you?'

'Why, sure.' But she was more puzzled than ever.

'I could never smoke Americans,' Palfrey went on. He walked slowly to the window, his movements casual and lazy, and stifled a yawn. 'By George, I'm tired!' He waved towards the door, urging her to hurry out, and she quickened her step, but at the door she turned and looked at him. He sat on the arm of a chair near the heavy curtains, and yawned again.

Stella went out.

Palfrey stretched out a hand and thrust the curtains aside. A man, crouching in the corner, uttered a sharp exclamation and tried to dodge. Palfrey pushed him with the flat of his hand. The man struck the window heavily. He was gasping for breath, and his thick lips were parted, his small brown eyes looked terrified.

He was a mulatto, and Palfrey felt sure that he was one of the men who had been a jailer at Randall City.

'Hallo,' said Palfrey, lightly.

The man licked his lips and his right hand went to his coat. Palfrey ignored it. The man gripped his lapel; beneath his armpit, Palfrey felt sure, there was a gun in a shoulder holster.

153

'Aren't you feeling so well?' asked Palfrey, cheerfully. 'You shouldn't hide behind curtains if——'

The man thrust his hand beneath his coat, and snatched at his gun. Palfrey struck him a ringing blow on the head, then took him by the coat and thrust him against the wall. Next he slipped his hand inside the man's coat and pulled out the gun, which was lodging against the top of a shoulder holster. Palfrey weighed it in his hand while the man crouched there, staring at him as if terrified.

'So you haven't deserted us,' said Palfrey, and felt really pleased at this apparition. 'Where's Casado?'

'I—I doan know.'

'But Casado gave you your instructions, didn't he?' asked Palfrey. 'He's a great one for instructions. When did you last see him?'

'Way—way back.'

'It wouldn't be true if I said I didn't want to hurt you,' Palfrey said, and the man licked his lips again ; there was an excuse for his fear, for Palfrey looked as if he would like nothing better than to lay about him. He struck the prisoner gently on the side of the head. 'That's a sample,' he said. 'When did you last see Casado?'

'I doan know, Boss, I swear——'

'Stand back, Palfrey,' came a voice from behind them.

Palfrey stood quite still, his hand tightened about the gun. The man in the window lunged forward. Palfrey raised his foot, and his assailant ran into it and staggered back, gasping.

'I spoke to you,' said the man behind Palfrey.

The voice was Casado's.

He was near the door which communicated with Stefan's and Bruton's room. Palfrey thought: 'So he must have slipped in there as soon as the others left.' He knew that he must somehow deal with both men before Stella came back ; he wanted no harm to come to Stella.

'Turn round,' ordered Casado, 'and drop your gun.'

Palfrey retained his hold on the gun, which was pointing downwards, and turned slowly. Casado was standing by the door of the wardrobe. There was a long-barrelled gun in his hand, the gun which fired the darts, or one very like it. Palfrey remembered the needle in Lannigan's eye, and watched Casado closely. Casado's gun was pointing towards him, but he did not fire. Palfrey felt slightly easier ; had the man wanted to kill him out of hand, it could have been done by now.

154

'You heard me,' Casado said.

'I'm deaf to reason,' said Palfrey.

Casado was watching his gun-hand. If he raised it, he would shoot; he would not take chances.

Palfrey sat on the arm of the chair. It would not be so bad if the other man were not present, a man who was feeling vindictive to say the least of it; and, judging from his expression now, he would not pull his punches.

Casado glanced at the mulatto.

'Take his gun,' he said.

The man was still rubbing his stomach and crouching; but he advanced slowly, as if it were more than he dare do to disobey Casado. How far could he go? wondered Palfrey. If he fired a shot at the floor it would raise an alarm, but it would also draw Casado's fire. His problem was to get out of this scrape alive.

Nervously, the mulatto stretched out his hand.

'All right,' said Palfrey, and handed the gun over, butt first. The man took it, and then punched him in the side of the face, a blow which sent him reeling into the chair, his legs waving. The mulatto followed up and by accident Palfrey's foot caught him in the face. He gasped and staggered back again, clutching his nose. Palfrey saw the blood streaming from it as he straightened up.

'Now don't spoil the carpet,' he said.

Casado drew a step nearer.

'This is not funny, Palfrey,' he said.

Why had the man held his fire? What did he want? Was he waiting for Stella? She would not be long downstairs.

Of course, she would know that he thought something was amiss! He would have rung for the floor-waiter for cigarettes otherwise. Hope began to rise.

'How much did Karen's wife tell you?' asked Casado.

'How to get away,' said Palfrey.

'You're lying to me,' Casado said. He moved nearer again, with his gun raised. Palfrey watched him closely, reckoning the chances of an attack; he ruled it out, Casado would not allow himself to be taken at a disadvantage; the only weapon he had was bluff. Once the man thought he had learned all the truth he would shoot and get away. He must be aware, too, that Stella might be back at any moment.

Seconds were important.

'How much did she tell you?' Casado repeated.

Palfrey said: 'Nothing.'

There was a sudden sound outside; a gasp, muffled sounds as of a struggle, and then a door closed. Palfrey stared towards the passage, his hands clenching. There were footsteps in Stefan's room. The communicating door opened, and Stella was thrust in by another mulatto. Palfrey did not waste time trying to guess how that had been contrived, but his heart sank.

Stella's hair was tumbled, her dress was torn at one shoulder. The man thrust her forward, and Casado said. 'Stuff her mouth.'

Palfrey watched, helplessly, while the mulatto gripped Stella's wrist so that she could not struggle, and thrust his hand into his pocket. The man whose nose was bleeding walked unsteadily to the girl, and held her arms behind her; his coat and shirt were caked with blood.

The man who had brought Stella in pinched her nose and thrust her head back. Her mouth opened involuntarily and he crammed something that looked like putty into her mouth. She retched and heaved, but little sound escaped her lips. The man released her, then thrust her into a chair. Her face had gone scarlet, but now the blood receded from her cheeks. She sat upright, trying to recover from the sudden attack, fighting desperately for breath. It seemed a long time before she was anything like normal, and breathing through her nose.

On the floor was a packet of cigarettes.

Casado turned to Palfrey.

'Listen to me,' he said. 'She can't make a noise—she can't even croak. It doesn't matter how badly she gets hurt. And she'll get hurt some if you don't talk. How much did Karen's wife tell you?'

Palfrey said: 'Nothing.'

'You were lying with her, and she told you plenty.'

'All she told me was how to escape——'

Casado motioned to the men standing near the girl. He took Stella's right hand and bent back her little finger. She jumped with the pain, but still no sound escaped her lips. There was a little cracking noise; it seemed to send a shiver of pain through Palfrey. Stella dropped her head against the back of her chair.

'Light a cigarette,' said Casado. He did not remove his eyes from Palfrey, but for the moment all Palfrey could do was to stare at Stella's left hand. The little finger was sticking up at an odd angle; he had not imagined that crack.

'You know what to do,' said Casado.

The man had lit his cigarette. Now he ripped the torn shoulder of Stella's dress to the waist and tore off a flimsy brassiere.

'If you don't want her hurt, talk,' said Casado. 'How much did Karen's wife tell you?'

Palfrey turned away from the girl.

There was so much at stake; more than would justify saving Stella, if by sacrificing her it would help to bring success. The mulatto was mauling her and drawing at the cigarette.

'Burn her,' said Casado.

The cigarette was pressed against the creamy flesh.

Palfrey snapped. 'What do you want to know?'

'That'll do,' said Casado, and motioned to the man with the cigarette. There was an ugly little black mark on Stella's skin. 'Now, Palfrey,' Casado continued, 'you'd better be sensible from now on. Did she tell you about Alaska?'

It took all of Palfrey's self-control not to start, and to answer quickly: 'Alaska?'

'So she didn't,' Casado said, and for the first time he smiled, a flash of white teeth against his dusky skin. 'That's fine, Palfrey, because you can't have told anyone else.' He put his right hand to his pocket, keeping Palfrey covered with the gun in his left hand, and took out a small box. He went to a table, put the box down and took off the lid. It was padded with cotton wool. Next moment, Palfrey saw something glisten; it was a hypodermic syringe. Still moving slowly and deliberately, Casado took it and turned to the man watching Stella.

'Take my gun,' he said.

The man obeyed quickly, and kept Palfrey covered. Casado handled the hypodermic syringe as if he loved it, his spatulate fingers, with their yellow half-moons, seemed to caress it. It was filled with a colourless liquid; and by its side was a capsule also filled with what looked like water.

Casado said: 'Now you'll forget all right, Palfrey. Karen doesn't want you to die. He just wants you to forget—that's all. It wouldn't count much if you remembered; you can't do him any more harm now, but—he'd rather you didn't remember.' He came forward slowly. 'Take off your coat.'

Stella was sitting bolt upright. She tried to get up from the chair, but the man standing behind her put his hand on her shoulders and thrust her back.

He might throw the coat at Casado; he might make him drop the syringe and break it. That would be something gained.

Suddenly Casado struck him in the stomach. The blow was so unexpected that Palfrey could do nothing to avoid it. A sharp agonizing pain surged through him, and he collapsed into the chair. Casado grinned and quite calmly took his right hand and held the syringe poised. Palfrey hardly realized what was happening, the pain was so great. He had forgotten the syringe. He felt the sharp prick of the needle.

He flung himself forward. Casado was taken so much by surprise that Palfrey sent him swaying back, and the syringe fell from his hand. Palfrey stamped on it, smashing it. He was fully conscious; he felt no immediate effect. Of course he felt no immediate effect! Casado was backing away, the man with the gun was coming forward. Palfrey thrust out his hands and took Casado by the shoulders and flung him into the approaching man.

The gun fell!

Nothing mattered, only vengeance. The man behind Stella jumped forward and stooped for the gun. Palfrey stamped on his hand. The squeal of agony must have reached the passage and the nearby rooms—it was a high-pitched, ear-splitting scream. Palfrey snatched the gun from the floor, and the man behind Casado rushed at him.

Palfrey fired.

A needle struck into the man's face, and he screamed in turn and tugged at it, but it had gone in too deep to come out easily. There were footsteps in the passage. Stella was on her feet, gesticulating wildly, spluttering. A man banged on the door and shouted at the same time:

'What's going on in there? What's going on?'

Stella turned away and rushed to the hand-basin. Palfrey saw that she was putting her hand to her mouth and spitting out the 'putty'. The man outside opened the door.

Palfrey said: 'Fetch the police!'

He kept Casado and the other man covered.

The fit of blind fury had spent itself. A moment more and he would have shot Casado, but now he was glad that he had not done so, for Casado was wanted alive. He looked at the mulatto's set face. Casado took the defeat well, and was standing quite still with his hands by his side. Palfrey thought of other things; why had there been no one on duty at the hotel? Three men should have been on that floor. He had known there was danger outside, but had not dreamed that there would be any in the hotel itself.

None of those things greatly mattered.

Two more men hurried into the room, one of them flashing a badge. Next, a moon-faced man, whom Palfrey had seen before, came rushing in. He had been on duty downstairs.

Palfrey said: 'There's Casado. Make sure he doesn't get away.'

It was so difficult to think clearly.

He knew the others were watching him curiously; the moon-faced man actually stood still and stared for a moment before he turned to Casado. Palfrey motioned to him irritably. Why should they stare? What did he matter now?

He looked down at the puncture in his arm. The flesh was red and swollen. *Fool!* He had lost his wits! There was a chance of taking action, simple action. He snapped:

'I want a stick or a ruler.' The men gaped at him. 'Something for a tourniquet,' said Palfrey. There was a glint of desperate excitement in his eyes. If he could stop the drug from spreading—surely it would be better even to lose his arm than his memory. The fierceness of that sudden hope made him feel sick. 'Get me a stick!'

A man came to him.

'I'm a doctor,' he said, 'and——'

'Tourniquet,' Palfrey snapped. 'Treat that as a bad cut or a snake bite.' He touched the puncture. 'Hurry!'

He was hardly aware of what was happening in the room, of the men who crowded in, some of them familiar—men who should have been watching. From somewhere a short, ebony ruler was obtained, the doctor set to work. The pressure about Palfrey's arm above the elbow grew tighter and tighter.

'Make an incision,' he said, and he was surprised that he could speak calmly. 'A deep one.'

The doctor hurried to his case near the door and took out a lancet. Stella was still washing out her mouth. A man had flung a towel over her shoulders, and as the lancet went into Palfrey's arm, Stella turned round. Her mouth was lathered as if she had been eating soap, and her voice was pitched on a high note.

'Sap, don't go to sleep,' she begged. 'Don't go to sleep; that's the main thing, don't go to sleep!'

SIXTEEN

'KEEP HIM AWAKE'

STELLA had gripped the doctor's arm and was saying something that Palfrey could not hear. He was vaguely aware of people staring at him. There seemed faces all round him—nothing but faces. And there was Stella's voice, an insistent murmur. Someone else was speaking, he did not know who it was. He closed his eyes. The desire for sleep was overwhelming. Just forty winks—if he could have forty winks he would wake up a new man.

A new man!

Alarm flooded through him; he was conscious enough then to realize his danger. Did Stella know what she was talking about? If he went to sleep, would the harm be done?

Someone slapped his face.

Again; then a third time; the slaps were gentle, but they pushed his head from side to side and forced him to open his eyes. The 'someone' was the doctor. Stella was turning and talking to those faces. The doctor stopped slapping, another man took his place. Even the slaps seemed soothing. The doctor was putting something on his arm—a bandage, of course, a bandage round the cut. Why had he been cut? The injection, oh, yes, he remembered the injection and the fury which had possessed him, but a single injection could do him no harm. If they would only let him sleep he would wake up fresh and there would be nothing the matter with him.

He felt a sharp prick, and flinched.

The doctor had given him an injection—*another* injection. The doctor was really Casado; he must make the others understand that he could not stand another injection; *that* might do irreparable harm.

The men began to march him round the room again. Vaguely he was aware of others shifting the furniture so that he should not stumble over it. He passed the bed. The pillows looked soft and tempting. Yes, if he could lie down, if they would leave him alone only for ten minutes, just ten minutes, it was all he wanted. It was as if he were back at the bungalow and could see the eyes watching him there. Dark, reddish-brown eyes like Casado's. Casado! Where was Casado? He came to a standstill.

'Casado!' he exclaimed.

'Don't you worry,' said one of the men, pulling again at his left arm, while the other propelled him by the shoulder. Suddenly he saw Stella quite close to him. The doctor was holding her hand. He could see the blister where she had been burned.

There was a disturbance at the door.

He saw a huge man who had to duck beneath the lintel; ah, here was Stefan! Bruton was just behind him. Well, they were all right, they would understand. Stefan was standing by his side now and talking.

'Don't go to sleep, Sap.'

He had always credited Stefan with common sense. How could he go to sleep while they were frog-marching him about the room like this? It was absurd. And surely Stefan, who was his friend, knew how desperately he needed a nap? He tried to say something, but the words did not make sense.

'Don't go to sleep, Sap.'

Then suddenly something happened. Palfrey did not know what it was, was aware only of a commotion. A man was running away, others were following him. He did not know who it was.

'Stefan, Casado——'

'Corney's after him.'

'Oh.' Palfrey's mind went blank again, and his eyes closed. Sleep seemed closer than ever now. His feet felt like cushions. He was sailing through the air, walking on air. He felt pressure on his left arm—a very tight grip. Then he winced. He opened his eyes. Stefan was gripping his arm and twisting—Stefan, deliberately hurting him. Had he gone mad?

'Don't!'

The pain grew worse. Stefan seemed to be leering at him.

The commotion had subsided, but he could not see Casado or Bruton. He could see the others clearly. Stella was standing by the hand-basin, and the man who called himself a doctor was beside her. He was doing something to her hand. Oh, he remembered again—her finger. So they were at last paying Stella some attention. Surely she deserved it more than anyone else in the room. He looked about him more intently. The eyes had gone, the faces had gone. There was a man on the floor with something sticking out of his face; one of Casado's darts had found the right home. Palfrey remembered firing at him.

'Don't go to sleep, Sap.'

Someone came into the room carrying a tray. The coffee pot

on it glistened in the light. The door closed behind the man, and someone came over and poured out coffee. For the first time since he had been pulled out of his chair he was allowed to stand still. His head was reeling, but he did not feel quite so tired.

'Drink this,' said Stefan.

Palfrey forced himself to sip the scalding liquid, and hardly had he moved his lips away from the cup when they started to march him about the room again. He was sweating now. Little beads of sweat ran from his forehead to his cheeks, and his eyes seemed to be swimming in water, but his head was clearer and that overpowering desire to sleep was easing.

'Sap,' said Stefan. 'You mustn't go to sleep.'

'I know,' said Palfrey. He grinned. 'I won't.'

He understood now.

They marched him off again; but the ordeal did not last much longer, for the assault of weariness receded. Although he felt bodily exhausted, his mind was now crystal clear. Stella had warned the doctor not to let him go to sleep—bless the girl! Had he succumbed, the drug might have taken full effect. But the incision had been made, most of the poison had probably been drawn off, and he was past that awful temptation. He felt limp, his feet still dragged over the floor, but he was in no immediate danger.

'You'll be all right now,' said Stefan.

'Yes, thanks.' He looked round. 'Where's Stella?'

'She'll be in soon.'

'How's her finger?'

'It's all right, the doctor set it.'

'Good!' exclaimed Palfrey. He laughed. 'Give me a cigarette, will you? What happened outside?'

Stefan lit his cigarette and then told him what had happened. The three watching men had been distracted by an alarm at the end of the passage, and each had been shanghaied. Casado had been working in the kitchens of the hotel with his two men. Once the watchers had been dealt with, he had been able to get into the room next to Palfrey's with a master-key. One of them had hidden in the room to distract Palfrey's attention so that Casado himself could be sure of an effective surprise.

'It was smart,' Palfrey said, slowly.

'Don't worry about it,' said Stefan.

'We shouldn't have allowed it to happen,' insisted Palfrey, 'but I suppose it doesn't matter now. Where's Casado?'

'He killed himself,' Stefan said.

'Oh,' said Palfrey.

He felt a rush of disappointment; but he had delayed asking that question because he had been afraid that Casado had escaped. It was really worse that he had killed himself, because now he could not be made to talk. But it could not be helped, and at least they had confirmation of the importance of Alaska ; that mattered above everything else.

And he had not lost his memory.

Palfrey and the others anxiously awaited a report from the White House next morning. It arrived a little after midday.

A watch was being kept all over the world. Hundreds of messages had come in and were sorted out, all from observers of the great agricultural regions ; and there were no fresh reports of black earth. That news was enough in itself to cheer them up, and Palfrey began to think clearly and logically.

The incident of the previous night had been of little importance except for the one result. For the rest, his interview with Hoffner had been much more important. Stefan had told him that inquiries were being made in United American, searching inquiries which were causing some trouble among the directors. There were no results yet. Karen Jorgensenn, it was established, was still their chief foreign sales adviser. A clearer picture of Karen was built up in their minds. He was not, as far as it could be established, an executive of United American; but Palfrey did not think he had boasted vainly of the other members of the syndicate. There was no certainty that the executive of United American were involved, but a close watch was kept on all their foreign agencies. United American used air travel and kept a fleet of small, private machines for special delivery and for their sales agents. Each machine was traced, the staffs were watched, and they were forbidden to take off, in whatever corner of the world they were.

The executives of the Corporation were being closely watched. None of them appeared to have had much to do with Karen personally. He had been an unusually able representative, and there had been no occasion to complain about his work. His fanatical hatred of the black race was well known, but this was not uncommon among southerners ; Karen appeared to have kept it within reasonable bounds.

One fact had materialized which made Palfrey thoughtful for a long time.

Karen had married the daughter of the Corporation's Indian agent; and soon after their marriage the agent had died in unusual circumstances. No one appeared to have guessed at the way Karen treated his wife; no one was prepared to say that he had any interest in United American beyond that which he was known to have. His salary was good, but nothing like good enough to account for the vast sums of money he must have spent in research, in reconstructing the bungalow and, presumably, in paying his men. There were big financial interests behind Karen, and the immediate preoccupation was tracing those interests.

Palfrey wondered if Grayson could help.

The millionaire's aircraft had been forced to land in Canada after being driven off its course by a storm, but there was no suspicion of foul play. Palfrey felt reasonably certain that Grayson would carry out his share of the bargain, and tell them what he knew. Would it be appreciably more than they had already discovered?

Brett had flown back to England, to take his report to Whitehall.

American, Canadian and Russian agents were working along the Alaskan seaboard; Palfrey wished he were with them, but his arm incapacitated him, and if there were fighting there would be no room for a man who was not fit. Bruton was fidgety in the two days following the raid on the hotel, and although Stefan did not put it into words, Palfrey felt that he, too, was eager to join in the hunt in Alaska.

On the second morning, after a good night's sleep, Palfrey went into the Russian's room.

'When are you going north?'

Stefan looked at him. 'Am I going north?'

'My dear chap, yes! You'll have to go and look after Corney. He won't be able to rest in peace down here much longer.'

'I think I understand you,' said Stefan, his eyes crinkling at the corners. 'I am not sure that we ought to leave you alone.'

'I shall be guarded as if I were bullion,' Palfrey said. 'What happened once certainly won't happen again.' He tugged at a few strands of hair at the front of his head. 'It won't do me any harm to have a few days in the dark to think quietly,' he said. 'I haven't really been able to do that since we started. The pressure's been too great, one way and another.'

'What do you advise about Stella?' asked Stefan.

'She'd better stay here,' said Palfrey.

164

'Yes.' The Russian hesitated, and then chuckled. 'All right, Sap! Go and tell Corney!'

'I'll leave that to you,' said Palfrey.

At breakfast, Stella joined them and made the party complete. She looked startled when Bruton talked of flying to Alaska after breakfast, and glanced at Palfrey.

'Am I going?' she asked.

'Not this time,' said Palfrey. 'Sorry.'

'Oh, well,' said Stella, 'I suppose I ought to admit I've had plenty to do.' Yet she was not happy about the decision, and the high spirits of the breakfast party were dashed. Only Bruton seemed unaffected, and he finished first and got up, dabbing his lips. Then he patted Stella's arm.

'You look after Sap,' he said. 'Come on, Stefan.'

Stella sat quite still, looking at Palfrey. There was a new expression in her eyes. 'Aren't you going?'

'Not yet,' said Palfrey; and Stella's eyes glowed.

Outside the door, Bruton looked up into Stefan's face, and said: 'I'm not so happy about Stella, are you?'

'I'm not at all happy,' Stefan admitted.

'It's a case,' said Bruton. 'And when a girl falls for Sap, she falls heavily. Maybe if she knew Drusilla——'

'She knows all about Drusilla,' Stefan said. 'I told her last night, my friend. Sap will know how to handle the situation; there is no point in our worrying.'

Both of them found it difficult to get Stella out of their minds as they flew north-west through the clear sky, with the peaceful country unrolling beneath them.

In Washington, Palfrey tried to put his increasing disquiet about Stella out of his mind. Yet he found her company restful, and always before him was the extent of the debt he owed to her.

He was uneasy about other things.

Much had been explained; but he had hoped—and even thought—that they had found the distribution organization in the United American Cereals Corporation. The inquiries into the Corporation's work gave them no reason for thinking that Karen had used it in any way, however. Reports from the White House on the records of the chief executives seemed to rule them out as conspirators. Hoffner had identified Karen, but it seemed that Karen had been working with other interests unknown to United American. It was almost too much to believe that a responsible American company would lend itself to such

165

a scheme as Karen's. That worried Palfrey more than anything else.

He was sitting in the sun-lounge of the hotel looking out on the white buildings and the gently waving trees, and Stella was lounging on a settee opposite him, with a magazine in her lap. Both had an arm in a sling, but Palfrey was finding his forearm less painful. A new dressing had been put on that morning, and the inflammation had been decidedly less.

He had put in a call to Drusilla, and had been waiting for it to come through for half an hour.

Stella looked up, and saw his frown.

'A penny for them,' she said.

'Oh, odd thoughts,' said Palfrey. 'Chiefly about distribution. That aircraft did fly over Texas and do its work. There are almost certainly others. It doesn't look like United American. I can't really convince myself that an American corporation would lend itself to the thing. Anyway, that would mean that, apart from the executives, employers in comparatively minor positions would have to be heart and soul in the foul business. It doesn't add up. There would be a leakage of some kind. One man at least would find it weighing too heavily on his conscience. Don't you think so?'

Palfrey glanced up when a man and woman entered the sun-lounge, and wished them a hundred miles away. But he smiled at them amiably.

The man stood on the threshold, and touched his wife's arm. The woman looked round. The man whispered something, and the couple turned away. Palfrey raised his eyebrows.

'Unexpected discretion,' he said.

'What do you mean?' asked Stella. She had grown pale, which surprised Palfrey, for the incident seemed trivial. He was a little uncomfortable because it had seemed to him that the intruders had assumed that they were breaking in on a romantic *tête-à-tête*.

'Well, wasn't it?' asked Palfrey, and wished that Stella did not show her feelings quite so clearly. 'I——'

'I'd like to break their necks!' snapped Stella.

Palfrey stared. 'But why?'

'So you didn't hear him,' said Stella, who was sitting nearer the door. She forced a smile. 'They went out because they know you're——' she paused.

'Go on.'

'English,' said Stella.

'My dear girl!'

Stella pointed to the papers which were folded on a table in the window. Palfrey had already glanced through them, and had been mildly amused. The story of a man-hunt for British Secret Service agents, which was supposed to have started near the atomic plant in Arizona, had raged right across America in the daily newspapers. The Liberal and international political papers had made no editorial comment: isolationist papers had not been so reserved, but until that moment Palfrey had not understood the possible consequences.

He got up, glanced at a headline, and then chuckled.

'I don't think it's funny!' snapped Stella. 'That anyone should do that to *you*——'

'Oh, come!'

'If they had an ounce of sense they'd realize what nonsense it is, they——'

'But we don't want them to realize it,' said Palfrey. 'It will all work out later ; just now we want everyone to be convinced of British villainy.'

'I think it's foul!' cried Stella.

She gripped his arm. Her eyes were suddenly filled with tears, and Palfrey realized that the incident had simply added flame to her emotions—emotions which were centred about him. 'If only they *knew* you,' she said. 'If they knew you as I do.'

'I think——' began Palfrey.

Her grip tightened.

'I don't think anyone knows you as well as I do,' she declared, and the statement took his breath away. 'You *think* they do,' she added, 'but—you don't remember the nursing home, not all the time. You don't remember how you behaved when you thought everything was lost, and you don't know how you acted under a strain that I didn't believe anyone could endure.'

'You managed,' said Palfrey, gently.

'*My* share didn't count!'

'Stella, *please*,' said Palfrey, in great distress.

'I've *got* to tell you,' she said, and caught her breath. 'You know, don't you? It's only a matter of putting it into words. You know, Stefan and Corney know. I'm in love with you.'

'Yes,' said Palfrey. 'I know, Stella. I'm at once so very sorry —and very proud.'

She drew in a sharp breath. They stood looking at each other for what seemed a long time, and then a page boy appeared, a bright-faced youngster who grinned, tapped ostentatiously on a table and then said: 'Your call to England's waiting, sir.'

SEVENTEEN

'WORLD CITIZEN'

WHEN Palfrey returned to the lounge, he was smiling faintly, and for a moment he had forgotten Stella.

He went slowly into the sun-lounge and found her standing by the table. She turned abruptly ; and her smile was radiant!

'Was it all right, Sap?'

'Perfectly clear,' said Palfrey.

'That's splendid. Sap, isn't there anything I can do to help? I feel as if I'm only on the fringe of things now.'

Palfrey sat down on the arm of a chair, greatly relieved.

'So do I,' he said. 'Help me to think. Distribution is the great problem which Karen had to overcome, and which he succeeded in doing—and we've got to follow his thoughts, follow his reasoning, and thus reach the same conclusion as he did. A world-wide network for distribution which no one is likely to suspect and in which he need have no fears about the loyalty of his agents. That's our problem. Think about it as you've never thought before.'

'I will,' promised Stella.

A page came hurrying to the lounge ; a different lad, excited and eager. 'There's a call from the *White House* for Dr. Palfrey!'

'Thanks,' said Palfrey. 'I'll take it upstairs, I think,' he told Stella, and hurried up to his first-floor room.

His step was lighter, and it was not wholly due to Drusilla's voice. Stella had fought her battle and won it ; there would be no further need for disquiet or anxiety about her.

The authoritative voice which had once summoned him from Montreal sounded in his ears.

'Is that Dr. Palfrey?'

'Yes.'

'I should be glad if you would come here at once,' said the secretary. 'Mr. Grayson arrived ten minutes ago.'

Grayson got up from an easy chair, looking small against the tall figure of the president and the others in the room. He looked at Palfrey and then put out his hand. His fingers were clammy and yet warm. He looked old, and his voice was unsteady when he spoke.

Grayson, it appeared, had heard stories of the experiments with black earth through Mallory. Mallory had come to him for financial backing; Grayson had at first refused it. As he said that, Palfrey saw the old man's eyes narrow, and thought from his complexion that the shock of seeing 'Diana' and the strain of the flight to and fro across the Atlantic had been too much for him. But there was something else. Grayson admitted, freely enough, that for many years he had been evading heavy taxation; in the United States the offence was more serious even than it was in England. Mallory had discovered it and used it as a form of blackmail. He had been trying to make Grayson finance him for some months . . .

Palfrey remembered Hoffner's story, and how that fitted in with the change that 'Diana' had noticed in her father, her anxiety, her suspicions of Mallory—yes, they all fitted into the picture.

Grayson went on. He had stood out against backing the research and had threatened to make a disclosure to Washington. Within a few hours of that threat his daughter had disappeared. After that, he had been like clay in Mallory's hands. He had gone to Randall City.

Grayson paused for a moment when he reached that stage, and then said slowly: 'Mr. President, I've been wrong—very wrong, I guess. But I had no idea what they were doing. I did what I was told without arguing. I advanced money—in big sums, I guess. I did it because I thought if I didn't my daughter would suffer. Maybe I was wrong.' He paused again, and then sat down heavily. 'Sure, I was wrong,' he said. 'I know all about that now. But I had no idea it was a serious matter. I thought——'

He stopped again.

The President's voice was harsh.

'You thought these people would use their black earth as a commercial weapon, isn't that so?'

'Yes,' muttered Grayson. 'I didn't think they would use it over a wide area.' He shivered. 'I know what a fool I've been,' he said, 'but I'll ask you to remember that the only person in this world I cared a rap for was my daughter. It's always been that way. I'm not sure, if I had to face it again without knowing what was at stake, that I wouldn't do the same thing.' He looked at Palfrey. 'All I can hope to do now is to try to help you in some way.'

'A month—even a week—ago, this would have helped plenty,' said the President, 'but it doesn't help now. You're too late.' There was no pity in his voice. 'And that's all?' he demanded.

'Yes, that's all.'

'I will send for you again if I want to see you, Mr. Grayson.' The President's voice was cold, aloof.

Grayson nodded, got up and went to the door. He seemed older even than when Palfrey had entered the room. A secretary opened the door, and Grayson went out. The President was staring towards the window, with a bleak expression on his face, and did not relax when he turned to Palfrey.

'We have got no further help from him,' he said. 'He knows nothing about the Alaskan cannery. I hoped we could get something more. There is no news from the north. I understand that Andromovitch and Bruton had gone to join the workers up there.'

'Yes,' said Palfrey.

The President went to his great desk and sat down. There were heavy lines on his forehead and about his lips. He said: 'I've had some worries while I've been here, Dr. Palfrey, but none has affected me like this. The one hope is still Alaska.'

Palfrey left the White House soon afterwards, and something of the President's depression had fallen upon him. As he was driven to his hotel, he went over the main points of Grayson's story. The picture was getting clearer.

Palfrey wanted Hoffner and Grayson to meet. Not once had 'Diana' been mentioned, and he wanted to hear from Grayson's own lips the story of the identification of his daughter. From his room he telephoned the two men.

He was leaving hurriedly when Stella called: 'Can you spare ten minutes?'

'Not right now, unless it's desperate,' Palfrey said.

'How long will you be gone? I've been thinking.'

'An hour at the most.'

She waved agreement, and Palfrey hurried on, smiling.

He was in the taxi driven by the long-jawed man when the real meaning of Stella's words struck home. 'I've been thinking.' She had gone off to set her mind to the question which Palfrey had posed to her, to himself, and to everyone—the problem of distribution. If Stella had a new line, it would be worth hearing. He wished he had spared her five minutes.

The cab pulled up outside Grayson's hotel. A man whom Palfrey had seen before on the case was waiting near the steps. He looked blankly at Palfrey, who hid a smile and hurried inside. Grayson was not at the desk, as he had promised, and Palfrey looked about him. The old man was nowhere in sight.

Palfrey waited for five minutes and then called the millionaire's room. There was no answer. Palfrey waited no longer, but hurried upstairs. He remembered Grayson's face when he had first seen him at the White House ; and the way he appeared to age in front of his eyes. He would certainly not put it beyond Grayson to kill himself. He reached the landing, saw a moon-faced man who had worked with him in Randall City, and felt relieved at the sight of another familiar face.

'Has Grayson come out?' he asked.

'Not lately,' said the agent. 'I followed him from the White House, and he's been inside ever since. What's your worry?'

'Have you a key to his room?' asked Palfrey.

The man grinned. 'Yes, sir, I can supply everything!' He took a master-key out of his pocket and handed it to Palfrey, then followed him to Grayson's room.

It seemed an age before the door was opened and Palfrey stepped inside. He was surprised to see a small room, long and narrow, with a single bed facing the window. The window was wide open. There was no sign of Grayson.

The moon-faced man said sharply: 'What's this?' and rushed to the window and leaned out. They were so high that the hum of traffic seemed to come from a long way off. Palfrey joined the agent and stared at the sidewalk. Everything seemed normal ; had Grayson flung himself out of the window, a crowd would have gathered by now, and the ambulance siren would be screaming.

Palfrey looked out again and bent his gaze upwards. The face of the building seemed to reach up an illimitable distance into the sky.

The agent said slowly: 'A girl came along ten minutes ago. She was quite a dame. She was friendly. I kidded her along for a few minutes, and most of the time I had my back to the door. I guess it's just possible that he went out and into another room. Some of these rooms have doors to two passages.' He talked as they hurried down the stairs. 'Shall I fix the call for him?'

'Yes,' said Palfrey.

He went into a telephone booth, called Hoffner, and told him that he would not be coming after all. Hoffner sounded disgruntled.

He left the booth and was joined by the moon-faced man, who looked at him ruefully, and said: 'I guess I asked for what I got, but I got plenty. I'm relieved of duty.' He lit a cigarette and tilted his hat to the back of his head. 'I was hoping to see this thing through,' he said. 'Put a word in for me if you can.'

'Of course,' said Palfrey.

He was driven to his own hotel in a state of uncertainty bordering on alarm. It was probable that Grayson was determined to kill himself. He would have known that he was watched; there would be nothing surprising in him attempting to dodge his trailers. But there was an insidious doubt in Palfrey's mind. Was it possible that Karen had stretched out an unseen hand and kidnapped Grayson? Karen worked through unexpected people, had agents in unexpected places.

The moon-faced man had talked of the good-looking girl who had been friendly. That would be an old, simple move, but one that was often effective; first distract the guard's attention, then act. Grayson could have been taken out of the room and put into one of the suites which opened on to two passages without the slightest difficulty in five minutes. He wished he had asked the moon-faced man to describe the girl; but the man was now on his way to Headquarters and would give a full account there.

Palfrey began to feel another doubt.

Was the moon-faced man reliable?

There was a crowd of people about the bookstall just inside the hotel. Palfrey caught sight of a headline in the *New York Daily Mirror*.

He drew in his breath, for he read:

SPIES BLAMED FOR CORN ROT

BIG AREA LAID WASTE

He bought a paper and read it on his way upstairs. He should have realized that sooner or later one of the newspapers would connect the mystery of the Texas corn belt with the sensational story about the British spy-ring. The *Mirror* made a veiled suggestion that the two things were connected, and most people who read it would jump to that conclusion. The British were not going to be popular while this lasted.

Whitehall must have agreed, or it would never have happened.

He called Scriebner from a telephone booth, and put in his word for the long-chinned man, chiefly because he wanted to hear Scriebner's opinion of him.

'He's okay,' said the Police Chief. 'He's too fond of curves. I won't be too rough with him.'

'Thanks,' said Palfrey.

He went upstairs, and, as he opened the door of his room, Stella jumped up from a chair.

'Karen's been at work again,' she cried. 'In Canada and India.'

Palfrey leaned against the door, sick at heart.

'How did you learn?'

To his astonishment she picked up a newspaper and held it out.

WE ACCUSE ENGLAND! There it was, in black and white, and nothing could be calculated better to work up anti-British feeling, to catch the eye and send a revulsion of fear and hate through the length and breadth of the country.

He glanced at the top of the page and stared. The paper was the *World Citizen.*

'It's making a good start,' he said. He went to a chair and sat down, glancing through the story. It was much as he expected after that headline. Without any of the vagueness of the *Mirror,* it accused England both of organizing a network of spies throughout America and of experimenting with a 'plague', which had laid waste vast stretches of the Texas corn belt. The outbreaks in Canada and India were not mentioned.

'Back page,' Stella told him, before he spoke.

A single column, printed in red, smeared, arresting, carried the story. The news, it said, had come from the *Citizen*'s correspondents. Since the news of the Texas disaster, the *Citizen,* in the interests of the people of the world, had sent special correspondents to the great wheat and corn districts of the world.

Palfrey turned to the editorial page. Comment there was more restrained, but tart enough. No one suggested that Great Britain was deliberately destroying the world's harvest ; a small group of financiers were probably chiefly responsible. There had been suggestions that the sensational reports of British Secret Service activity in the United States were connected with the wheat disasters. This might prove to be the case, but, said *World Citizen*, further proof should be awaited.

Palfrey put the paper down and went to the telephone. He was quickly connected with the White House. As he waited for the President's secretary, Stella said:

'There have been several calls for you from the White House, Sap.'

'Probably about the new visitation,' said Palfrey, and the President's voice sounded in his ear.

'Hallo, sir!'

'Have you seen the *Citizen*?' asked the President, abruptly.

'Yes.'

'Well?'

'There isn't much to say yet,' said Palfrey. 'When did you first hear of the trouble abroad?'

'Ten minutes before I saw the *Citizen*,' said the President.

'So they move faster than we do,' murmured Palfrey, and laughed again. There was no comment from the great man at the other end of the line. 'Sorry, sir. Have you heard that Grayson has disappeared?'

'Yes,' said the President.

'I suppose there's no news from the north?'

'Nothing at all.'

'Is there anything you want me to do at the moment?' asked Palfrey.

'What can I say?' asked the President, and added, almost despairingly: 'We *must* get results.'

'Yes,' said Palfrey. He began to toy with his hair. 'I won't sleep on it, I assure you.'

He rang off, and looked blankly at Stella, who had not moved during the conversation. He took a step from the telephone, but it rang again. He lifted the receiver.

'A call from England, sir,' said the operator.

'Thanks.' Although Palfrey was not expecting the call, he was not surprised to hear Brett's voice.

Brett had little to say that the President had not already said. Whitehall had been informed of the trouble in Canada and India; the same grave view was taken of it—there could only be the one view. Brett was alarmed, too, by the growth of the anti-British feeling in America. He rang off after ten minutes, and Palfrey put the telephone down with the feeling that Brett felt frustrated and had almost given up hope of getting results. Time was so short.

He glanced at Stella.

'Hadn't you been thinking?' he asked, idly.

'It doesn't matter now,' she said.

'It might. What's the bright idea?'

'You've taken it for granted that the men who drop this stuff know what they're doing,' said Stella, and paused. Palfrey eyed her with sudden attention. 'You said that dozens of men and dozens of aircraft would be needed to make a really big attack,' she said. 'I suppose you're right. But supposing the pilots *didn't* know what they were carrying. Wouldn't it be possible for the stuff to be loaded in the aircraft without the pilot knowing? It could be released automatically. The pilot might just have his instructions to fly over a certain area and have no idea of what was really happening.'

'You're quite right,' Palfrey said. He went to a chair, sat down, and closed his eyes. 'It would be in keeping with what we know of Karen if he were using innocents, wouldn't it?'

'That's what started me thinking about it,' Stella said, and then exclaimed sharply, 'Sap, how *are* we going to stop this hatred of the English?'

'By solving the puzzle,' said Palfrey.

'I'm beginning to wonder whether Karen told you everything. I'm beginning to wonder whether he wasn't as anxious to break Anglo-American relations as much as anything else.'

'Breaking them would be an integral part of his scheme.'

Palfrey sat up abruptly.

'What's on your mind?' Stella demanded.

'The explanation I've been looking for,' said Palfrey. 'I may be wrong, but—the *Citizen*'s behaviour is curious, isn't it? It's been preaching love between the nations, and suddenly comes out with a full-blooded attack on England. Its editorial is all over the place, it's forsaken logic, it's twisting everything it can to work up feeling against the English. Not a good thing for the *World Citizen*.'

'No,' said Stella, in a strained voice.

'And they got the news of the trouble in India and Canada before the White House,' said Palfrey. 'Curious fact. The White House was likely to be informed direct and Whitehall certainly would be, but the *Citizen* got its blow in first from men on the spot.

'And it's got agencies throughout the world,' Palfrey said.

'It's boasted time and time again that it is the only world news-paper and has representatives everywhere. A pretty hot news-paper! Financed by men from different countries—just the kind of organization we're looking for. Right?'

'Right,' said Stella, and her voice was hardly audible.

'To cover the world, it needs aeroplanes,' Palfrey said. 'Foreign correspondents fly everywhere. The news-service organization is as good if not better than any commercial organization. You don't know the names of the owners, do you?'

'Only that it's a syndicate,' Stella said.

'They'll know at the City Hall,' said Palfrey.

They went up several flights in a fast-moving lift to Scrieb-ner's office.

'Well, what's all the rush about?' asked Scriebner.

'Any news of Grayson?' asked Palfrey.

'Not yet. There isn't all that hurry about him, is there?' Scriebner was a slow-speaking man.

'I think I know where he might be,' said Palfrey. 'Do you know who owns——' he paused, for he caught sight of a familiar headline on a newspaper on the desk. He touched it. 'This,' he added.

'So that's got under your skin,' said Scriebner, 'and I don't say I blame you, Palfrey. I don't know the names of the owners, but it's a syndicate which——'

Palfrey said: 'Will you find out the Americans who are part owners, and have them watched?'

'Sure,' said Scriebner. He picked up a telephone and gave orders laconically. Palfrey found he was sweating freely and sat down, mopping his forehead.

A little later, Palfrey asked Scriebner to get him a call to Washington.

'The Great Man?'

'Or his secretary.'

'Sure.' Scriebner picked up the telephone again and in a few minutes Palfrey was talking to the man with the deep, authorita-tive voice.

He told the secretary what he had already told Stella ; and, after the first few sentences, Scriebner leaned forward and picked up another telephone. Palfrey could hear snatches of what he said. Stella seemed to be trying to listen to both of them at once. Palfrey talked in quick, crisp sentences ; the secretary at the other end of the line kept saying: 'I've got that.'

Palfrey finished as Scriebner said into his telephone:

'Sure, get the men in position right away.'

The secretary said: 'Will you hold on, Dr. Palfrey.'

It seemed a long wait to Palfrey. Scriebner was as cool as ever, but he was sitting forward with his hands resting lightly on the desk and his shrewd eyes were sparkling. Stella began to move restlessly about the room.

The telephone came to life with the now familiar voice.

'I've had your message, Palfrey. Where are you now?'

'With Captain Scriebner.'

'Tell him to speak to me,' said the President. 'Whether you're right or wrong, we must act right away.'

Palfrey beckoned, and Scriebner leaned forward to take the telephone.

Things moved quickly then.

Scriebner said twice: 'Yes, sir, at once,' and then replaced the receiver. He rubbed his hands together. 'I'm in on this,' he declared. 'Are you coming?'

EIGHTEEN

DISCOVERIES

THE *World Citizen*'s offices covered three floors of the Krufeld Building, which towered over the sky, exceeded in height only by the Empire State and the Chrysler Tower. It was a corner site on Broadway.

A man with a long jaw was standing near the entrance. He winked at Palfrey. So Scriebner looked after the small points as well as the big. They hurried to the hall, where men whom Palfrey recognized were lounging about.

A lift shot them up to the forty-first floor, to the main editorial offices. The hall leading to them was dotted with men. A few people were coming out of the doors on which *World Citizen* with written in gilt lettering, with a map of the world beneath it. A stenographer looked in some surprise at Palfrey, and then hurried back abruptly to the doorway through which she had just come.

Scriebner stretched out an arm. 'You'll stay outside,' he said.

He nodded to one of his waiting men to make sure that she

did not leave, then they made a complete tour of the outside of the offices. Palfrey was smiling faintly; the girl had recognized him and had intended to take the news: Scriebner missed nothing.

They reached the front hall again.

'We're all set,' said Scriebner. 'Come on.'

They went inside, Scriebner leading, Palfrey, Stella and two other men with them. There was nothing unusual in the office. A few dozen girls, each at a small desk, were working, mostly on typewriters and comptometers. Scriebner went to a door marked *Editorial*, but before he reached it two men appeared from the side of the room.

'What's your business?' asked one.

'Private,' said Scriebner.

'You'll have to send in your name.'

'I'll take it with me,' said Scriebner, and flashed his badge. He opened the door and went in. There was another large office divided into sections, all with glass partitions. Two or three people were in each 'room'. At the end of a passage down the centre was another door, marked *Editor*. Scriebner and his party strode along, and Palfrey glanced about him, still wearing a look of mild surprise. He saw a man get up from the desk and go towards the door. He smiled faintly: the man would find plenty waiting for him outside.

He touched the policeman's arm.

'Now what?' asked Scriebner.

'There'll be a house telephone system here,' Palfrey said. 'They might be able to send word to the other floors once we start moving. That system should be put out of order.'

Scriebner passed his hand across his chin.

'You're right,' he said, and shot a glance at one of his men. 'Get cracking.'

Scriebner pushed open the door marked *Editor*, but they had not reached the editor's office yet. Here were two partitioned offices, with two men and a girl in each one.

Then he saw another door, marked *Managing Editor—Leopold Mangus.*

Two people moved from the outer offices and blocked the way to Mangus's room. They were tall, wary-looking men who stood in front of the little party determinedly.

'You've an appointment?' one asked.

'This is it,' said Scriebner, showing his badge again. He pushed the man aside and Palfrey thought they were going to have trouble. Then he saw one of the men kick gently against the door of the editor's room. A buzzer sounded inside.

Scriebner tried the door and found it locked. He banged on the glass. 'Open up,' he ordered, in a voice which must have reached whoever was in the room.

'*Open up!*' Scriebner shouted again and took a gun from his pocket. He pointed it at the lock. From inside the room came sounds, as of men moving quickly and of drawers being opened and closed.

Scriebner fired. The shot echoed loudly in the confined space and the door sagged open. Scriebner kicked it wider and dodged inside. Palfrey pushed Stella behind him, not knowing what to expect.

A door at the far end of a long room closed.

A man was sitting at a huge, flat-topped desk in front of the door. Palfrey saw his white hair, his thin, handsome face. The room was the largest office that Palfrey had yet seen in the *Citizen*, but there was only one desk. Several rows of filing cabinets stood against the walls.

'Hallo, Mangus,' said Scriebner.

'What does this mean?' asked Mangus. He did not look up, and his voice was pitched on a low key—the husky voice of a southerner.

'Who did you have in here just now?' asked Scriebner.

'My secretary, who——'

'Secretary nothing,' said Scriebner. He looked over his shoulder. His men were filing into the room, lining the walls. Mangus must have been impressed by the strength of the raiding party, but did not show it. Scriebner motioned to the door behind him. Mangus remained expressionless as two men hurried out of the room. They said nothing; presumably the room beyond was empty.

Someone cried: 'No!' The sound seemed to come from a long way off, but was high-pitched—the cry of a man who was terrified. '*No, no!*'

'You'll pay for this,' said Mangus, slowly. 'What do you want?'

'I think you know,' said Scriebner, 'and——'

Mangus said: 'I think I know.' He looked at Palfrey. 'You've taken the word of an English secret agent—do you think I don't know Palfrey? He's been protesting against the stories we've printed. Listen to me, Scriebner; those stories are gospel truth.'

'*No!*' screeched the man who was out of sight, and this time there was a new note of terror in his voice.

There was a shot.

Scriebner snapped to his men: 'Watch him,' and rushed into the next room. Palfrey followed, motioning to Stella to stay behind. Another door was opening. A second shot echoed loudly, and Scriebner and Palfrey ran into the third room. It was small, lined with steel cabinets, and dark, for there was only a small window. Two men were struggling there. One of Scriebner's men was on the floor, lying very still; the other was at the window, grappling with someone *outside*.

Scriebner went forward.

Palfrey looked round for another door, but saw none; this was a strong-room. He looked back and saw Mangus still at his desk, but with his head turned to watch the raiding party.

Scriebner shouted: 'Hold him!'

'Hold him,' thought Palfrey, vaguely, and then saw that there were *three* men at the window, besides Scriebner. Scriebner grabbed a chair and jumped up on it, then leaned out.

His man had arrived to find two others struggling in the window; one was obviously trying to push the other out. Scriebner watched as his man clutched at the arm of the man hanging dangerously over the small safety ledge. Forty storeys below was Broadway, crowded with hurrying people, all unaware of what was happening up here.

A man screamed.

Scriebner saw that one of those outside had lost his hold. His head disappeared, his arms swung into sight, and the scream grew louder; and then he disappeared. Scriebner's man was still holding on to the other fellow, although his grip on the window frame was slipping. Palfrey craned his neck to see more clearly . . .

He saw Grayson!

Scriebner's man was holding Grayson, but if he released his hold Grayson would have no chance. And there was nothing Palfrey could do except support Scriebner, who was leaning forward and staring down and clutching Grayson.

Scriebner said: 'It's okay, Bennett.'

'Bennett' released Grayson, but Scriebner had his hands under the man's armpits, and hauled him in. Palfrey did not release his hold on the detective until both were safely in the room. 'Bennett', his face chalk-white, was leaning against the wall. Cool air came in at the window.

180

Then Palfrey heard Stella cry out.

'*Sap!*' Her voice seemed to echo about the small room, and Palfrey, gasping for breath, turned round. She was rushing towards the safe-room. He caught sight of Mangus's face; the man was smiling, as Karen might have smiled in a moment of great triumph.

The door between the two offices was closing—a sliding-door which moved slowly. Stella reached it; so did two men behind her. They exerted all their strength to keep it open, but it was nearly a foot thick, and slid on remorselessly.

Stella was caught between it and the wall. She was struggling now to free herself. Scriebner jumped forward and took her arm, pulling her. Men were pulling from behind.

'*Let her go!*' shouted Scriebner.

They must have heard him, for suddenly she lurched forward almost into his arms. Her skirt ripped apart as she came. The door was only six inches from the wall. A policeman on the other side thrust the back of a chair into the gap, and Palfrey swung round, looking desperately for something stronger than wood to prevent it from closing.

There was nothing; but he saw something which made him stop thinking about it——

A steel shutter was sliding across the outside of the window, making the room dark. The only light came from the gap at the door and the gap at the window. The men in the outer room were still struggling, but the door had reached the chair; the wood began to splinter.

Scriebner raised his voice again.

'Get Mangus! Treat him as rough as you like, but make him open this door.'

Someone said: 'Okay, Captain——'

Palfrey moved slowly towards the door and groped for the light-switch. He pressed it down. A powerful bulb lit up in the centre of the ceiling. It cast a blueish-white light over them all, and added to the pallor of their faces.

Grayson was lying on the floor, unconscious. The man who had saved him was standing up against the wall, looking dazedly about him. Scriebner's collar and tie were awry, and his dark hair was falling into his eyes. He brushed it back. Stella was pinning up her torn skirt.

'What happened?' asked Scriebner.

'There was a row at the other end of the office,' Stella said, 'and some men tried to break in. All of us looked towards it.

Then I saw Mangus with his hand on his desk, pressing a button. He——' she paused, and added tensely: 'He was smiling. And the door was closing.'

'I wonder what they intend to do,' Scriebner grunted.

Palfrey said: 'Let's not wonder. We might as well look round for what we can find.'

The steel cabinets were locked, but there were keys in the table drawer. Scriebner took one out, and Palfrey selected another. Scriebner opened one of the cabinets first. Stella went to join him as he took out several sheaves of papers. The man by the wall suddenly moved forward and said abruptly: 'I don't like this.'

Scriebner chuckled.

'You're dead right, Bennett,' he said. 'Get one of those cabinets open. And you, sister.' He patted Stella's shoulder. 'We'll learn all we can before we get out, it will save time.'

No one said: 'If we get out,' but it was in all their minds.

Palfrey glanced at Grayson. The old man was stirring, and would come round in a few minutes.

Palfrey unlocked one of the cabinets, and found more papers. Scriebner looked up.

'What have you got?'

'Chemical formula,' said Palfrey, after a quick glance. He paused, then added: 'Interesting formula, too.'

They watched him as he stood reading; he could follow the formula closely enough to understand it. He saw how easily the *bitua* product could be manufactured.

'Well?' asked Scriebner.

'I suppose they've got copies everywhere,' said Palfrey. He leaned back and narrowed his eyes, then caught sight of the papers in Scriebner's hand. The first words he read, on the top left-hand corner, were: *Strictly Confidential*. There was the royal coat of arms on the centre of the page, and in one corner, *10 Downing Street, London, S.W.1*.

Scriebner smiled wryly.

'Photostat copies of the documents borrowed from the British Embassy,' he said, and passed them over.

Palfrey began to compare them with the papers which he had studied. There were differences, but the basic principles of manufacture were the same.

Scriebner opened another cabinet. Stella began to go through the papers. She uttered a sharp exclamation, and they joined her.

There were lists of the places throughout the world where *Citizen*'s representatives were ready to take flight. There were statements on the loads of *bitua* already delivered to them. It was clear, as they studied the sheet, that Karen was preparing a single devastating swoop, using in all nearly fifty aircraft. The places where the ruin was to be spread were marked: these included wide areas in every wheat-growing country. Karen had not boasted in vain.

'They don't give the date when they plan to start,' Scriebner said, and his voice was hoarse.

'They—do,' said Stella, and pointed to a single sheet of paper on which were the words:

Operation A—Worldwide—25th July

'Tomorrow,' said Scriebner.

They looked at one another helplessly.

They *had* to get out.

Palfrey had not allowed himself to contemplate that thought seriously before, but now he faced it. Whatever happened to them, they had to get the papers out of the room. Mangus surely had some way of ensuring their destruction; the look of triumph would not have been on his face but for that.

Bennett turned from the steel-shuttered window.

'What—what are we going to do?'

'They'll come for us,' Scriebner said, quietly.

'How do you know they'll come?' asked Bennett. His nerve was giving way.

Grayson stirred again.

'What are the chances of getting through the floor?' asked Palfrey.

'None,' said Scriebner. 'I saw this building going up. We'll have to wait.' He was still going through the papers, and stopped abruptly. 'This is another thing we wanted,' he said, 'the names of the *Citizen* syndicate.' There were names of two Americans, two Englishmen, a Frenchman, and others—in all seven different countries were represented; and all the men had world-wide reputations, all were financiers controlling millions.

Now it was easy to understand how Karen had got his money.

Stella exclaimed suddenly: 'Look at this!' They swung round towards her. 'The Alaskan cannery address,' she said, 'it——'

Bennett suddenly raised his voice.

'What does it matter?' They turned to face him and saw his eyes had a feverish gleam; his lips were working. 'What the hell does that matter? We're trapped, we'll never get out of here. Don't you understand—we're trapped! We'll never be able to tell anyone about those papers. Throw them away; start thinking about how we're going to escape.'

Scriebner went to his side.

'Take it easy,' he said, and rested a hand on Bennett's shoulder. 'The boys are just on the other side of that door.'

Bennett wrenched himself free.

'It wouldn't matter if they were a thousand miles away, they can't help us! Do you think he would have locked us in here if he thought we'd get out? He wants to destroy those papers—answer me, doesn't he want to destroy them? He must want to —he—he'll blow us up!'

Scriebner's voice sharpened.

'Don't be a fool,' he said, 'you're talking like——'

Bennett struck him on the face, knocking him backwards against the table. Scriebner went down. Palfrey jumped forward as Bennett leapt to get the papers and snatched them out of Stella's hands. He tore them across and across before Palfrey could get at them, and he screamed: 'They don't matter! Get us out of here! Get us out!'

Palfrey drew back his fist and struck him on the side of the jaw, a blow which shook him but did not knock him out. Palfrey thought: 'I've got to stop him.' Then he saw Bennett snatch at the gun in his shoulder-holster; the man's brain had given way.

Palfrey was too far away to stop him.

Stella flung herself at him!

The gun pointed upwards. A single bullet hit the ceiling, and then Palfrey wrenched the gun out of the man's hand. But Bennett could use both arms and Palfrey was able only to use one.

Palfrey glanced at Scriebner; there was blood on his forehead, where he had struck the desk; he was only half-conscious. Bennett thrust Stella aside. Palfrey turned the gun in his hand, and, as the man rushed at him, hit him on the temple with the butt. Bennett swayed. Palfrey struck again, trying to judge the blow so that he would only knock the crazed man out.

Bennett collapsed.

184

Stella said: 'Scriebner's hurt.'

'Yes,' said Palfrey. 'I——'

He turned to look at Scriebner, but saw something else. Smoke was coming into the room beneath the door. Thin wisps of it curled upwards and he smelt burning. Stella saw the smoke, too. They exchanged quick glances, but neither spoke.

Palfrey turned to Scriebner. Stella helped him, and together they sat the man with his back against one of the filing cabinets. Scriebner grinned weakly and rubbed his hand across his eyes. Then he sniffed. The smell seemed to act as a stimulant. He stiffened, glanced at Palfrey and then at the door. Palfrey nodded.

'I get it,' said Scriebner.

The office outside was on fire. Palfrey did not doubt that it was deliberately contrived. The fire would spread rapidly. It might be held back by the steel door for a while, but it would reach them eventually. He touched the wall and found it warm. Then he turned back—and someone clutched his foot. He thought it was Bennett coming round, but it was Grayson, who had stretched out a hand to get his attention.

He had forgotten Grayson.

He bent down and raised the man with his one good arm.

Grayson licked his lips. 'We—we've got to get out.'

When none of the others answered, he raised his voice; he was going to be another Bennett. 'We've got to get out!'

'Soon,' said Palfrey.

'Don't be a damned fool! We'll be blown up! I——' Grayson paused and winced, as if he were in pain, and then went on: 'I tell you we'll be blown up; I heard them talking. And they left me in here with the door open. They said that if there were a raid they'd close the doors and blow the room up and they'd fire the rest of the floor. They're doing it, and there's explosive in here, there must be——'

'I wonder if he's right?' asked Scriebner, in a far-away voice.

'Of course I'm right! I heard—I heard them, the explosive —Palfrey!'

Palfrey said: 'Yes?'

'I heard them talk about a key, *a key in this room*; there must be one.'

Palfrey said: 'We'll have a look round.'

They opened drawer after drawer of the desk.

'It's getting hot,' Scriebner said, and glanced at the door. Palfrey passed his hand across his damp forehead.

'Two left,' Stella said, standing back from an open drawer. She pulled her hair back wearily and tried to open another, while Palfrey felt inside the drawer.

He touched a box. It was of steel, quite small; there was a lock on it. He picked the box up and found it surprisingly heavy. He carried it to the table and studied it for a moment. The others moved towards him.

'Open it,' said Stella, sharply.

'No key,' said Palfrey, but he tried the lid, and it opened.

Inside was a small detonator with an electric coil and a small dry battery. They stared at it in tense silence, which was broken by a cry from Grayson.

'What is it? What have you found?'

Slowly and deliberately, Palfrey disconnected the detonator. The charge of explosive was a small one in a tiny wooden box. He did not even look at it, but he did at the door. He had no idea how fierce a hold the fire had taken outside. He only knew that if this room got really hot, it might touch off the explosive. He lifted the box cautiously and took off the lid. It was nitroglycerine, he thought. He left it in its tiny glass container—enough explosive to blow them to pieces, and put it carefully against the outside wall, where it was likely to keep cool for some time.

Grayson croaked: 'Does—does anyone know we're here?'

'Yes,' said Palfrey.

With Scriebner, he collected all the papers in a bundle on the table. There they were, with all the information that could be wanted, with the weapon with which to stop Karen from striking, in their hands—and a few inches of steel and concrete between them and——

Fire!

'*Look for the key*,' croaked Grayson.

'There isn't a key,' Scriebner said. He turned away from the old man. 'This looks like ours, Palfrey. It wouldn't be so bad if we thought they'd get inside in time to save those papers.'

The room grew hotter and the smoke thicker until Grayson's face was just a vague shape against the far wall. Moving about was an effort. Palfrey thought: 'So this is the way it's going to happen.' An hour passed since the door had shut, half an hour since they had found the nitro-glycerine. It was such harmless-looking stuff, and——

A stab of yellow flame came into the room with a fierce roar. Palfrey swung round. Grayson screamed. Stella clutched

Palfrey's arm, and Scriebner said: 'Here it comes.'

Palfrey cried in a loud voice: 'The door must be open!'

The words had hardly left his lips before men staggered into the room, wearing asbestos suits and fire-fighting masks. They were carrying a small hose. Palfrey grabbed the papers, Scriebner stooped down and picked Bennett up. He had not the strength to carry him, but dragged him to the door. Grayson staggered out, across the flame-filled room, towards the clear, cool air of the big outer office.

Among the people in the room in the White House when Palfrey returned from having a bath and changing clothes, were the President and his secretary. Hoffner and Grayson were also there. For hours, Palfrey knew, radios had been sending out messages ; codes had been used to make sure that Karen's agents, waiting for final instructions, could not be warned of what was impending. North, east, south and west the call had gone out. Police and military had moved into what remained of the offices of *World Citizen* ; most of the 'reporters' were under arrest by now, as were the syndicate members.

The President had a slip of paper in his hand.

Palfrey smiled at him. 'Progress, sir?'

'Everything's fine,' said the President, and thrust the paper towards Palfrey. Palfrey glanced at it, and his eyes shone. The brief message read: *'Karen's had his—all over—Bruton.'*

'Not bad,' said Palfrey. 'I'm glad they were in it to the end.' He lit a cigarette, and smiled rather foolishly. 'Nothing more to worry about, sir. I hope you're discouraging that anti-British story.'

'I'm talking about it on the radio tonight,' said the President. Never had Palfrey seen him in so happy a mood. The man even bent his gaze on Grayson with some amiability. 'I understand that Mr. Grayson warned you of the high-explosive,' he said.

'That's right,' said Palfrey.

Grayson raised a hand.

'I am daring to hope, Mr. President, that—that you will think I have done something to expiate my—my folly.'

'We realize how much we owe to you,' said the President, 'and it will not be forgotten.'

Grayson closed his eyes.

'Thank—thank you,' he said, and turned towards the door. He was near it when his knees bent beneath him, and he fell. Hoffner rushed forward and helped him up.

'We'd better get him to his hotel, sir,' he said.

'I wonder,' said Palfrey, and went forward, looking at Grayson thoughtfully. The man was leaning heavily against Hoffner, and everyone else in the room was watching. 'I wonder if we ought to let him go at all,' he said. 'Karen's people weren't careless. I'm not sure that they would have let anyone overhear where the nitro-glycerine was stored.' He was smiling faintly.

Grayson had stopped shivering, and there was a sharp glint in his eyes.

'What do you think, Scriebner?' Palfrey asked.

Scriebner looked bewildered.

'They were trying to throw him out of the window,' he said.

'Were they?' asked Palfrey. 'Would you have much difficulty in throwing Grayson out of a window? And would you let him remain conscious before you did it? Wouldn't you have knocked him out first?'

'There wasn't time for that!' Grayson exclaimed. 'They were questioning me at my hotel when a warning came. I tried to get away, but they took me to the *Citizen*'s office and dragged me to that window. What are you driving at, Palfrey? What do you mean?'

Palfrey said slowly: 'I mean I don't think you're telling the truth, Grayson. Supposing you weren't kidnapped, but walked from your hotel to the Krufeld Building to the *Citizen* office. Supposing you went to get reports *from* Mangus and, when the raid came, he pretended to be having you thrown out so as to save *your* skin.'

Grayson said: 'They wouldn't have left me in that room to be blown up if I had been one of them.'

'Mangus had no choice,' said Palfrey. 'Events moved too quickly for him. He had to get that room shut off and the fire started by pressing a button; it was all prepared to make sure we weren't rescued. The detonator would be adjusted every so often so that the room would blow up at the right time. You were unlucky, that's all.'

Grayson said: 'You're crazy!'

Palfrey snapped: 'Grayson, you were in at the beginning of this affair. The first incident was when your daughter disappeared. I don't think she was ever kidnapped. I think she discovered the truth about you, knew that you were planning this scourge. You had to silence her. You would not kill your own flesh and blood, but you allowed Mallory to destroy her memory and to change her identity. Afterwards you heard of the documents sent to America through our Embassy. You managed to steal them and planned to blame Kennedy Lee. There's more yet. You wanted a try-out in America, and you selected Hoffner's land. It was evident that whoever did that had reason to hate Hoffner. You did. He made your daughter fall in love with him. Because of him, she took life more seriously. She stayed around more, and she learned the truth about you. That's why you hated Hoffner.'

Palfrey paused, but no one spoke. 'It's all clear once we have the key,' went on Palfrey. 'You wouldn't co-operate with the police after the girl's disappearance, but you hired Lannigan for appearance' sake. He learned too much, and Casado killed him. Lannigan would soon have realized that you didn't want to find your daughter. When you were told she was in England, you sent another man in your place, and he removed his disguise and disappeared among the crowd on board the *Adua Star*. Only when Stefan came to see you were you persuaded to fly to England. You thought it time, then, to identify Valerie. You thought it all over bar shouting.'

'It is a foul lie!' Grayson cried, and turned towards the President, his face scarlet, his eyes flashing. 'Haven't I admitted my error? Haven't I suffered enough without being insulted by a damned Englishman?' He drew in his breath and then launched into a diatribe against Palfrey and the British. He seemed hardly sane.

This man was voicing Karen's sentiments—the sentiments of the members of the *World Citizen* syndicate.

It was the voice of hatred and the awful pride of a race which had instigated the attempt to destroy the Old and rebuild the New World. This was the real Grayson ; but could the charge against him be established in *any* way?

The President turned to Palfrey, and asked quietly : 'Can you prove your charges, Dr. Palfrey?'

'Haven't we had proof?' asked Palfrey.

'No.'

It was true. There *was no proof*. Grayson's name had not been on the lists found in the strong-room. He had worked cunningly and cleverly, always careful of his own safety. Even to the last he had appeared a 'victim', but had been really fighting to preserve himself.

Mangus must know!

He snapped : 'Where's Mangus?'

'He killed himself,' said Scriebner, laconically.

'After he had tried to kill me!' cried Grayson.

Silence fell again. Palfrey sensed the feeling of them all. Grayson must have known what they were thinking, but felt secure in his position. There was one chance, thought Palfrey —that Karen had been caught alive. He remembered how Casado had committed suicide; and now Mangus; it was expecting too much that Karen still lived.

There was a tap at the door. The secretary opened it, and a man spoke in a soft voice. The secretary turned with a slip of paper in his hand. He looked transfigured; it was the first time Palfrey had seen him as a man, not as a machine serving the President.

His voice was unsteady. 'There has been a radio message from Alaska, Mr. President. It reads: *'Karen's talked. Hold Grayson'*.'

When Karen was brought in, late next day, Palfrey hardly recognized the broken, battered hulk of a man.

He had fought desperately when the cannery had been raided, but Stefan had prevented him from killing himself. Stefan and Bruton brought back reports of the cannery, which was genuine enough and did plenty of canning. There was news, too, of the underground workshops where *bitua* was converted into the black dust. The *bitua* deposits were a few miles from the factory, on the banks of a river, where for many years there had been a derelict gold mine. The mine had been taken over, ostensibly for gold; Karen would never have lacked raw material.

Arrests throughout the world were being made every few minutes, and a constant stream of reports came in. Gradually, one fact emerged: none of the men who were to have dropped the black dust knew what they were carrying. Stella's theory of automatic release was right. Correspondents were to have been told to fly in a certain direction. As they spread destruction beneath them, they would have been quite unaware of it. And, had they finished their task, few, if any, would have returned alive. In every aircraft inspected, a tiny container of high-explosive was secreted; the aircraft would have exploded in mid-air. There was no longer any mystery about the wrecked aircraft in Texas.

Stefan and Bruton had brought back some papers from the factory, and with Palfrey and Stella they were sitting round a table in the hotel comparing notes.

Bruton broke a short silence. 'What's this?' He had taken up a slip of paper with a small photograph attached. 'Diana *Leeming*,' he added, and looked at Palfrey as he pushed the photograph towards him.

Palfrey drew in a sharp breath.

'That's Löis!' he exclaimed.

It was clear, from the papers which they found later, that the Leemings had discovered the truth about their daughter's work with Karen, and Karen had engineered the plane crash in which they were killed. Diana had not been on the plane. She had lain low, as Löis, until she was needed. Karen had kidnapped Valerie Grayson and put it about that she was Diana, recovering from the crash in his care. He took her memory away and altered her appearance. If anyone who had known Diana saw Valerie, he would have accounted for her changed appearance by saying that she had been badly injured and her face re-made. If Karen had had his way, Valerie would have been eliminated after she had discovered what her father was doing, but Grayson would not allow that. It had been Grayson who had been behind the financing of Kennedy Lee, when Lee fell in love with Valerie—as Diana—so that he should take her to England, away from Karen, to look after her.

'I think that covers everything,' Bruton said.

Palfrey nodded.

'When are you going back?' asked Stella.

'Quite soon,' said Palfrey, and smiled at her. 'I hope you'll come with us; I'd like Drusilla to meet you. She wants to say "thanks", too.'

Hoffner also travelled to England with them, and Palfrey and Drusilla were with him when he met 'Diana Leeming' again. She recognized him as Karen's one-time visitor, but her mind was still blank about her earlier past. Hoffner took her hands. She flushed a little, as if she were puzzled, but Palfrey and Drusilla exchanged glances. There were no serious breakers ahead for that couple. Research was being made to find a cure, but specialists were not hopeful; Hoffner would see that she did not brood over the past, however.

Brett was coming from London to Brett Hall later in the day. Stefan and Bruton were strolling in the sunlit grounds. Hoffner and 'Diana' went out, and passed the window, walking close together.

Drusilla stood by Palfrey's side, and they clasped hands.

They did not notice Stella, who looked in, stood for a moment on the threshold, and then withdrew. Stella's eyes were misty, but she was smiling ; Palfrey would have been glad to see that. She caught her breath a little as she hurried to the front door, but before she reached it, a shy voice sounded softly.

'Hallo.'

Stella swung round. Hilary, long-legged and a little bashful, stood by the morning-room door.

'Why, hallo!' exclaimed Stella.

'I do hope you don't mind me speaking to you,' said Hilary.

'Of course not!'

Hilary put her head on one side. 'Are—are you American?'

'That's right.'

Hilary raised her arm and touched a healing scar.

'There was an American here not long ago,' she said. 'He saved my life. I liked him *very* much, and——'

But Hilary broke off, astonished ; for the American girl with the sunlight in her hair suddenly pulled her close and hugged her and—yes, she was crying.